THE RECKONING

Also by M.J. Trow

The Kit Marlowe series

DARK ENTRY *
SILENT COURT *
WITCH HAMMER *
SCORPIONS' NEST *
CRIMSON ROSE *
TRAITOR'S STORM *
SECRET WORLD *
ELEVENTH HOUR *
QUEEN'S PROGRESS *
BLACK DEATH *

The Grand & Batchelor series

THE BLUE AND THE GREY *
THE CIRCLE *
THE ANGEL *
THE ISLAND *
THE RING *
THE BLACK HILLS *

The Peter Maxwell series

MAXWELL'S ISLAND
MAXWELL'S CROSSING
MAXWELL'S RETURN
MAXWELL'S ACADEMY

* *available from Severn House*

THE RECKONING

M.J. Trow

This first world edition published 2020
in Great Britain and the USA by
Crème de la Crime an imprint of
SEVERN HOUSE PUBLISHERS LTD of
Eardley House, 4 Uxbridge Street, London W8 7SY.
Trade paperback edition first published
in Great Britain and the USA 2021 by
SEVERN HOUSE PUBLISHERS LTD.

British Library Cataloguing in Publication Data
A CIP catalogue record for this title is available from the British Library.

ISBN-13: 978-1-78029-129-1 (cased)
ISBN-13: 978-1-78029-699-9 (trade paper)
ISBN-13: 978-1-4483-0424-0 (e-book)

All Severn House titles are printed on acid-free paper.

Severn House Publishers support the Forest Stewardship Council™ [FSC™],
the leading international forest certification organisation.
All our titles that are printed on FSC certified paper carry the FSC logo.

Typeset by Palimpsest Book Production Ltd.,
Falkirk, Stirlingshire, Scotland.
Printed and bound in Great Britain by
TJ International, Padstow, Cornwall.

ONE

The light filtered in through gaps in the canvas and the dust motes dancing there shone like stars. The very sound of breathing was muffled and the men's heads, close together, made a mosaic in a fitful beam of winter sun. Black curls, bronze curls and blond locks mingled with a skull beneath the skin. Freckles, tan, the pasty white of a man who rarely saw daylight, all moved in a slow pavane and their voices, muttering low, seemed to stay in the circle, the words melding and melting together until no single one could be heard.

The mice in the wainscoting shuffled and chewed. They knew that after this strange meeting there would be crumbs to be had, bedding to drag home to their children. This happened now and then and only men knew why; mice sorted out their squabbles and disagreements with a swift, sharp stab of razor teeth and then it was over. But these men were still muttering, trying to jockey for position, to get the upper hand.

Eventually, one voice rang out from the others. 'For the Lord's sake, Shaxsper!' it said, exasperation in every syllable. 'Can you please just draw a straw and be done with it? I for one don't want to be here all the live-long day. I have places to be.'

'All right, Ned.' The nasal tones of the Warwickshire man were peevish and whining. 'I just don't want to be cheated, that's all.'

'Come on, Will.' The next voice had mastery and music in it. 'Do as Alleyn says and choose a straw. I believe he has a widow just coming to the simmer down in the Vintry and he doesn't want to miss the tide, if I may mix my metaphors for a moment there.'

There was a sigh and a voice the mice recognized above the others. This belonged to the one who dropped the most crumbs, made the most curls of wood and the lovely sawdust for their babies. He was there all day and half of most nights. The mice listened intently. 'I don't know why we do this,' Tom Sledd said. 'I always pick the . . .' there was a pause and a rustle and some chuckles in the sun-pocked dark '. . . short straw.'

And with murmurs of 'Bad luck, Tom,' the others melted away.

'The Lord Chamberlain's Men?' Philip Henslowe snarled. 'Never heard of them.' The impresario didn't even bother to look up at his stage manager. In Henslowe's world view, if you didn't acknowledge something, it didn't exist. He found this worked particularly well with actors asking for money.

Tom Sledd had known that this would not go well. Philip Henslowe may have his finger in many pies – not all of them that savoury – but his heart lay in the Rose, the theatre he had built from the ground up with the sweat of everybody else's brow. Tom Sledd owned two of those brows, but he was merely stage manager at the Rose, something on Henslowe's pattens.

'Ssh!' Sledd hissed, flapping his hands as if he was talking to his little daughter when she was having a tantrum. 'It's very hush-hush.'

'What is?' Henslowe hadn't finished his weekly accounts yet and his little counting house under the theatre's eaves was filled with piles of tickets, earthenware pots and small change. The Queen looked haughtily up at him from the floor with a hundred identical faces.

'The troupe,' Sledd whispered, as if the word were blasphemy. 'The Lord Chamberlain's troupe.' By now, he wasn't even whispering; he was just mouthing the words in an exaggerated mime.

Henslowe put an inky finger down on the page to mark his place. 'One hundred and ten,' he murmured to remind himself of the running total. Tom Sledd, Henslowe would be the first to agree, was a good functionary but he could irritate for England. No one could build the towers of Ilium like Tom Sledd; nor the ghetto of Malta; nor the killing grounds of Paris. But he was still a pain in the arse. 'We are talking about the Lord Chamberlain?' Henslowe checked. 'Henry Carey, Baron Hunsdon? Queen's cousin? Good jouster back in the day?'

'The very same,' Sledd nodded. He hadn't wanted this task, breaking the news to Henslowe, but he had, as always, drawn the short straw. And here he was, facing the ogre in his lair. Whenever Sledd had to confront the gorgon that was Henslowe, he kept reminding himself that the man was not a scholar or patron of the arts; he could make money, that was all his skill. But each time, it didn't work. The philistine's finger rings alone could buy the stage manager twice over.

'I didn't know that Hunsdon had any theatrical leanings,' Henslowe said. 'He liked putting down rebellions in the North if memory serves. Oh, and Italian mistresses, of course; dark ladies and all that. Before your time, I expect. But the theatre? No, I hadn't heard that.'

'Oh, it's all the rage now, isn't it?' Sledd toyed with pulling up a chair to engage in conversation but thought better of it. Besides any other consideration, to move anything even an inch in this room under the eaves would be to invite an avalanche of paper and coin that might be impossible to stop. 'Lord Strange. Effingham. They're all at it.'

'Yes,' Henslowe grunted. 'Effingham. You got that right.'

'It's only a short run,' Sledd went on. 'A couple of weeks at most. Croydon, Guildford; Scadbury, maybe. Nowhere . . . unpleasant, you know. Nothing Northern.'

Henslowe nodded. He was grateful for that at least. 'What's the play?' he asked.

'Er . . . something by Tom Kyd, I think. *The Spanish Tragedy.*'

'You *think*, Sledd?' Henslowe repeated. 'You're the stage manager, for God's sake. Don't you *know*?'

'Yes, all right, then. It is. Kyd. *Spanish Tragedy*.'

Henslowe's brain whirled for a moment. 'Right. So, you're taking the walking gentlemen, right? People like Skeres? Frizer? Shaxsper?'

'Oh, probably,' Sledd shrugged. He was edging towards the door. He lifted a paint-spattered hand to his mouth to stifle a sudden cough. 'And Ned,' he said.

Henslowe held up a hand and the stage manager froze, like a sparrow in thrall to a weasel. 'Pardon?' the impresario said, his head on one side and a glacial smile on his lips.

'Yes, sorry.' Sledd cleared his throat. 'I beg your pardon. Bit of a frog in my throat. So, I'll be off now, then . . .'

'No, I mean, pardon, what did you say?'

'When?' Sledd smiled brightly. He could still just about get away with ingénue parts if the light was right.

'You said Ned.' Henslowe was still smiling. It was like a basilisk but a basilisk on the verge of a very serious tantrum.

'Hmm?' Sledd raised his eyebrows and inclined his head, trying to recall. 'Oh, yes, I did. And Ned. So, if that's all . . .?'

Henslowe was suddenly not smiling. He was on his feet, leaning forward on his knuckles, paper and ink going everywhere. 'Ned Alleyn?' he roared.

'He insisted,' Sledd told him.

'*He* insisted?' Henslowe knew Ned Alleyn. The man believed that the sun shone from his arse and that all London loved him. *And* he was constantly flirting with Henslowe's daughter. He would no more go on the road in the dead of winter than fly to the moon.

'Well, actually, it was Kit.'

'Kit?' Henslowe was repeating things a lot this morning and his stage manager knew that was a very bad sign. 'Kit Marlowe?'

'That's the one,' Sledd grinned. It was hard to imagine there could be another.

'What's he got to do with it? It's Kyd's play.'

'Ah, I think he might have to do the odd rewrite. You know Tom Kyd – bit weak on the rhyming couplets.'

'That's a Merchant Taylor's schoolboy for you,' Henslowe nodded. 'So Marlowe's going too?'

'Yes.' Sledd's hand was on the latch. 'And Richard,' he said to the door, in an almost inaudible voice.

'No!' Henslowe's ears were attuned now to Sledd's subterfuge. He was out from behind the desk in what seemed to Sledd a preternaturally short time for a man of his age and condition. The impresario drove his patten into the door so that it stayed shut. 'You're not taking Burbage as well. You can have Marlowe, Shaxsper and even Alleyn. But I'll die in a ditch before I let you have Burbage.'

Tom Sledd knew the very ditch he had in mind – it ran along the embankment past the Bear Pit where the great black beast that Master Sackerson believed himself to be usually failed to entertain the crowd. Master Sackerson, according to Kit Marlowe who was one of the bear's favourite people, had a rather subtle sense of humour, but this was largely lost on the passing playgoers and pleasure seekers who peered down into his Pit.

'Did you hear what I said?' Henslowe shouted, his face purple above the ruff. 'No Burbage!'

'What do you mean, "no Burbage"?' Kit Marlowe asked.

Tom Sledd didn't know how many other ways he could say it. A genius like Marlowe, all fire and air, probably had a hundred ways. But Tom Sledd was of the common clay. He had nothing.

'I need Burbage for the king,' Marlowe shouted.

'Don't shoot the messenger, Kit,' Sledd pleaded. 'You know what Henslowe's like. If you wanted it to go differently, you shouldn't have rigged the straws.'

Marlowe looked shocked. 'Rigged? Tom, you cut me to the quick. As if we would . . .' he caught a glimpse of Sledd's face. 'All right, so there may have been a little sleight of hand. But you know Henslowe the best. You can manage him, Tom, you know you can.' He smiled and punched the stage manager's arm lightly. 'Anyway, what did you tell him about the play?'

'Like you said,' Sledd told him. 'Tom Kyd's *Spanish Tragedy*. He seemed all right with that.'

Marlowe chuckled. 'I'm not sure Tom will be,' he said. 'I may be looking for a new lodger after this.'

'Kit.' Sledd always whined a little when something was bothering him. And something was bothering him now. 'I don't really understand this. Why all the secrecy?'

Marlowe looked at the man. He and Tom Sledd went back a long way and he knew that the stage manager would walk through the fire for him. But there was no need to tell him more than he need know. 'The Lord Chamberlain's a strange man,' he said. 'Cousin to the Queen, Privy Councillor; they don't come much higher up the tree than that.'

'So?'

'So, he has to run with the hare and with the hounds. At heart, I suspect he's an old Puritan, like the rest of them. And you know how the hard hats and stiff collars feel about the theatre.'

Sledd did. There wasn't a Puritan in the land who wouldn't cheerfully burn the Rose – and the Curtain – to the ground. And if the actors were inside, that would be even better. He'd listened to a Puritan preaching at Paul's Cross once; he'd never heard language like it.

'But recently,' Marlowe went on, 'Carey has immortal longings in him. He likes poetry, Tom. Some of us do.'

Sledd nodded.

'So he's putting a toe in the theatrical water. Taking a show on the road, rather than opening here in London. As for the play . . .'

Sledd screwed up his nose. 'I've read better, if poetry is his passion.'

Marlowe smiled. He knew a hawk from a handsaw, did Tom Sledd, but no one could call him a connoisseur of words. But he was right on the money this time. 'There may have to be . . . adjustments, shall we call them?'

'Does Kyd know?'

Marlowe looked at his friend from under his lashes. 'Not as such,' he murmured.

'By that you mean "no", I assume.'

'Look on the bright side. There may not need to be any.' Marlowe would be the first to admit he was no actor and the line certainly failed to convince. 'But if there *are*,' he added, hurriedly, 'they won't be obvious, no, not by any means.'

There was a silence between the two. They were both running a few lines of Kyd's play through their heads.

'But *if* there are,' Sledd said for them both, 'there's no need to let Kyd know in advance, is there?'

'No, no, indeed.' Marlowe gave a stagey shake of the head. 'Not at all. And . . . if all else fails, well, I expect I may have . . . something.'

Sledd's ears pricked up. 'Something new?'

'Unperformed.'

'Hmm . . .' Sledd racked his brain. He couldn't think of what it might be.

'Allegorical.'

Sledd shook his head.

'It's best you don't know,' Marlowe said. 'If you don't know, you can't tell, can you?'

Sledd's eyes widened. 'Not . . . not Master Topcliffe?'

Marlowe laughed. 'Good Lord, Tom, what do you take me for? I wouldn't imagine that a simple play would interest the Queen's dungeon master. No, I just mean, you can't accidentally tell Tom Kyd. He is my lodger, don't forget. And a friend, of a sort. Be reputed wise, Tom, for saying nothing.'

Sledd shrugged and turned away, cannoning into Shaxsper as he went. 'Sorry, Will, didn't see you there. Can't stop – things to do, you know.' And indeed he did. He had timber to buy, carts to hire. A travelling troupe doesn't float on air, after all. At the door, he paused and turned. 'And don't forget – and you're my witness, Will – there is no way in Hell that I am playing Queen Dido, Zenocrate, Catherine de Valois or Helen of bloody Troy! You know Ned Alleyn's not my type.'

Shaxsper and Marlowe watched him go, with a grin.

'Anyway,' Shaxsper said, having listened outside the door for long enough, 'you don't know where he's been. Who *is* playing the female lead, by the way?'

Marlowe looked at the erstwhile playwright and stroked his chin. 'Ever thought of losing the beard, Will?' he asked, thoughtfully.

Philip Henslowe may have reluctantly allowed some of his actors to go on the road with the Lord Chamberlain's Men, but he had refused point blank to allow them to use his theatre to audition for other parts. He knew, he told Marlowe in no uncertain terms, when he was being taken for an idiot. So Marlowe was sitting on a settle at the sign of the Mermaid across the river – he wouldn't put it past Henslowe to listen in and then put a spoke in his wheel. The man would stop at nothing, even as he paid lip service to the idea of going on the road. There was a goblet of wine before him, a sheet of paper beside him, a list of names on it, largely scratched through.

'Who?' Marlowe wasn't quite sure he'd heard.

'John Foxe,' the actor said. 'With an "e".'

'What have you done?' Marlowe asked. 'Would I have seen you in anything?'

'*Ralph Roister Doister*,' the actor said proudly.

Marlowe grimaced. *Everybody* had done *Ralph Roister Doister*. 'Anything good?' he asked.

Foxe smiled. '*Tamburlaine*,' he said.

Marlowe sat up straighter. 'Really? Where?'

'For the Queen,' Foxe told him. 'At Nonsuch, two years ago. When my Lord Chamberlain announced the tour, I leapt at the chance, Master Marlowe. And may I say what an honour it is . . .?'

'Yes, well, of course. Tamburlaine, eh? What did you think of the Scythian shepherd?'

'A part to die for, if I'm any judge. There is one thing, though. I understood from my Lord Chamberlain that we were doing *The Spanish Tragedy*. But only yesterday, I heard . . . I didn't realize . . .'

'Nobody does,' Marlowe smiled. 'Tell me, Master Foxe, can you keep a secret?'

'But there's nothing wrong with it!' Tom Kyd was insisting. It was largely the ale talking. In his heart of hearts, he knew the *Spanish Tragedy* needed work, but Ned Alleyn was a man who got right up his nose and Kyd was a man who didn't take criticism well.

'Oh, come on, Kyd,' Alleyn sneered, a girl on each arm. 'It's unworkable. I *do* have a reputation.' He winked at the blowsier one on his left.

'I can see that,' Kyd muttered.

'John, you're a new face to us,' Alleyn called across the table. 'Honestly, what do you think?'

Foxe held up both hands, faced as he was with the theatre's greatest tragedian and a tall, gangly playwright on the defensive. 'And it's precisely *because* I'm new, I have no comment,' he laughed. 'You boys work it out.'

Tonight wasn't the time for serious conversation. Mrs Isam's Ordinary in Dowgate had opened its slightly grubby doors to the gentlemen and players of the Lord Chamberlain's Men and the ale and the women flowed freely. Tom Sledd was happily married, but parties like this, before a troupe took to the road, had no rules. Everybody knew that the next couple of weeks would be hard, even assuming they actually had a play to perform and letting down a little hair in Dowgate wouldn't come amiss. So Tom Sledd slumped in a corner with one of Mrs Isam's girls on his lap.

Kit Marlowe sat in another corner, his back to the wall as it so often was. His was a difficult situation. Tom Kyd was not just a friend; the pair shared lodgings in Hog Lane. He knew that Alleyn was right, but he couldn't say it openly. A balding man slumped into the chair next to him. What little hair he had curled over his ears and the little goatee beard he had recently allowed to grow longer was pomaded to perfection.

'It *is* December, isn't it?' he asked Marlowe.

'It is,' Marlowe confirmed, catching the glazed look in the man's eye. 'And you're William Shaxsper and one day you'll be a passingly average playwright. Perhaps.'

'Huh!' Shaxsper grunted. 'Better than Kyd, anyway.' And he smiled at what he assumed to be the man across the smoke-filled room and raised his cup in a toast.

'Now, Will,' Marlowe chuckled. 'You know I couldn't possibly comment. Why are you asking what month it is?'

'Well, correct me if I'm wrong,' Shaxsper was trying to light his pipe but the damned thing wouldn't keep still, 'but who in their right minds takes a show on the road in the middle of winter? We won't be home until Twelfth Night.'

'Two things,' Marlowe had been patronizing Shaxsper for years now; he was getting pretty good at it. 'First,' he held his colleague's tinder box steady, 'there is still plague floating over the city and our own, our very own, Master of the Revels might close the theatres on a whim any moment. Second,' the flame burst into life, blinding Shaxsper temporarily and singeing his beard, 'oh, sorry.' Marlowe patted at the falling specks of burning hair that settled on Shaxsper's burgeoning paunch, 'Second, the Lord Chamberlain is only now putting his aristocratic toe in the theatrical waters – damn, the metaphor thing again – and he doesn't want it noised abroad in London. The man's a Puritan.'

'Aren't we all?' Shaxsper puffed gratifyingly on his pipe-stem as the smoke drifted upwards. He was smiling and nodding at Alleyn drowning in women and John Foxe cavorting with a dark-haired beauty.

'Indeed,' Marlowe smiled. 'And talking of that, how is Mistress Shaxsper and all the little Shaxspers?'

'Well, as far as I know,' the Warwickshire man told him. 'Susannah's ten now. Stratford seems eternity ago. Where have all the years gone, eh?'

'Where indeed?' Marlowe nodded.

A solid-looking walking gentleman loomed over Shaxsper, looking down at him. 'Is this right, Will?' he asked.

'Is what right?'

'That we're going to Croydon? Bloody Croydon?'

Shaxsper and Marlowe looked at the man. They had no idea that Ingram Frizer had such an aversion to Surrey. Frizer may have had a few already, but he caught their look of surprise. 'Let's just say,' he tapped the side of his nose, 'that Nicholas and I . . .' on cue, his friend Skeres arrived, '. . . are not exactly welcome in that borough.'

'. . . On account,' Skeres explained, 'that the last view we had of it was from the cart's tail . . .'

'. . . where we had been tied, on wrongful charges, of course, by an over-zealous Constable of the Watch . . .'

'. . . who in turn was working at the behest of a rather Calvinistic Archbishop of Canterbury who has always, I understand, had rather a soft spot for Croydon . . .'

'All this is fascinating,' Marlowe said, breaking into their flawless narrative, 'but Croydon isn't our idea. You'd have to talk to the Lord Chamberlain.'

'Oh, right,' grunted Frizer. 'I'll just pop round and see him. Hold my drink for a moment, would you?'

'Well, his man's here,' the playwright told him. 'Master Foxe . . . oh, too late, I fear.'

John Foxe was making his way a little unsteadily up the

rickety stairs to the first landing, guided tipsily by the flame-haired girl.

'Anyway,' there weren't many conversations of a theatrical nature that Tom Sledd didn't manage to overhear. He held a girl's head out of his way. 'You don't have to go, you know. Walking gentlemen like you and Skeres are ten to a groat; know what I mean?'

'Did you hear that, Nicholas?' Frizer stood to his full five foot three.

'I did, Ingram,' Skeres was a head taller, 'and I am frankly appalled.'

Marlowe and Shaxsper laughed. This was what it was all about, what drove them to the wooden O every day – the camaraderie of the cast, the fellowship of the fair.

And the ale flowed and the smoke drifted and the laughter echoed into the night.

The rats along the river lifted their noses and smelt the dawn. The tide at Dowgate was on the turn and the eddies whirled along the jetties and rope-moorings of the Queen's wharves. There was no light yet on this December morning and the Night Watch had long ago hung up their lanterns and blown their candles out.

Tom Sledd was already cursing himself for the amount he'd drunk the night before. This was nothing new, but every time he promised himself he wouldn't do it. He was stage manager of the Rose – next to the Lord Mayor of London there wasn't a higher office in the capital. And in the pursuance of that office he had to wake everybody up ready for an early start on the road. Pack horses didn't pack themselves; neither did wagons load their own flats.

One by one, he kicked them into life. Skeres and Frizer had forgotten all about their fear of Croydon and the slight they'd received from Sledd. They growled at him as they felt his patten thud into their respective backsides, slumped as they were over the furniture. Shaxsper still cradled his pipe, head down on a table. Alleyn wasn't there; neither were Marlowe and Kyd. They'd be upstairs in reasonably soft beds with bugs and, in Alleyn's case certainly, at least two women to keep them warm.

Sledd rapped on the first door he came to. No answer. No surprises there, then. He lifted the latch. John Foxe was lying on his back in the middle of the tester and the room was lit only by the light that Sledd had brought with him, a candle that guttered in the sudden draught.

'John?'

Nothing.

'Master Foxe?' Louder this time, more formal. There was no telling with actors – if they thought you were being too familiar, they would ignore you without batting an eye. 'Oh, for the love of . . .' Sledd hauled the covers off the man. Foxe didn't move. He was pinned to the mattress by a blade, the tip of which protruded through his chest. Dark brown blood had run from his sternum down both sides of his naked body. His arms were by his side, slightly splayed out. Sledd's heart was thumping in his chest, his bleary eyes suddenly sharp and focussed in the half light. He held the candle close to the dead man's face. Foxe's eyes were wide open, staring at the ceiling as though in disbelief. His lips were peeled back from his teeth in a terrible grin, as though John Foxe, in his last moments, had recognized an old friend and was happy to see him.

'Jesus!' Sledd was not a religious man but he crossed himself now and stumbled backwards. After the name of his Lord, there was only one name he could think of. 'Kit!' he shouted. 'Kit Marlowe! Where the Hell are you?'

TWO

Marlowe stood in the doorway, peering in as Sledd had done but without the shock of the new – although a dead body is never pleasant, being told by a gibbering stage manager that one was to be found in the third room on the left made it easier to handle. Foxe still stared at the ceiling, his bright hair somehow dulled and the same colour as the rusty blood which pooled beneath him and ran in a thin stream from one corner of his grimacing mouth. Watching where he trod, Marlowe crossed the room and threw back the curtains which had been pulled roughly across the window.

The thin, cold light of a winter's dawn flooded the room and bounced off the dry surfaces of the dead man's staring eyes and his bared teeth, giving highlights which Tom Sledd and his limelight would have died to achieve. The tip of the dagger, wickedly sharp, glinted at the man's chest, like a diamond brooch in the cleavage of a duchess.

Marlowe looked around the room, standing in the window bay. The noise from the street was growing, but even so, it seemed dulled by the dead man on the bed, who drew all attention. He was dressed in just a shirt, the rest of his clothes thrown anyhow all over the room, the jerkin across the foot of the bed, his hose on a chair, his venetians on the floor, the legs akimbo. Marlowe could retrace his last actions just from this. One leg of the breeches was near the door, pushed aside as Sledd had opened it. The other was near the bed, as if Foxe had shed them a leg at a time, as he strode into the room. But why was he so excited to be there? Who could have been with him?

Marlowe's eyes flickered from side to side and he lifted the jerkin with finger and thumb. He smiled wryly. The Bishop of Winchester's Geese were well versed in the arts of love but no one had ever called them tidy. A lacy nothing that had once enhanced a milk white bosom was caught up in the buttons and when he lifted it to his nose, it brought with it a scent of patchouli and exotic flowers. It was an unusual scent and one he had smelled before. He would follow that clue later. If he had guessed right, the lady in question wouldn't be going anywhere until well after noon.

He bent over the body and looked at it carefully. There was no sign of any injury except the one, single thrust which had emerged through the man's chest. The look of amazement on his face showed that he had not expected this, that he had not been arguing with anyone, was in nothing but a happy state of anticipation, now gone, leaving nothing but wrinkles behind, dangling between his thighs. He had run into the room, shedding his clothes as he went and then had fallen onto a knife.

Marlowe straightened up and stroked his chin. Unless there were a dozen knives hidden in the bedclothes, how could he have fallen just by luck – or bad luck, perhaps that should be? Carefully, the playwright felt along the bed, patting the covers gently in case more blades were waiting. But there was nothing. The other question was how the knife had stayed upright. If it had just been propped in the feather bed, then as soon as the actor fell on it, it would simply be flattened; it most certainly wouldn't have gone through his chest like a hot knife through butter, no matter how sharp it was.

He knelt by the bed and doubled over, so he could look beneath it. Mistress Isam, though no doubt a woman of parts, was no housekeeper and here she had done Marlowe a service. There was a track in the thick dust to a point just below where the dead man lay. A few drops of congealed blood hung on the bed strings, like a grisly stalactite. The gleam of a knife handle showed where it had been twisted into the stringing, a cat's cradle of death. Marlowe tested the tension. The knife was held tight in the tangle, pushed up through the mattress. Before Foxe had fallen back onto it, it would have been hidden in the plump depths of Mistress Isam's best goose down. It was ingenious, there was no doubt about that. All Marlowe needed to find out now was why – or perhaps the question was more a case of 'how' – Foxe had thrown himself back to his death.

* * *

The house where the playwright found himself was in a short alley off The Vintry, one of many that leaned in at the upper storey so that gable almost touched gable, blocking out the light. The girls in residence changed with the wind, but there were usually at least six at any one time, some living there permanently, others by the hour. Sometimes it was by the minute; the staying power of their visiting gentlemen had a lot to do with that. The door was opened by a bleary-eyed blonde, with her breasts exposed in her open gown.

She looked Marlowe up and down and bit back her snappy retort. It wasn't often that one of his stamp knocked on this door. Here was one she wouldn't throw out in a hurry. She rearranged her deshabille to look more like art than accident and smiled. 'How can I help you?' she asked, fondling a nipple casually. She had found that a nice pink, perky nipple could often seal the deal, especially with the young ones.

'Is Moll in?' he said, looking into her eyes, much to her surprise.

'Moll?' She stopped in mid-fondle and tucked her breasts away. 'She had a special last night, far as I know. Don't know if she's back yet.'

Marlowe smiled. 'Could you go and see?' A coin had suddenly materialized between his fingers and he twirled it absentmindedly.

The blonde made as if to release her breasts again and he stopped her with a raised hand. 'No, really, I've had a sufficiency. But if you *could* fetch Moll, I would be grateful.' The coin stopped its spinning and she held out her hand.

'I'll fetch her,' she said, catching the coin as it fell. 'Come through here and if she's in the house, she will be here in a moment.' Never had a groat been earned so easily.

She went through a door in the back wall of the room she led him into. All around the walls were soft couches, with much used cushions, flattened by the activity of many bodies. Some men just didn't have the time or money for privacy, but that was no reason not to get comfy. Marlowe lowered himself gingerly onto a couch and sat as upright as possible. Some of the geese, he knew, could strike like a cobra and he didn't want to be mistaken for something he wasn't. He heard the blonde shouting from the room beyond the door.

'Moll!' Then a pause. 'Moll? You up there?'

Silence.

'Moll? Anybody?'

A voice from above answered, but he couldn't hear the words.

'Well, get her down here now. There's . . .' she dropped her voice and even Marlowe's keen ear couldn't catch what she said. Then, louder, 'Yes. That's what I said. Just tip a jug of water over her if that's what it takes.'

Then the door opened again and a blonde head peered round it.

'She'll be down in a moment, Master . . . umm?'

Marlowe smiled. 'Thank you,' he said.

She came into the room. 'Are you . . . comfortable?' she said, with a predatory gleam in her eye.

'Quite comfortable, thank you.' Marlowe sat more upright, trying to make his lap as unwelcoming as he could.

'You wouldn't have to pay again,' she said. 'It's all part of the service.' She reached into her bodice once more. Her breasts were on and off stage more often than any walking gentleman.

The door behind her swung open and a girl slid in. Next to the blowsy blonde, her dark looks were delicate and finely drawn. She was tiny, with a pointed chin and large, brown eyes like a doe. Like the deer, her skin was freckled as a thrush's breast and her clothes were discreet and, to Marlowe's relief, modestly drawn up to her chin. There was only a finite amount of breasts that anyone could take so early in the morning and Marlowe had exceeded that some time ago.

'Master Marlowe!' Moll came into the room on a gust of patchouli and exotic flowers. 'How can I help you?'

The blonde took herself off on a resounding snort. She never would see how that tart Moll was so successful with the gentlemen. There was nothing to her. No wonder she wore clothes that didn't show anything; she had hardly anything to show. And yet, she had had more gentlemen than any other of the girls in the house, at better prices, too. And all of them had all their teeth, eyes and limbs – something the other girls could only dream about. Except Nancy, but then she did make something of a speciality of men with bits missing. Popular with the sailors, was Nancy.

Marlowe and Moll waited until the door had closed and he answered her question. 'You can tell me about last night, Moll,' he said gently.

She tossed a raven curl. 'That's not like you, Master Marlowe,' she said. 'Wanting dirty talk.'

He frowned. 'You know that's not what I mean, Moll,' he said, sternly. 'I want to know how Master Foxe comes to be as dead as mutton, impaled on a knife in one of Mistress Isam's best bedrooms.'

'It's no good looking at me like that, Master Sledd.' Eliza Isam was not a woman to be put off when her dander was well and truly up. 'I don't suppose a fine gentleman like yourself would know how much a fine goose feather mattress costs, but let me tell you, it's more than I am prepared to spend, just because one of your actors chooses to bleed all over it. I've had all sorts over my best goose feather mattresses, let me tell you, but never . . .'

Tom Sledd was a patient man. He had learned patience at the knee of his adoptive father, the great and, sadly, late, Ned Sledd, actor manager and all-round rogue. Anyone who could live in his shadow and not go stark staring mad had to learn how to plumb depths of calm unknown to mere mortals. It had made him the perfect stage manager for Philip Henslowe who, though less volatile than Ned Sledd, still could try the patience of a saint. But this woman had done what most had failed to do and so, Tom Sledd, without warning, lost his temper. It was as if a fluffy chick newly hatched had suddenly turned into a fighting cock, complete with steel claws. He leaned forward, a vein throbbing in his forehead. The words came out between his clenched teeth.

'Mistress Isam,' he said, evenly, 'Master Foxe did not *choose* to bleed all over your best goose feather mattress. He was stabbed by what looked to me like a knife, hidden in the bed.

Now,' he leaned in more so he was nose to nose with the brothel keeper, 'who do you think the magistrate would blame for that? Would it be Master Foxe, for foolishly falling on a knife hidden in your bedding and dying horribly, *or* . . .' he paused for effect, '*you*, for providing the bed as described and also for providing . . . how many girls was it? Five? Six? And what do the magistrates call it? "Keeping a bawdy house"? That's the one!'

Eliza Isam was brazen about her girls and usually got away with it. The Constable of the Watch in Dowgate was not averse to a quick one on a cold and stormy night once in a while and she had managed to avoid trouble, by and large. But she could tell this man meant business. She backed away, hands up, capitulating. 'I have spare mattresses, Master Sledd. Let's say no more about it.'

Sledd smiled but it was humourless. 'That's wonderful for you, Mistress Isam. But do I have a spare actor I wonder?' He put a theatrical finger to his chin and rolled his eyes skywards. 'Hmm. Do you know, I don't believe I do. And do Mistress Foxe and all the little Foxes have a spare husband and father?' Sledd had no idea whether Foxe was married, but he was well into his narrative now and there was no need to let a little thing like the truth get in the way. 'I don't believe they do.'

Eliza Isam's eyes were huge, fixed on Sledd's face. 'I . . . I hadn't thought of that, Master Sledd. I . . . I'm so sorry. I . . .' Tears spilled down her cheeks, perhaps the first ever since she was about three years old.

Sledd was staggered. He had been about to go into more detail. About being dragged at the cart's tail. Whips. Flails. Swingeing fines. But there appeared to be no need. She had taken the wind out of his sails and he patted her on the shoulder, awkwardly. 'Well,' he muttered, 'don't let it happen again.' He turned on his heel and swept out of the room.

Eliza Isam watched him go and wiped away the tears with the back of her hand. With one sniff, she dismissed Mistress Foxe and all the little Foxes. 'I shall be sure not to,' she said to the air. 'Goose feather mattresses don't grow on trees, you know.' And as for that Moll – she could keep to her own side of the river; those Geese had never known how to behave in a respectable house.

Kit Marlowe was a favourite with the Geese. He would stand them a drink whenever he saw a girl looking thirsty, but he never asked for more. Which was a shame because most of them would have happily accommodated him for free. Moll sat looking at him, tears swimming in her eyes. She had done some things in her life of which she was scarcely proud, but last night she had gone lower than she ever had before and she had spent the night wondering if she would ever sleep again. Her one consolation was that only she and God knew what had happened. And now, here was Kit, gentle and kind, who could see right through her and her lies.

'I didn't know he was going to die, Master Marlowe,' she whispered. 'The gent who gave me the money just told me to tease him a bit, get him, well, you know, get him very excited.' She caught a glint in Marlowe's eye and smiled through her tears. 'More excited than usual. I was to start . . . teasing . . .' having found a word that seemed to do the trick, she decided to stick with it, '. . . as we went up the stairs. The gentleman told me that Master Foxe liked it that way. I was to know him by his red hair and I was to sit in his lap, all the usual things, but not to ask him for money. He told me Master Foxe didn't go with girls like me, so I was to make it seem as though I . . . well, as if I was just a loose girl out on the town, doing it for pleasure.'

Marlowe was amazed yet again by the hubris of actors. John Foxe was nice enough looking, but nothing to write home about. He had a groat or two in his purse, but not enough to attract even a very loose girl doing it for pleasure. But he was an actor, hence the centre of the world.

The girl sniffed and wiped her eyes on her sleeve. She was into her narrative now and was calmer. 'I must tell you, Master Marlowe, he wasn't a hard one to tease.' She smiled at her unfortunate pun. 'He was up and running almost as soon as my arse touched his thighs. His hands were everywhere and for a man who didn't go with girls like me, he knew where everything was and how to use it, that was for certain. I hardly got him into the room before he had almost all his clothes off and all of mine.' She suddenly realized something. 'You found my kerchief, I suppose.'

Marlowe nodded. 'If you want to stay anonymous, Moll, you will have to change that perfume. You might just as well write your name on the wall as leave a thread behind smelling of it.'

'Only you notice it, Master Marlowe,' she said.

'And a few wives, I have no doubt. But carry on.'

'The gentleman said I was to play it coy once I was in the room. Let him chase me as far as the space allowed. Then, when he was good and ready, I was to push him onto the bed. Hard. And it had to be in the middle of the bed. He said, he said he liked it like that. That he could only . . . you know . . . when . . .'

She started to cry again, her face reddening and her mouth contorting. She could hardly get the words out.

Marlowe leaned forward and patted her arm. 'Moll,' he said softly, 'Moll. It isn't your fault. You've done madder things than that. Do you remember that one you told me about?' She sniffed and looked at him with big eyes. 'The one with the pig?'

She laughed through her tears. 'I remember.'

'Well, who would blame you for believing that a man likes to be pushed down on a bed. There are worse peccadilloes.'

No one knew better than Moll that that was true. The pig was only the half of it.

'But tell me,' Marlowe continued, 'who was this gentleman who paid you to treat Master Foxe? Was he someone you know?'

'I've never seen him before, or since.'

'Can you describe him?'

'I can describe parts of him,' she said, honestly. 'But I don't think it would be helpful. He came up to me in the dark, about a week ago. I was waiting on a corner for . . . well, a friend. Someone who doesn't have to pay, if you follow.'

Marlowe nodded. Even the Geese had to have friends who didn't have to pay.

'This gentleman, he came up behind me and tapped me on

the shoulder. He held out a crown and gestured to an alleyway behind him. My friend was late and I didn't see the harm. We went down the alley and afterwards . . . that's how I can describe some of him, you see, and I thought he was just a customer . . . he said I could have three more coins like it if I treated a friend of his. As a present, you might say. He said I was just the kind of girl he would like. The gentleman could tell because . . . well, he could tell.'

'There you are, then,' Marlowe said, extracting another coin like it from his purse and handing it to the girl. 'It wasn't your fault. You weren't to know.'

'But . . . he's dead, Master Marlowe. Nothing can change that.'

The playwright leaned forward and kissed her gently on the cheek. He tasted her salt tears. 'Yes, Moll, he's dead and we can't change it. But we can try and find his murderer. Leave it with me. And just for a while, don't wait on any street corners. We don't want your gentleman to come tapping you on the shoulder again, do we?'

She shook her head. 'I'll stick to the house, Master Marlowe,' she said, her hand to her cheek. 'I'll be careful.'

'See that you do.' Marlowe extricated himself from the deep cushions and made his way outside to the winter street. He took with him a scent of patchouli and exotic flowers.

'Master Marlowe,' Henry Carey smiled. 'Welcome. My son speaks highly of you.'

Henry Carey was the first Baron Hunsdon, cousin to the Queen and Marlowe had once written a masque for the man's son, George, at his castle in Carisbrooke.

'I am flattered, my Lord,' Marlowe bowed.

Hunsdon looked like George through a dark mirror. His eyes were smaller, his hair greyer and he seemed to have less affinity with jewellery. A goshawk flapped and squawked on his left wrist and he was feeding a dead chick to it. 'I must admit,' he said, 'I didn't expect to see you here.' He nodded to the man alongside him. 'Master Kyd, I assume?'

'My lord,' Kyd bowed too.

'And this?' Hunsdon peered at the third man.

'Thomas Sledd, my lord.' Sledd bowed even lower than the others. He *had* played Queen Elizabeth herself once, briefly, but he was, by and large, unfamiliar with the court.

'Somebody's man, are you?' Hunsdon queried.

'Tom is stage manager of the Rose theatre, my lord,' Marlowe explained, 'and stage manager to your very own Men.'

'Yes, well,' Hunsdon scowled. 'That's dead in the water, clearly.'

'Not necessarily, my lord.' Kyd felt he had to step in to save his play.

'John Foxe *is* dead, isn't he?' Hunsdon passed the squawking bird to a lackey. 'My man informed me.'

'He is, my lord,' Marlowe nodded, 'and we're looking into that.'

'Looking into it?' Hunsdon frowned. 'Some sort of affray, wasn't it? Knife in the dark, that sort of thing?'

'A knife in the dark, certainly,' Marlowe said, 'but an affray? I don't think so.'

'Hmm.' Hunsdon clicked his fingers and another lackey passed him a cloth to wipe his fingers. He turned his attention to Kyd. 'What do you mean, sir, not "dead in the water"?'

'Well,' Kyd shuffled his feet. 'We could find another actor.'

'Foxe is the only actor *I* know,' Hunsdon said. 'Can't call yourself the Lord Chamberlain's Men if none of the men are actually mine. Man was a servant of mine for years.'

'Are you determined, my lord,' Marlowe said, 'to take the show on the road?'

Hunsdon looked narrowly at him. 'What do you mean?'

'If we could find a great house, perhaps?'

Hunsdon thought for a moment. 'It would have to be a great house outside London,' he said. 'These wretched Puritans are making life very difficult. And then, there's the plague.'

'I was thinking of Scadbury, my lord,' Marlowe said.

'Scadbury?' Hunsdon was scratching his head. 'Oh, yes, Tom Walsingham's place. Know him, do you?'

'I do, my lord.'

'Hmm. Scadbury. Yes, that would do. That would do nicely. Now, Kyd, this play of yours . . .'

'*The Spanish Tragedy*, my lord, or *Hieronimo Is Mad Again*.'

Hunsdon's mouth hung open.

'It's a working title, my lord,' Marlowe said, ignoring the frosty look that Kyd gave him.

'Thank God,' Hunsdon said. 'It doesn't exactly trip off the tongue, does it? All right, consider it done. I'll give you a letter, Marlowe, for Tom Walsingham, so he knows it has my approval. Keep in touch with me, now. I'll be there for the opening night.'

THREE

Rehearsals were not Tom Sledd's favourite time. He had often sat in the back row of the better seats and watched with horror as his beautifully designed and painted flats transformed themselves from a realistic scene to a lot of ill-drawn and worse painted scrawls. He listened to the voices of the boys playing the women's parts break catastrophically in the final run through before the first performance. He remembered when it had happened to him and although of course the balls dropping was not altogether a bad thing – in fact it had made a man of him – it still often meant a promising acting career gone west, in a single second. He had sat there while rain poured in and flooded the groundlings' pit. He had sat there as snow piled up against the flats. But he had never sat there through such arrant drivel as he was listening to now.

'How's it going, Tom?' Marlowe's voice suddenly breathed in his ear and made him jump.

Sledd didn't answer, just sat, slumped miserably, his eyes unfocussed in the direction of the stage.

'Tom?' Marlowe poked him in the ribs. 'I said . . .'

'I know what you *said*,' Sledd replied. 'I don't have your vocabulary, Kit. I'm trying to think of the right word.'

'Ah.' Marlowe leaned back and folded his arms. 'As bad as that?'

'Worse, if by "that" you are thinking of that version of *Ralph Roister Doister* that Alleyn tried to make us do with real women in the female roles.'

'The naked one?'

'That's the one.'

'It would have got bums on seats,' Marlowe pointed out.

'And it would have got us dragged out of town at the cart's tail. This . . . well, it's only being put on at Scadbury, I know, but I have my pride!'

'No one will blame you, Tom,' Marlowe said. 'No one blames the stage manager.'

Sledd snorted. 'Don't be ridiculous, Kit, if you don't mind me being blunt for a moment. *Everybody* blames the stage manager. If their costumes don't fit. If their dear old grey-haired mother doesn't get the best seat in the house. If they forget their lines – yes, even then. They can't remember their own bloody lines and whose fault is it? Hmm?'

Marlowe knew how this conversation went. 'Theirs,' he said, on cue.

'No, not theirs. Oh dear me, no. It's the stage manager's fault. So when this pile of horse shit hits the stage at Scadbury, it will be my fault, just as always.'

Marlowe knew that this was the point where the listener unfortunate enough to get the rough edge of the 'stage manager's fault' speech simply waited while Sledd simmered down, so he turned slightly in his seat to give his friend room to twitch and grumble and waited until normality could resume.

What he saw on the stage was not much consolation. All of the cast, even the walking gentlemen, seemed to be carrying sheaves of paper, lines copied at the last minute by the room full of scholars fallen on hard times which Philip Henslowe kept in virtual slavery at the back of one of his warehouses. The pages were unlikely to all be the same, but most actors learned quickly that near enough was good enough. But by now, most actors were relying on their memories and the somewhat random help of a small boy, preternaturally early at learning to read, who was stuffed into a box under the first row of seats. During the performances he was invisible behind the groundlings, but for rehearsals he served well enough.

Amyntas, the newest walking gentleman, stood out like a sore thumb. Not only was he standing with his arms straight out from his body at a very strange angle, a rictus grin on his face, he was also a head taller than anyone else. As far as Marlowe had been able to tell, Kyd did not call in his dramatis personae for a giant, but it was hard to know. Even Kyd didn't really have a complete grasp of what was required, though he had sat for hours with sheets of paper covered in spidery writing, trying to explain to Marlowe just who was doing what to whom, and why.

Ned Alleyn was centre stage as the two watched from the dark. He was usually quick to learn, but he was struggling with his lines, holding out the paper at arm's length and squinting furiously at it.

Marlowe judged that Sledd was feeling calmer and leaned in with a question. 'I assume that this is where Hieronimo is mad again.'

Sledd sighed and closed his eyes. 'If only it were,' he said. 'He's stone cold sane at this stage. It only sounds like gibberish because . . . well, because it is.'

The two men looked at the stage, where actors seemed to be randomly walking around. Ingram Frizer had just wound back his arm and landed a nasty one on the nose of the actor playing the king, a replacement for Foxe.

Marlowe stood up and shouted. 'Oy! Frizer! What was that for?'

Frizer muttered into his chest.

'What?' Marlowe bawled.

'He trod on my foot,' he said.

'That's not much of a surprise,' Marlowe observed. 'How many people are on stage? It looks like hundreds.'

'Thirty,' said Alleyn, stepping forward and looking into the dark. 'It feels like more, I grant you. Look, Kit . . . can we talk? The lads and I . . .' he turned round for support and there were mutterings from behind, especially from the boys laced into women's dresses, '. . . we're not happy.'

'Any particular reason?' Even as he spoke, Marlowe knew he had made a mistake. The stage erupted with yells and gesticulations. Pages of script went up in the air like goose feathers on Michaelmas Eve. One voice rang above the rest, the grating tones of Walking Gentleman Skeres.

'It's a load of pizzle, Master Marlowe, that's the reason. Nobody knows who they are or what they're doing. All respect to Master Alleyn, but we can't tell when he goes mad because he talks rubbish when he is and when he isn't. And what with so many of us having more than one part,' everyone behind him nodded and murmured to each other, 'we none of us know who we are from one minute to the next.'

Skeres subsided and the stage was enveloped in an ominous silence.

A voice came from the back, high in parts, with a warble at the ends of the sentences. Sledd's head snapped up.

'Isabella's on the turn,' he muttered to Marlowe. As if things weren't bad enough already.

'Why can't we do one of your plays, Master Marlowe?' the boy quavered. 'We know the words to them.'

'Yes, Kit,' Alleyn added his voice to the throng. 'Something we know.' He smiled smugly. It didn't matter which one it was, he knew he would have the leading role.

'Or I could write something,' Shaxsper's Midland tones were soon smothered by catcalls and slow handclaps.

Marlowe picked his way down to the groundlings' pit, carefully stepping from tier to tier. 'Well,' he said, 'I do happen to have a new play we might consider. Easy to learn.'

There were cries of 'huzzah' from the mob.

'With a king in it.'

Alleyn bowed solemnly.

'And you can have the parts by this evening.'

The stage was suddenly full of beaming faces. A small boy, almost hidden by an enormous farthingale and ruff, stepped forward.

'Will we all have parts, Master Marlowe? Only, I gave up a job in the fish market for this.'

'Of course, . . . umm . . .'

Sledd had arrived at Marlowe's shoulder. 'Andrew.'

'Andrew. I don't know if you will all have lines . . .'

Skeres and Frizer glanced at each other, looking mutinous. It had been some years since they had been merely silent Walking Gentlemen and it wasn't their way to accept demotion.

'But I am sure we can spread them around, if needs be. There may be a niece or two involved. Now, I suggest that you all go and take your costumes off, get them to the seamstresses and tell them I will let them have the requirements soon. Then take the rest of the day off and come back at sunset for your pages. And . . . Mr Finch?'

The big man raised his head, a query on his face.

'If I may have a word?'

'Can I take this stuff off first, Master Marlowe?'

'Of course.' There was no noticeable difference between what he was wearing and what he had had on when Marlowe saw him last, but it was best he was comfortable when he got the bad news.

Marlowe turned to Sledd. 'He's got to go. There are too many people in this damned project, and I use the word advisedly. He was the last of the gentlemen to get a part, it's only fair he is the first to go. And I don't have parts for everyone as it is.'

'You can't get rid of anyone, Kit,' Sledd said, shaking his head.

Marlowe raised an eyebrow. 'Can't I? Whyever not?'

'Because Skeres and Frizer will raise Hell. They have a kind of . . . I don't know what to call it, really, but they have made some kind of guild where everyone pays them a farthing a play and they look after them. It won't catch on, but at the moment, I can't get worried about it. Just leave Finch where he is. Or offer him something else. If you can give that lad a niece, surely Finch's worth a nephew.'

Marlowe sighed. He didn't know what the theatre was coming to. He looked at Sledd. Was it a trick of the light, or was the man starting to grow a little grey at the temples? Ever since they had known each other, Sledd had taken on the worries of the world and was still looking for more. So if Finch had to be kept on, then so be it. But there was no way on this earth that it would be on a stage. He decided to talk about something else.

'So . . . all is well?' Lord Burghley sipped his wine. Outside, beyond the leaded windows of the palace of Whitehall, the sleet of December was driving from the west, pounding on the thick glass and trickling onto the lead.

'As well as it can be, Father.' Robert Cecil, the Queen's spymaster was only now beginning to feel his feet again. Whitehall was a huge place, spreading like a small village from the parliament houses to the Strand and to cross it, a man had to brave the elements, even on a bleak winter's afternoon. 'Except that Marlowe is with the troupe.'

Burghley raised an eyebrow. Both men knew Marlowe. He had done the Queen inestimable service since Francis Walsingham, Cecil's predecessor, had recruited him from Cambridge. Even so, the man was tricky, mercurial; as fast with his dagger as he was with his brain. All fire and air, the Muses' darling, but not a man to be trusted; not completely. All projectioners had that quality; it was what made them indispensable. An honest man was predictable, boring; you always knew which way he would run. But Marlowe? He was a different question. And with him, you knew one thing only – that he wouldn't run at all.

'Will that be a problem, Robert?' the old man asked. Burghley had watched the Queen's back now for more years than his son had been alive. And for most of those three decades, she had been the Jezebel of England, the target for any demented Papist west of Rome. Problems were what Lord Burghley did; his son had inherited them too.

'I shouldn't think so.' Cecil poured himself a glass of Rhenish. 'Our man would have been careful.'

'But Marlowe will investigate?' Burghley wanted to know.

'When a man is found murdered under the same roof that covered him, albeit briefly? Count upon it.'

'Is our man up to it?' Burghley squinted at the spymaster. 'Keeping one step ahead of Marlowe, I mean?'

Cecil sat himself down by the fire, warming his feet. 'We may have to send someone else, you know, to keep an eye.'

'Who?' Burghley asked.

'I thought perhaps . . . Nicholas Faunt.'

'Faunt?' Burghley paused, in mid-sip. 'I thought you'd dispensed with his services.'

'There was a parting of the ways, yes,' Cecil said, 'but I believe that various members of the Privy Council use him from time to time – Howard, Hunsdon; Faunt has his uses.'

'Won't Marlowe be suspicious?' Burghley asked. He knew his son to have a mind like a razor, for all he only reached most men's shoulders, but he would always be the old man's little boy and the father in him couldn't quite let go.

'Undoubtedly,' Cecil nodded, crossing one leg over the other as the fire warmed his buskins, 'but he both likes and trusts Faunt. We can give him a cover story that even Marlowe will accept.'

There was a silence. 'Shame about Foxe, though,' Burghley said. 'I liked him.'

'Hmm.' Cecil stared at the crackling flames. 'The world, Father, is full of people we like. The trouble is, we can't live with them, can we?'

'I found the girl, by the way,' Marlowe said.

'Girl?' Sledd still had vague worries about the all-naked *Ralph Roister Doister.*

'The girl who was with Foxe when he died. It was Moll. You know the one.' Marlowe sketched in with quick fingers the tiny girl with the face like a flower and hair like spun coal.

Sledd looked dubious. He was a happily married man.

Marlowe laughed and punched him on the arm. 'I know you do, Tom, so don't give me the happily married man look. She was paid to push him onto the bed.'

Sledd was outraged. 'So you took her to the Watch?'

'Of course I didn't!' Marlowe sometimes wondered whether people knew him at all. 'She isn't a murderer. She was no more to blame than a musket ball is if it is fired into someone's heart. She didn't know the knife was there.'

'Well, the man who paid her, then.' Sledd wasn't going to let this go, but at least he now had something else to be irate about.

'I don't know who that was,' Marlowe conceded. 'Moll said she could describe him, but only . . .' He let the silence speak the rest of the sentence for him.

'Only? Oh, I see.' Marlowe thought that it was one of Sledd's most pleasant features that he could still blush like a girl.

'I suppose we could check every one in London, but it would be a difficult task and I'm not sure even Moll would be up to it. I'll have to try other methods. Now, where's Master Finch?'

'I'm disappointed, Master Marlowe, I can't deny.' Amyntas Finch slumped in front of Marlowe but still managed to be a head taller than anyone else. 'I've been practising and everything.'

'I could tell you had been,' Marlowe said and that at least was true. No one could walk like that unless they had put in a lot of work on the art of Acting Natural. 'But with this sudden change of play, poor Tom has so much on his plate that he needs a good, reliable man to help him redesign and paint the sets, move everything around, co-ordinate the move of everything to Scadbury. And it strikes me that you are the kind of man who is good with his hands.' Marlowe inclined his head and Finch obligingly bent his to meet him. 'Just between us, I don't think Tom is feeling as young as he was. Tempus fugit, you know. He's been in this game a long time now and needs an assistant who can help with the heavy lifting.'

Finch stepped back and nodded. 'I see what you mean, Master Marlowe,' he rumbled. 'I don't mind what I do, I just want to be in the theatre. It's what I always wanted, even from a little 'un.'

Marlowe could hardly believe that Finch had ever been little, but he took his word for it. He was also rather relieved. Men who thought they had the theatre in their blood, no matter how misguided that belief might be, tended to be a little testy and quick with their fists. And a clout from this man would be no small matter. 'Well, that's excellent, then,' Marlowe said, slapping a bicep like a tree trunk in a friendly fashion. 'Tom will be in the room at the back, seeing what scenery will be suitable, what needs changing. If you go and find him, he'll give you something to do.'

'Will do, Master Marlowe,' the big man said and ambled off, amiability coming off him in waves.

'That went well,' Shaxsper suddenly materialized at Marlowe's elbow. 'I hung around in case you needed help.'

Marlowe looked at the man from Stratford and tried to think of any way in which he could have been useful. He was beginning to run to fat and his slightly protuberant eyes were beginning to look more than a little myopic. At best, he could have bored the man to death. 'Thank you, Will,' Marlowe said. 'That was thoughtful. Can I help you with anything?'

The would-be playwright blushed and looked down at his feet, one toe drawing an arc in the dust of the groundlings' pit. 'I just wondered . . . well, if your new thing still needs work . . .?'

Marlowe looked at the man and wondered yet again at the man's unshakeable confidence in his own tiny talent. 'Thank you, Will. I wish I had thought of that, but the copyists have it already and it's almost complete. When we are rehearsing though, who knows . . .'

Shaxsper looked up happily. 'I'll read it through and mark up any places, shall I?'

'What an excellent idea,' Marlowe said. 'Let me know.'

Shaxsper slid off into the shadows and Marlowe slumped into a seat, pushing aside a half-crushed turnip as he did so. Sometimes, he wondered why he was in the theatre at all. He looked up and saw the grey winter sky above the pit, the clouds still heavy with sleet scudding overhead. He smelled the mud at his feet, pocked with half-rotted vegetables which had either never been thrown or had been hurled back by a walking gentleman who had had as much as he could take. He heard the sawing already coming from behind the stage as Tom Sledd gutted his scenery to make his new play come alive. A London street, the king's palace, Tynemouth Castle, Paris and the open country – he'd need the lot. He also heard a brief shriek as Ned Alleyn took full advantage of being fitted for a new costume. He smiled up at the sky – he never wondered why for long.

Despite what many people thought of him, Kit Marlowe didn't actually like confrontation. If he had been able to choose his perfect day, it would be one spent doing a little writing between breakfast and a light dinner, then a walk somewhere pleasant, preferably alongside some running water, singing softly to him as he wandered. If he had company on his walk, it would be with one of the few people he loved in the world, swapping ideas, gentle rhymes, memories and laughter. The day would end as the sun went down on a gilded day, with soft limbs entwined, golden in the fading light. He had had perhaps one or two days like that in his whole life, but they sustained him on days more like the one he was living now, when he had to give good people bad news. Finch had taken it very well, all things considered. He doubted Tom Kyd would be as accommodating.

His wool-gathering had taken him across the river, his cloak wrapped around him against the flurries of the sleet, returned as dusk began to threaten. Now, he turned into Hog Lane in Norton Folgate, hoping to see the windows of his house dark. That would mean that he could put off the evil hour. But no; every window showed golden. Tom Kyd had his muse, such as it was, on him again and was wandering the house, muttering and declaiming in equal measure and making the maid mad with annoyance as she ran behind him closing doors, trying to keep the heat in.

Marlowe pushed open the door and nearly knocked the girl over.

'Oh, there you are, Master Marlowe,' she gasped. 'He's at it again. Opening and closing doors. Out in the street shouting things at the sky. Traipsing all the mud in, letting the heat out.' She lowered her voice. 'I know he's a friend of yours, sir, but why do we have to have the mad thing in the house? He treats it like a barn.'

'I'm sorry, Annie,' Marlowe said, closing the door carefully behind him and hanging his cloak on a peg near it. 'It's lovely and warm in here, though; well done for keeping the fires in.'

'It's not easy, Master Marlowe,' she said, but her dimples came back under the glow of her master's thanks. 'We're going through coal like nobody's business. I wish you'd speak to him . . .'

Speaking to him was just what Marlowe was trying to avoid, but there was no help for it. He didn't feel he was speaking out of turn as he told Annie that she wouldn't have to worry about Master Kyd and his profligate ways much longer.

Wreathed in smiles, she scurried back to the kitchen, to bank up the fire and get the roast on the spit.

Marlowe stood in the dark hallway and listened. The house seemed full of noises. Whispering fires, with the coals settling gently together, snuggling down in their red ashy beds, made the timbers of the old place creak and mutter. But above all of that, he could hear a voice rise and fall, underscored by the tread of heavy feet above his head. He took a deep breath and climbed the stairs.

'Tom, I wonder . . .' he threw open the door to Kyd's room and the sentence died unborn. The chamber was empty, except for a cat, stretched out on the hearth enjoying the blaze. The animal looked at him accusingly. If it wasn't one thing, it was another, it seemed to say. People kept calling his name and then didn't even have the courtesy to give him even a tiny morsel of fish. 'Sorry, Tom.' Marlowe wasn't a natural pet owner, but it pleased the maid and did no harm to have the creature in the house. It may even keep the mouse population down, though he had seen no proof of that.

He tried another room, his own. This time, he was more successful. Tom Kyd was standing in the window bay, leaning dramatically against the wall and gazing out into the darkening street, the black expanse of Moor Fields stretching into the distance. He was muttering under his breath and then scratching down words on a scrap of parchment in his hand. His shirt was splattered with ink and he had a wild look in his eye. He took no notice of Marlowe as he walked around the bed and went to stand beside him in the window.

'Tom?' Marlowe said. He raised his voice as though speaking to a deaf man. He had learned since Kyd had been sharing his lodgings that speaking low and sweetly when Kyd was in full flow was of little use.

Kyd looked around and then went back to his muttering, as though he had seen no one there.

Marlowe was wise to this. He found it supremely annoying that Kyd behaved like a caricature of a poet and playwright here, in this house. He wanted to remind him – often *did* remind him – that he was a poet and playwright himself and didn't go around behaving like a crazy person. When reminded, Kyd would turn gentle eyes on Marlowe and would pat him gently on the arm, as if comforting a confused child. Thomas Kyd had a hide like a rhinoceros. He was going to need that now, and more.

'Tom!' Marlowe swung him round, plucking the quill from his fingers and throwing the parchment onto the bed. 'We must talk and I can't stand this play-acting any longer. Annie is threatening to give notice for one thing, but also there is a pressing matter which can't wait. I need to get back to the theatre within the hour, so sit down and listen.'

'How is the rehearsal going? Perhaps I should . . .' he looked around vaguely. 'Some of the actors seem confused about their motivation . . .'

Marlowe sighed and pushed Kyd down onto the bed, a sudden grisly image of Foxe impaled on Mistress Isam's best goose down flitting briefly before his eyes. 'Tom,' he said, holding him down with a hand on each shoulder, 'there is no easy way to say this. Your play is . . .' what should he say? Too confusing? Too difficult?

Kyd's eyes were wandering past Marlowe's shoulder, still looking out into the night. 'Yes,' he murmured. 'I should be there. I should not have left it to you, I realize. It needs a poet to understand . . .'

Marlowe was grateful. He had not known what to say and suddenly, he did. 'Your play is rubbish, Tom,' he said and was pleased to see Kyd's eyes snap into focus on his face. 'Utter, unadulterated, unmitigated drivel. No one knows who anyone is. The mad people make more sense than the sane people. Someone may have been murdered, but we can't work out who or why or even, despite Tom's best efforts with his scenery, where. And only God knows how. So, the cast have rebelled, they refuse to do it.'

Kyd smiled slowly and poked Marlowe in the belly. 'You, Kit!' he chuckled. 'You will have your little joke.'

Marlowe let go of the man's shoulders and blew out his cheeks in exasperation. 'I'll put this simply, Tom,' he said. 'I tried to be nice and it didn't work. So, a long story cut very short. Your play is rubbish. We're not putting it on. And . . .' he looked around at the mess Kyd had made of the room, '. . . I'll give you till the end of the week, but after that, I must ask you to find lodgings elsewhere.'

Kyd looked at him. 'So, what are you saying?'

Marlowe went to the door and turned. 'Play rubbish. You leave.' He stepped outside on the landing and nearly bowled over Annie for the second time that afternoon. She was clapping her hands and dancing a little jig.

As Marlowe put on his cloak to brave the weather on his

way back to the Rose, the cat wound himself around his legs, purring. 'Well, Tom,' Marlowe said, pushing him gently aside with a buskined foot, 'I think that went well, don't you?'

'Whose idea was this, exactly?' Henry Carey was stamping his feet and tucking his hands under his armpits. The brazier on the poop deck was achieving nothing apart from sending black smoke drifting across the dock at Deptford. At least the freezing rain had stopped.

'I'm sorry, Hunsdon,' Howard of Effingham said, 'it just so happens that I am Admiral of her Majesty's bloody fleet and that means that I have to set foot on the odd warship now and then. And when I say "now", I mean now. Today.'

'Yes, all right,' Hunsdon shivered, 'but isn't there anywhere warmer?'

Effingham sighed. He was the wrong side of sixty and, if truth be told, was far too old for all this roping and tarring. But he was the hero of the Armada, for God's sake – there *were* standards and he still accepted his annual supply of rum in lieu of actual payment. 'Claverton,' he called to the *Vanguard*'s captain, 'we'll go over the ordnance later. His lordship and I have things to discuss.'

'Very good, my lord.' And Claverton watched the two old men clatter down the steps below decks. He shuddered to think what their ages would add up to if combined; and these men ran England!

Below decks was not much warmer than above, but at least, among the creaking timbers, the wind wasn't blowing around the bend in the river and neither man could see the towers of Placentia, the Queen's palace downstream. The *Semper Eadem* standard floating overhead told them she was there and anywhere within the Verge, where the Queen was, members of Her Majesty's Privy Council were on constant duty.

'So,' Howard poured a ruby glass for his guest, 'what's all this about?'

'Do you know Nicholas Faunt?' Hunsdon asked him as the feeling slowly returned to his feet.

'Never heard of him,' Howard said. Unless a man commanded a ship of the line, he barely crossed Effingham's mind.

'Cecil suggests he acts as a sort of go-between for us, given the situation.'

'The pygmy?' Howard snorted. 'What's he got to do with the price of fish?'

'He *is* a member of the Council, Effingham,' Hunsdon reminded him, 'albeit a short one.'

'He's a deviant,' the Admiral assured his friend. 'Anybody as deformed as he is has a deformed mind. Trust me.'

'I do, Effingham,' Hunsdon sighed, 'but not in this. Whether we like it or not, little Cecil, the Queen's imp, is the future.'

'God help us,' Howard grunted.

'What?' Hunsdon frowned.

'Figure of speech,' the Admiral said, 'How's the rum?'

'The what? Oh,' Hunsdon took too large a swig and instantly regretted it. 'What the Hell is that?'

Howard laughed. 'Probably beyond the palate of landlubbers like you,' he said. 'I had some in Cyprus years ago, but it was hard to get. This one's from Jamaica, imported by a Portuguese fellow I know.'

'Where's that?' Hunsdon asked. 'Up river somewhere?' He took another sip and pulled a face. 'It hasn't travelled, wherever it's from.'

'Never mind.' Howard sipped his drink with more relish. 'Now, about this Faunt . . .'

'Well, it's about Foxe, really,' Hunsdon said.

'Ah, yes,' the Admiral's face darkened. 'Bad business.'

'Cecil thinks it could get worse.'

'Really?' Howard leaned forward. 'What does Burghley think?'

'Same as his son,' Hunsdon assured him. 'The apple doesn't fall far from the tree.'

'So, are we safe?' Howard asked.

Hunsdon chuckled. 'You are, Effingham, you've got a bloody navy at your back. As for the rest of us . . .'

The Admiral was shaking his head. 'The navy can't save us from the axe, Hunsdon,' he said. 'I thought Foxe was the end of it.'

'We all did, Effingham,' he murmured. 'We all did.'

FOUR

Marlowe got back to the theatre, stopping off for his usual chat with Master Sackerson. The bear had been old when the poet was born, living a hand-to-mouth life in a forest somewhere south of Linz. He had been captured to be trained as a dancing bear, but his sense of rhythm had let him down and he had been rescued by Philip Henslowe, who knew a bargain when he saw one. Now, he was a little moth-eaten in parts and couldn't always remember what he had had for breakfast but he was always pleased to see Kit Marlowe peering over the wall of his Pit and yawned a greeting from the dark depths of his bedding, piled against the far wall. Marlowe threw him an apple, wizened now and almost the last of the store. Winter would soon be upon them and the bear would hunker down, sleeping away most of the day.

First read through was always an exciting time. The main leads like Alleyn had nothing to worry about, but everyone else had a lot to prove and it was by no means a given that they would have a speaking role or even a walk-on part. But this time, Marlowe had promised that there would be something for everyone so there wasn't quite such an electric atmosphere with sharp elbows and sharp glances everywhere. The cast from Kyd's aborted play were sitting, standing, lounging on the stage, waiting for Marlowe to arrive. The parts had been delivered, some with the ink still wet and smearing on the last pages. They were stacked on the apron and everyone was watching them as if they might get up and walk off otherwise. Alleyn, his sight growing longer with age, thought he could see his name on the top copy and he was trying to judge from a distance whether it was significantly thicker than anyone else's. The erstwhile Isabella had been gargling with honey all afternoon and he hoped that by keeping to non-lascivious thoughts and not using his voice too much he would manage to make it through the performance at Scadbury without embarrassing himself.

Marlowe slipped in and watched and listened for a while, partly because being a projectioner was in his blood and partly because he simply liked to see his people relaxing and enjoying each other's company. As soon as the parts were handed out, there would be little enough of either. After a few moments, he stepped forward and clapped his hands for quiet. Every head swivelled towards him and silence reigned.

Tom Sledd picked up the parts and went to stand behind Marlowe, waiting to hand them out. There didn't seem to be many, but anything set in royal circles could be infinitely stretched by adding courtiers to taste; ladies and attendants for the use of.

'Thank you for coming back,' Marlowe said, raising his voice so that the minor players at the back could hear. 'The play we are to perform is *The Troublesome Reign and Lamentable Death of Edward the Second, king of England.* As you may have noticed,' and he gestured to Tom at his side, 'there are fewer parts than in the Spanish Tragedy. But not to worry!' He held up his hand to quell the mutterings, 'By sharing parts, everyone who had one before will have a speaking part. And you may also be glad to hear, the costumes are more comfortable and less . . .' he chose his words with care '. . . unusual.' The boys who had been girls cheered and punched the air. The wired farthingales had been giving them a lot of trouble, one way and another, especially when nature called. The seamstresses lurking in the wings smiled at each other and sagged with relief. They would have to work night and day as it was but it sounded as though they would at least be able to wave the company off with completed clothes, not have to go with them sewing as they went.

'I'll just give out the main roles first. Ned – you are Edward, the king.' There were titters from the walking gentlemen and cries of 'he knows that anyway'. Alleyn took the proffered part and went to sit in a front row seat, the copy held out at arm's length as was his custom these days.

'Gaveston would normally be Dick Burbage, of course,' Marlowe said, looking with exaggerated annoyance up to the eaves of the theatre where he knew Henslowe sat, looking down. The boys giggled and nudged each other. 'But circumstances being what they are, I had to recast.' He paused. Marlowe was no actor, but he could use timing better than anyone who trod the boards. Frizer and Skeres sat up rather straighter and tried their best to look even more important than they knew themselves to be. 'I know there are many of you more than up to the role and if we had been doing the whole tour, I would have shared the role out. But with our single performance at Scadbury – until we bring it back to the Rose, of course – I couldn't do that. So, the part goes to . . .'

'I feel there should be a drum roll here,' Sledd murmured in Marlowe's ear. 'Aren't you dragging it out a bit?'

'Of course,' Marlowe said out of the corner of his mouth. 'Otherwise, where's the fun?' He raised his voice and brandished Gaveston's part. 'The part goes to William Shaxsper.'

The man from Stratford walked forward, his hand to his chest and his face a picture of amazement. No one was fooled. 'Me?' he said, just managing to stop himself from snatching the pages from Marlowe's hand. 'Well, I hope I will give satisfaction.'

'He sounds like a maid in a new job,' Sledd murmured. 'Are you sure you've done the right thing, Kit?'

Marlowe shrugged. 'No. But if he has a biggish part, he might leave me alone about rewriting half of it. There's method in my madness, Tom. And anyway, he's dead by Act III, Scene II.'

'Who was Isabella before?' Sledd asked and without speaking and giving himself away, the relevant boy stepped forward and took his part. As he slid past Sledd, the stage manager grabbed his arm and pulled him close.

'If I hear so much as a single warble,' he said, through gritted teeth, 'you're out.'

The boy nodded furiously and pulled away.

'Say "Yes, Master Sledd".'

The boy swallowed and arranged his vocal chords with care. 'Yes, Master Sledd.'

Tom Sledd was a suspicious man with much to be suspicious about. 'Again.'

'Yes, Master Sledd.'

'Hmm. All right, then. But don't forget – just one warble.' He looked at the boy's face closely. 'Or spot. Or whisker.'

The boy nodded and fled. He wasn't sure he would manage another repetition without disaster and he could almost feel the spots and whiskers sprouting as he stood there. He looked down hurriedly at the papers in his hand. In Thomas Kyd's play he had been Isabella. In Kit Marlowe's he was Queen Isabella. What goes round, comes round.

Marlowe was handing out the other parts and soon everyone was quiet, thumbing through the pages, in some cases shared, looking to see how famous they might become in a few weeks' time. The playwright gave them some time and sat next to Alleyn, watching the faces of the others as they read their parts. He was watching for grimaces, secret mutters as they shared their displeasure with what they were being asked to do. But he saw nothing untoward. Skeres and Frizer were sharing the part which was once a single courtier. He would let them decide between them who said what. As he remembered it, neither of them had ever stuck to a script anyway, so he may as well have simply given them blank paper. But it was important to keep to the proprieties, as far as possible when working in the theatre.

Tom Sledd slid into the row of seats behind Marlowe and his leading man. He put his head between theirs, his chin almost but not quite resting on Alleyn's shoulder. The great man shrugged and moved away as far as he could without distancing himself from Marlowe. Really, the people one had to mix with these days! But it was important to stay in with Sledd, if one wanted to bring certain ladies with one on the road. Without turning his head, he lodged his request.

'Sledd,' he said, as if about to make an inconsequential comment, 'there will of course be room for guests on the theatre train?'

Sledd clapped his hand onto the man's shoulder. 'Of *course*,' he said, with false bonhomie. 'Mistress Alleyn will enjoy a change of scene, I am sure. Will all the little Alleyns be coming too?' He smiled at the actor and was rewarded with a muffled guffaw from the playwright.

'Mistress . . .?' Alleyn looked puzzled and a little pained.

'Oh, dear me, no, Sledd. Mistress Alleyn is indisposed at the moment, as I thought you knew. No, I thought to bring my . . . sister . . . along.'

'Your *sister*? Hmm? It might be difficult,' Sledd said. 'I only have a double palliasse for you and a guest, Master Alleyn. I had assumed that you would be bringing . . .'

'Mistress Alleyn, yes, I know. But don't worry about the sleeping arrangements,' the actor said. 'My sister and I are very close. Our entire family are famous for our closeness and we often share a bed.'

'Shaxsper has a single,' Marlowe put in his groatsworth. 'If he shares with Ned, Tom, Ned's sister can have a bed to herself.'

'Of *course*!' Sledd clicked his fingers and fished out a crumpled piece of paper and a stub of pencil from inside his jerkin. 'I'll just make a note . . . oh, but wait!'

'Yes?' Marlowe turned to Sledd with an exaggerated look of concern on his face. It was his way of stopping himself laughing aloud. Alleyn looked so crestfallen.

'I wonder . . . is this the same sister who tends to cry out in the night, Master Alleyn? If you recall, when we were last away from the Rose, she kept folks up till dawn.'

Alleyn twisted in his seat and glared at Sledd and then at Marlowe. That they were laughing at him seemed certain, but he could tell nothing from their expressions. Eventually, when their faces gave away nothing, he nodded. 'Yes,' he said, 'it is indeed the same sister. Poor, afflicted soul that she is. We . . . that is, the family . . . thought that a change of air . . .'

'Quite so,' Sledd said and made a note on his paper. 'Consider it done. Anything else, either of you?'

'No,' Marlowe said. 'No, I think everything is as it should be.'

'Master Alleyn?'

'Nothing, Sledd, thank you?'

'A pair of spectacles, perhaps?'

'Thank you, no. I have the sight of an eagle, as well you know.'

'An eagle. Yes. Well, if you're both sure, I have costumes to distribute.' And Sledd edged out of the seats and made his way to the sweatroom behind the stage where the final touches were even then being made.

After a pause, Alleyn turned to Marlowe. 'I wonder whether Sledd quite believed that the lady who will be accompanying me is my sister, Kit,' he said.

Marlowe liked a joke as well as the next poet, but this one had gone far enough. 'Ned, please; give us all credit where it's due. We know that your sister would no more sleep with you than a chimney sweep. Like the rest of us, she can't be sure just where you've been. Just bring the girl with you and be done with it. If you could manage to choose a quiet one, though, I think we'd all be grateful.'

'I'm appalled!' Alleyn gave the two words all the horror he could muster.

'I expect you are,' Marlowe said. He looked across the stage which was now almost empty. Two seamstresses were finishing the adjustments to Piers Gaveston's hose and Shaxsper was looking on aghast as one of them wielded her shears.

'Watch what you're doing, there,' he said, flinching. 'I felt the breeze just then!'

The girl clambered to her feet and stepped back, wiping her cheek with her hand. 'Sorry, Will . . . I mean, Master Shaxsper. It's just we're a bit upset. We've just had bad news about a friend.'

Shaxsper pulled at the crotch of his hose and limped theatrically away. The petty worries of a seamstress didn't really fret him unduly.

Marlowe was cut from different cloth. He stepped forward across the groundlings' pit and hopped up onto the stage. 'What's the trouble, Jane?' he asked, a kindly arm circling the girl's shoulders.

'Oh, Master Marlowe, I shouldn't have brought my worries here. It's just that . . .' she paused and dropped her voice. She wouldn't say this to anyone else, but this was Master Marlowe and it was all right. 'You know some of us . . . well, it's hard to make ends meet . . . some of us . . .' Even to him, it wasn't easy.

'I know,' Marlowe said gently. A seamstress's wage went nowhere in London and some of them had other mouths to feed. 'Who is your friend? Is she . . .?' There were lots of different kinds of bad news she could have had, from death to worse.

'It's Moll, Master Marlowe!' Jane couldn't keep her voice low any longer. It came out on a sob and she bit her knuckles to quieten herself.

'Moll?' Marlowe felt a cold hand at his heart. 'What about Moll?'

'Oh, Master Marlowe,' the girl sobbed and, proprieties or no proprieties, she buried her face in his shoulder, 'she's dead.'

It only seemed to be a matter of hours since Marlowe had been sitting on the overstuffed sofas in the house off The Vintry. There was still a faint scent of patchouli and exotic flowers and when the door at the back of the room swung quietly open, he almost expected to see Moll's gentle face peeping round at him. He was glad that it was the blowsy blonde instead; another little quiet brunette might have been more than he could bear. He had been racking his brain as he made his way across the river to see if he could remember telling anyone anything, anything at all, that would have put Moll in danger. He had given her all the advice he could to keep her safe but there had always been scant chance that she would take it; she would have told him that she had a living to earn.

The blonde girl sat down beside Marlowe, mercifully with everything tucked neatly away, in deference to the death in the house. She was tear-stained and her hair was simply strained back from her face under a kerchief. He wanted to tell her how much more appealing that made her, but this didn't seem to be the time.

She took an enormous sniff and wiped her eyes on her sleeve. 'I'm sorry, Master Marlowe,' she said, pulling at her bodice and patting her hair, forgetting the scarf. Old habits die hard. 'I can't believe she's gone.'

'What happened?' Marlowe asked, gently. 'Was she here?'

'Yes,' the girl said. 'She went out after you'd gone and did some decent business, from what she said. In this cold weather, nobody wants to linger, if you know what I mean. I've seen some of my best custom . . . well, I don't have to paint a picture, I'm sure. The cold takes some men funny ways. So you can get through a lot of business when the weather is on your side.'

She smiled a lop-sided smile. It was hard to think that Moll wasn't going to come in shaking snowflakes from her hood and jingling her purse, laughing and blessing the weather.

'But she must have brought someone home with her,' Marlowe said.

'No one saw anyone,' the blonde girl said.

'But do you usually see the men you bring back?' he asked.

'Sometimes,' she shrugged. 'Sometimes we don't want the others to see. We've all got someone . . . special,' she said, with a blush. 'Not always business, if you know what I mean. So we learn to turn a blind eye.'

'And did Moll have anyone special?' Marlowe asked.

The girl sat back, looking puzzled. 'I always thought it was you,' she said.

Marlowe blinked. 'Me?' he said. 'No. I'm friends with all you girls, you know that.'

'I think she wouldn't have minded, Master Marlowe. She would have given up this life for you.' She laughed mirthlessly. 'Mind you, it wouldn't take much for us to give up this life.'

Marlowe didn't know what to say. Moll had given up the life, of that there was no doubt. He thought perhaps a change of subject, however grisly, might help them both. 'How did she die?'

'We couldn't tell at first,' the blonde said. 'She was curled up on her bed and she looked as though she was asleep. Sarah went to call her because she had a regular come in and she shook her shoulder when she didn't answer and she . . .' the girl put her hands over her face and shook her head.

Marlowe patted her knee and waited for her to recover her control. Finally, she looked up, tears staining her cheeks.

'Her throat had been cut, Master Marlowe. From ear to ear.' She sniffed and looked up with swimming eyes. 'She didn't know about it, did she, Master Marlowe? She didn't feel any pain or anything? Any fear?'

Marlowe smiled softly at her. 'No, she would have felt

nothing,' he said, only lying a little. If this was the man who had rigged up the knife to kill Foxe, he would have struck like a snake and she would have felt nothing. He would have slashed her before getting his money's worth, that was certain; he wouldn't want her to recognize the only thing she could. The girl was beginning to cry again and Marlowe brought the conversation back to the here and now. 'I don't want you girls to have to bury her,' he said, reaching for his purse. He knew they always looked after their own.

'No need for that, Master Marlowe,' the girl said. 'A gentleman came by and left enough to bury her and pay for a wake, too.'

'A gentleman?' Marlowe asked sharply. 'Can you tell me what he looked like?'

She waved her hands vaguely in the air. 'Tall. Tallish, perhaps. Not fat. Unless he was only tallish, in which case he might be a bit on the heavy side.'

'Hair?'

'Yes. He had hair.' She twirled her hand around her head. 'Not like yours. Short. But definitely hair.' She looked up at the ceiling. 'Or it might have been a hat.'

Marlowe started to struggle out of the cushions.

'I'm sorry I can't be more accurate, Master Marlowe,' she said. 'But he was just a man who knew Moll, I expect. That's most of the men in London, if you think it through. We were upset. Crying, you know.'

'How long had she been dead?'

'When?' She was puzzled.

'When the gentleman called to leave the money for her funeral.'

She looked at him for a moment, then he saw the light dawn. 'Not . . . long. Master Marlowe, was he the man who killed her, then?'

'Unless he is in the habit of randomly paying funeral expenses for people he doesn't even know are dead, then yes. Are you *sure* you can't tell me more about his appearance?'

The girl shook her head.

'Well, if you can't, you can't.' Marlowe was finally on his feet, freed from the clinging cushions. 'If you do remember anything, then let me know. A message at the Rose will find me. But please, *please* don't tell a soul we have spoken.'

'Did Moll . . .?'

'I don't know if she went looking for him or he for her. But if you see a tallish man with hair then remember, least said, soonest mended.' Marlowe reached into his purse and took out two coins. 'One for Moll; buy her some flowers. The other is for you; stay at home today, on me. Think about Moll and don't forget her.'

She stood and watched him go then sighed, tucking the coins into her bodice. What did a girl have to do to catch a man like Christopher Marlowe?

The cranes swung in the Vintry that night, creaking in their chains and timbers. Along the Queen's wharves, the merchantmen rode at anchor, the sluggish Thames lapping against their tarred, clinkered hulls. The rats scurried along the cables, gnawing here and there at the hemp and skittering into the shadows of the planking on the quays, tails high and whiskers alert. Kit Marlowe followed them into the shadows, like a pied piper in reverse, driving the wet-furred creatures ahead of him. But he carried no pipe and his clothes were darkest black, so that he could vanish into the night.

The house he was looking for was typical of the dwellings north of the river. It was large and old, leaning towards its opposite number across the street. The lane gleamed silver for a moment under the fleeting moon, then the clouds closed again and it was lost in blackness. The first floor. Why was it always the first floor? He checked the window ledges. They were firm enough, so he shinned up the brickwork until the brickwork stopped, then he had to drag himself hand over hand from timber to timber, feeling the plaster cold on his face and hands. He peered in through the lattice window. Darkness. He didn't know – couldn't know – whether John Foxe's rooms had been re-let. He cursed himself for not having done this sooner and now, it might be too late. For all he knew, the nest into which this cuckoo was stealing was full of fledglings, all of whom would wake up screaming blue murder when he freed the casement. That was a risk he would have to take. In an instant, the dagger was in his hand and its blade-tip was springing the catch. He swung the window wide and peered in. The moon helped him now, lighting his way as clearly as a candle. There was no one there, but there had been. Foxe's travelling chest stood open and empty. His bed had been ransacked, the sheets and mattress torn with a blade. Even the curtains had been slashed and in one corner, the floorboards had had their nails ripped out, rattling as Marlowe stepped on them. Whoever had been here after John Foxe had carried out a very thorough job. His spare shirt and venetians lay strewn on the floor, his cloak, shredded, dangling from a peg behind the door. There was just one place left for Marlowe to look – the press which loomed dark against the far wall. But before he could reach it, he heard a rustle in the room's darkest corner and spun round, his dagger slashing the air and scraping on another blade, coming at him out of the darkness. A second clash and this time Marlowe struck home, feeling his knife rip velvet and skin and hearing a hiss of pain. A figure was stumbling backwards, clutching his arm and breathing hard. Then he hauled over the press in Marlowe's path and was gone through the now open door. Suddenly, the house was alive. Candle lights and lantern beams danced in the darkness. Dogs barked and shouts and screams sounded in the Vintry night. 'Who's there?' Marlowe heard somebody shout, but whether they were asking him or his mystery assailant, he didn't wait to find out.

Marlowe's bay clattered over the drawbridge at Scadbury, a little before noon. He had been riding hard since early morning, the wind at his back and he was frozen to the marrow despite the padding of his Colleyweston cloak. The great house had stood ahead of him for miles, like a grey ghost in the mist and he had trotted up the slope through the orchards and hopyards, dead and deserted now in their winter stillness, the poles and wires empty and waiting for spring.

Frost had sprinkled the hovels he had ridden past as he left London, but as the day lengthened, the ground had warmed and the hedgerows of the closed sheep pens stood stark and dripping in the morning.

The gates of Scadbury were thrown back and there was no guard. In a way, Marlowe expected more. Thomas Walsingham was not merely the Lord of the Manor; he was cousin to the late, lamented Queen's spymaster, Sir Francis, a man whose home had every concealed contrivance known to science secreted in its walls.

A priest in a white alb and Puritan collar was crossing the courtyard as Marlowe reined in.

'Master Marlowe?' he greeted him. 'I am the Reverend Richard Baines, priest of the parish of St Nicholas and chaplain to Thomas Walsingham. Welcome.'

'Thank you, Master Baines,' Marlowe shook the man's hand, gratefully swinging out of the saddle before handing his reins to a lackey.

'I'm afraid Sir Thomas is not at home at the moment. He was called to London unexpectedly. You may have passed him on the road.'

Marlowe had not.

'But if you'll come this way, Mistress Walsingham is expecting you.'

Marlowe followed the man up a twist of wooden stairs to the first floor, past the plodroom and what had clearly been a nursery. What was once the solar had been enlarged and extended to be a great brown parlour, its windows to the floor and allowing the cold light of December to flood the chamber. A wolfhound, shabby and grey, raised a tired old head from the Ottoman rug in front of the huge fire, but other than that, paid Marlowe no attention at all.

'Master Marlowe.' The lady near him stood up and crossed the floor. She was beautiful in a haughty way with a mass of auburn hair caught up in a snood of pearls and Marlowe imagined that this was probably how the Queen had once looked and how she still saw herself, despite the black teeth and sagging breasts. Audrey Walsingham would have many years to go before she found herself in that position. 'Welcome to Scadbury.'

'Thank you, my lady,' Marlowe bowed. 'The honour is mine.'

'Audrey, please.' She raised her hand for him to kiss and

held it against his lips for just a trifle longer than was strictly necessary. 'Baines,' she said to the priest, barely turning her head, 'see them in the kitchen, will you? Master Marlowe and I will take luncheon.'

The priest looked less than pleased to receive an order normally given to a steward but he bowed briefly and left.

'Puritans, eh?' Audrey murmured and patted the settle beside her.

Marlowe sat opposite her on a settle of his own, the great dog snoring between them.

'I'm afraid,' she said, 'poor old Padraig isn't what he was. Do you like dogs, Master Marlowe?'

'I can take them or leave them,' Marlowe smiled.

'Tell me, Master Marlowe,' she said, leaning back and resting one hand on the carved arm of her seat, the other caressing the smooth fabric of the cushion beside her, 'what play do you have in store for us?'

'*Edward the Second*, Audrey,' he told her, 'a little something of my own.'

'Edward the second,' she repeated. 'They killed him, didn't they? Rebellious earls, that sort of thing?'

'That sort of thing,' Marlowe nodded. Few women he knew had much of a grasp of history.

'And what made you write about that?' she asked.

'Its dramatic possibilities,' Marlowe said. 'To kill a king is a serious matter.'

'With a poker up his fundament,' Audrey said, without a hint of embarrassment, 'red hot, as I understand it.'

Marlowe blinked, but carried on regardless. 'I leave such directions to my stage manager,' he said. 'Thomas Sledd. I'll introduce you.'

'Christopher Marlowe,' she said, looking him up and down. 'The Muse's darling. They say you are the finest playwright in England.'

'They flatter,' Marlowe laughed.

'And what does Mistress Marlowe say?' she asked. She had already looked at his hands and saw no wedding band.

'Very little,' Marlowe said. 'She does not as yet exist. Unless, of course, you ask after my mother.'

Audrey laughed. 'Not the marrying kind, eh? Well, neither is Thomas but I am persuading him of the error of his ways. There is a great scandal in this house, Master Marlowe; Thomas and I are not man and wife. Are you shocked?'

'No, Audrey,' he smiled. 'I am not shocked.'

'Good, because Thomas speaks highly of you.'

'He is very kind.'

She stood up and he with her. 'Let me show you the great hall,' she said, 'before we eat. The weather is too unkind, I fancy, for an outdoor performance but I think your Master Sledd will be intrigued by the hall. It has . . .' she closed to him and hooked a finger in an errant curl, tucking it behind his ear as if putting a child to bed, 'nooks and crannies, confined spaces.'

Marlowe smiled and released the lock of hair to fall again with the others. 'Ideal for a conspiracy,' he said.

FIVE

'So, Kit.' Thomas Walsingham was a head taller than his mercurial cousin the spymaster and years younger. 'You've met Audrey. What do you think?'

He and Marlowe were sitting in the brown parlour as night settled on Scadbury. Whatever business he had had in London had been handled quickly and he had ridden back through the short December afternoon, his black flecked with foam and breathing hard as he clattered over the drawbridge. They had dined and Audrey had made her departure, leaving the men alone with a bottle of fine Rhenish and their pipes.

'A vision, Thomas,' Marlowe said. 'A face that could launch a thousand ships.'

'Ah, you poets,' Walsingham chuckled, freshening Marlowe's cup. 'That's *Faustus*, isn't it? My favourite, in fact.'

'I'm flattered that you recognize it,' Marlowe said.

'No, I must confess, this marriage lark intrigues me. How long have we known each other, Kit, you and I?'

'Four years, Thomas, perhaps a little more.'

'Exactly,' the Master of Scadbury said, 'and would you say that I was the marrying type, had I asked you, say, two years ago? One?'

'No,' Marlowe laughed. 'Horses. Dogs. The hunt.'

'Exactly,' Walsingham nodded. 'Then I met Audrey. Not a whirlwind romance, but she's grown on me. Believe me, I'm a different man.'

'Good for you,' Marlowe smiled.

'Now,' Walsingham leaned in closer, 'I've read the missive Hunsdon sent with you, obviously. But what's going on? Why this new play? And why here?'

Marlowe leaned back, sipping his wine. 'There's no mystery, Thomas,' he said. 'We playwrights have to put quill to parchment now and again to earn our crust. And there has to be something new. Otherwise we'd still be doing the miracle plays or *Ralph Roister Doister*.'

'Spare me!' Walsingham said.

'Quite. As to why Scadbury, that's a little tricky.'

'Come on, Kit, this is me; Tom Walsingham. You and my cousin, God rest him, were thick as thieves back in the day. You can tell me.'

'Baron Hunsdon is trying to raise an acting troupe.'

'Is he, by God?'

'It's all the rage at the moment. To be called the Lord Chamberlain's Men.'

'That makes sense,' Walsingham nodded, 'seeing as how he's the Lord Chamberlain.'

'We were going to travel with it,' Marlowe went on, 'despite the season. Unfortunately, one of our number was killed.'

'Not Burbage was it?' Walsingham asked, almost gleefully. 'Only, I can't stand Burbage.'

'No,' Marlowe laughed darkly. He'd heard that before. 'John Foxe, one of Lord Hunsdon's people.'

Walsingham shook his head. 'Don't know him,' he said. 'Baines might. My chaplain knows everybody.'

'I thought he was the parish priest,' Marlowe said.

'Well, yes, he's that too. Ambitious fellow, Baines. No doubt after the top job when old Whitgift leaves this vale of tears. Oh, no, that's a pity about the play and all. I was hoping for some sort of skulduggery. Nothing ever happens here at Scadbury.'

It was warm and comfortable in one of Thomas Walsingham's best beds that night. Christopher Marlowe always tried to do himself well, wherever he was, but he knew that whenever he was beneath a Walsingham roof, he would do himself better than well; he would be safe as well as warm and comfortable. There was something very relaxing in feeling safe for a man who spent most of his life looking over his shoulder. The mattress was soft, the linen smooth and scented with lavender. The pillows were, unless he missed his guess, stuffed to perfection with only the softest of goose down, hand-picked so that not a single needle-sharp feather remained to spear the unwary cheek. How typical, he thought, as he began to drift off to sleep, of Thomas Walsingham to think of every last detail.

The last threads holding the playwright to the day began to stretch and finally break. He hung in a hammock made of frost and starlight, his eyelids drooping as he gazed from his warm bed out at the night sky. The moon was almost full, circled with a haze of faint rainbows. The Pole Star sat beneath the moon, seeming to twinkle in the frosty air. Marlowe made a note to himself to include that star in a poem one day and let his eyelids drop over his tired eyes. It had been a long day. He stretched his legs out in the bed, feeling the cool linen against his warm, bare skin.

Suddenly, he was awake! His bare legs were no longer just touching cool linen; other bare legs were twining with his. He held his breath. This wasn't a dream he had had before, but there was a first time for everything. A hand snaked up his thigh and soft fingers walked their way across his hip and down; he stopped them just before they reached their destination and gripped them firmly. He knew without turning round to whom those sharp nails belonged. 'Good evening, Mistress Walsingham,' he murmured.

'Oh, Kit,' she purred in his ear. 'Audrey, surely?'

'No,' he said, decisively, turning over to face her, still holding her hand out of harm's way. 'I think it is definitely Mistress Walsingham, don't you?' Pressing her hand into the mattress, he hauled himself up on the pillows, making sure that his nightshirt didn't move with him. He wrapped his legs in its linen fastness and drew up his knees. Only then did he risk letting go of her hand. By the light of the hazy moon, he looked at her. Her hair was loose and hanging down her back. Her silk nightgown was cut low over her breasts and her skin glowed in the moonlight as her breath came fast and uneven.

'Master Marlowe,' she said, with much emphasis, 'I don't really mind what you call me. All I want is that you satisfy me. Thomas is . . . Thomas is a disappointment, shall we say? A well-turned calf is all very well, but the rest of him does not live up to his legs.' She made another lunge, but Marlowe was too quick for her. He had outmanoeuvred some of the best swordsmen in Europe – a love-crazed hostess stood no chance.

'And what makes you think that the rest of me lives up to my legs, Mistress Walsingham?' he asked.

He saw her teeth gleam in the moonlight. 'Let's just say, Master Marlowe,' she said, leaning forward so that her breasts swung free in her gown, 'that you didn't wake up quite as soon as you may think you did. My soldiers,' she walked her fingers up his chest and twisted them in his hair, 'had reconnoitred far and wide before you opened your eyes.' She knelt up with one movement and had her hands on his shoulders before he could stop her. 'What they found convinced me that you and I could become the best of friends before you leave my house.'

With a sudden twist, Marlowe pushed her back into the pillows and straddled her, holding her down. He leaned down, pinning her flat with the weight of his body. He felt her shudder and he put his mouth to her ear. 'Mistress Walsingham,' he said, soft and low, 'I would as soon lie with you as lie with Padraig. At least if I lay with him, the worst I would get up with would be fleas. So please, leave my bed, leave my room, leave me be. And as long as you do, I will say nothing to Thomas.'

'And what makes you think that I will say nothing to Thomas,' she said, pulling her head back so that she could look into his eyes.

He laughed down at her. 'And say what?' he asked. 'That I dragged you bodily into my bed?'

'I will say you burst into my room,' she said, defiantly. 'I will rend my gown. I will cry. He will believe me.'

'Will he?' Marlowe said. 'If I should shout now, who will believe that any of that happened. Your gown is unrent. I see no tears. What I see is a woman wearing a gown many would blush to wear for a husband. A woman who has brushed her hair, has rouged her cheek and . . . unless I miss my guess . . . other parts to take advantage of a poor Kentish boy unused to the wiles of the aristocracy.'

She laughed in his face. 'A poor Kentish boy? Would anyone believe that? You are Christopher Marlowe, to whom no sin is unknown, from what I hear.'

'You hear strange things, Mistress Walsingham,' he said, jumping off the bed and bringing her with him in a feat of athleticism that took her completely unawares. 'Now, do you want me to shout for help now, or do you want to go back to your chamber and hope that I am too much of a gentleman to tell a soul that this ever happened?'

She tried one more time to reach in for a kiss, but he still had her by the wrists and he held her at arm's length. She stared at him in the faint light through the casement and seemed to come to a decision. 'If you don't want what I have to offer,' she said, 'you are more stupid than I was ever led to believe, Christopher Marlowe. I just hope you don't live to regret it.'

'I hope to live, Mistress Walsingham,' he said, with a smile, releasing her wrists. 'And I doubt that I will regret anything. I never have so far.'

'Then may that continue,' she said, holding her left wrist with her right hand. 'I hope there will be no bruises tomorrow. Thomas will be worried if there are, I know.'

'There will be no bruises, as well you know,' Marlowe told her. 'Or perhaps you could visit Thomas now and have him hold you as I have.'

He heard her laugh softly as she slid out of the door. 'Oh, no, Master Marlowe; Thomas would never hold me as you have.' And with a click of the latch, she was gone.

The dark was useful for many things. Love. Secrets. Venom and spite. It was one of Audrey Walsingham's favourite things. It was dark now, as she met with her husband's chaplain later that night.

'Marlowe,' she said, leaning closer to Richard Baines. 'What do you know about him?'

'Cambridge man,' Baines said, 'Corpus Christi, I believe. Destined for the church, like most of us.'

'And before that?' she asked.

'Not much,' the priest said. 'He was born in Canterbury. Father was a shoemaker or tanner or somesuch. Went to the King's School – Marlowe, not the father. Choral scholar.'

'So, he's riff-raff?' Audrey checked.

Though it was dark, Baines knew his mistress well enough

to be able to picture the smile that was playing on her lips. ''Fraid so,' Baines nodded.

'That doesn't surprise me,' she sneered.

'Became the blue-eyed boy of Archbishop Parker – hence the scholarship to Corpus.'

'So he didn't actually earn his place?'

'Oh, he's bright,' Baines said. 'No doubt about that. He's probably our finest playwright, at least until somebody else came along. It seems unlikely, but Nicholas Udall used to bear that laurel.'

'Who?' Audrey Walsingham had little time for the arts.

'*Ralph Roister Doister*?'

He heard her draw in a breath, thinking. 'No. That means nothing.'

'Never mind,' he said. No one had ever accused Audrey Walsingham of having a sly sense of humour, or indeed any other kind. 'Long story short, he has a fine mind and is an excellent poet.'

'All that's on the surface,' Audrey said. 'What's underneath?' In the last of the moonlight before it went down beyond the stand of trees that marked the eastern extent of the lands of Scadbury her teeth and eyes shone as she turned to face the chaplain.

'Why do you want to know?' he asked. He knew there was no gainsaying her when she was in this mood, but he thought that he would at least ask.

'Let's just say I don't entirely trust Master Marlowe. Tom, of course, thinks the sun shines out of his venetians, but we all know what a soft touch Tom is.'

'Well,' Baines checked the coast was clear but leaned in closer just to make sure he wasn't overheard. She could feel his breath on her cheek. 'There *are* rumours, of course.'

'Ah.' She smiled like a viper. 'Now we're getting somewhere.'

'They say he's overfond of tobacco.'

'Baines!' Her slap rang around the room. Audrey Walsingham never stinted when it came to letting underlings know how she felt.

'All right, all right,' he gabbled. 'Not a hanging offence,

I know. I'm just trying to remember all that I've heard. Boys. He likes boys.'

'Does he now?' Audrey was smiling like a basilisk now. Only the dark saved Baines from a petrified future.

'I was with him in an inn once,' Baines told her. 'The Eagle and Child, it was, in Cambridge; not that the great and mighty Kit Marlowe remembers me at all. But I distinctly heard him say that people who don't like tobacco and boys are fools. But there's more. Much more.'

'That alone could hang him,' Audrey said.

'What I know could burn him,' Baines said. 'He'd go to the fire.'

'Say on.'

'He believes that Moses was just a conjuror,' the priest half-whispered. Audrey raised an eyebrow. This was getting altogether more interesting.

'That . . . that Jesus Christ and John the Baptist were bedfellows.'

Audrey Walsingham had no leanings to the Puritan persuasion and she crossed herself openly.

'The man is a damned atheist, Audrey,' Baines hissed. 'He, like the stage-fiend Tamburlaine he created, would dare God out of his Heaven. If he believed God existed, that is.'

'Audrey?' The mistress of Scadbury and all within its walls bridled. 'You would call me Audrey out loud? We need to keep to the proprieties, Richard.'

'Proprieties,' he said, sliding his arm from around her waist and running his hand down her thigh. 'Are any left to us, Mistress Walsingham?'

'Perhaps not,' she murmured, matching her action to his, with rather more attack. He gasped, then leaned into her; she was certainly not shrinking when it came to the arts of love and sometimes, when he was alone in his narrow bed, he cursed the other men she blessed with her body. He suddenly realized why she was asking so much about Marlowe and his face contorted with hatred and evil.

'All this is just a rumour,' he said, throwing his head back as her fingers did their work. 'Except . . . oh, God, Audrey . . . except the tobacco and boys bit. I heard that myself.'

'Rumours hang men, Richard,' Audrey said, pulling him towards her. 'And they burn them too. Will you write all this down? It might come in handy.'

'Now?' he hissed between clenched teeth.

'Perhaps later,' the mistress of Scadbury said.

Marlowe stood on Scadbury's battlements and watched the Lord Chamberlain's Men rattling out of the morning mist. At the head, jolting on the lead wagon, sat Tom Sledd, wrapped in a cloak against the cold. Assorted flats and timbers lay behind him, trailing coloured cloth, part costume, part bunting. The showman in Sledd couldn't help himself. Whenever an acting troupe was on the road, they pulled out all the stops, with shawms and viols, lutes and drums, dragons breathing fire and arquebusiers barking through the streets. Local children ran with them, dogs yapping and snapping at their heels, jinking in and out of the horses' hooves as the actors flaunted their wares.

The walking gentlemen walked; Frizer and Skeres and the rest in rich brocade, tossing skittles into the air and swallowing swords. None of it was real, but none of it was supposed to be. It was theatre. It was free. And the crowds that gathered at the roadside loved it.

Ned Alleyn never walked. He lounged on velvet on the second wagon, a girl on each arm and a flagon of ale between his feet. Every now and then, he threw a fake rose at a pretty girl watching from the roadside, but otherwise he was fully engaged with his own girls, neither of whom bore a strong family resemblance to any of the Alleyns.

Marlowe smiled to himself. He didn't think it would be long before the mistress of Scadbury got her claws into his leading man and he couldn't see Ned Alleyn being as resistant as he had been. Shaxsper with his new-found status as second on the playbills, rode in the third wagon. He was already wearing a natty little number he had chosen from costume for his role as Piers Gaveston, the ingle of Edward the Second. Every time he thought of it, he gave himself a shake. He was a happily married man – well, married, anyway – and a real actor had to cope with difficult parts sometimes. He'd get over it.

One by one, the troupe rattled under the archway that led to Scadbury's courtyard. Sledd, Alleyn, Shaxsper, the new assistant stage manager, Finch, various people Marlowe barely recognized, Nicholas Faunt . . . Faunt?

'I don't know what analogy to use,' Marlowe said. 'Bad penny?'

'Less than kind, Kit,' Faunt smiled and nodded, speaking out of the side of his mouth. 'Less than kind.'

'It's just that I hate to use clichés such as "What are you doing here?"'

Faunt glanced from left to right and twirled under the archway that led to the knot garden and the butts. He pulled Marlowe with him. 'Tom Walsingham,' Faunt hissed. The man had once been the secretary of Francis Walsingham, the late Spymaster. There was no one better versed in the arcane arts of espionage than Nicholas Faunt.

Marlowe was unimpressed. 'What about him?'

Faunt glanced back to the courtyard of the great house where the wagons were being unloaded and Lewknor, Walsingham's steward, was barking orders. 'Let's just say,' he said in the low, level growl he used in the passageways of Whitehall, 'that there are certain . . . irregularities, shall we say?'

'Nicholas,' Marlowe said at the same pitch, 'It's me – Kit. You're going to have to do better than that.'

'So, of course, I leapt at the chance to join the Lord Chamberlain's Men. Who wouldn't?'

One of Walsingham's lackeys walked past with a pair of his dogs on leashes.

'Quite, quite,' Marlowe smiled. 'What part had you in mind?'

Faunt was whispering again. 'The part that keeps us all safe in our beds,' he said.

'Sorry,' Marlowe shook his head, 'that still doesn't cut the mustard.'

Faunt waited until the dog-handler was a diminishing speck among the reeds that edged the moat. 'The Queen is old,' he said. 'Her friends are dying around her. There are whispers of the succession.'

'Ah.'

'Well, we all know about Anjou, Alençon, Dudley, all the others. Ralegh was the flavour for a while, more recently Essex. It was fun once. Now, between you and me, it's a little nauseating.'

'How does any of this involve Thomas Walsingham?' Marlowe asked.

'First,' Faunt said, 'Let me ask you what you nearly asked me – what are you doing here?'

'Performing my new play,' Marlowe shrugged. 'Edward the Second.'

'No, I mean, why *here*? Why Scadbury? Why not the Rose? I can't see Philip Henslowe objecting to a new play by Christopher Marlowe.'

Marlowe laughed. 'There are plays and plays, Nicholas,' he said. 'Henslowe likes the cash a play brings in, but he doesn't like adverse publicity. Kyd's play would have brought in a fine crop of not-so-fresh vegetables. My play, possibly something worse.'

'I had heard that *The Spanish Tragedy* is perhaps not the easiest play to sit through.'

'I'm interested to hear you say that,' Marlowe said. 'Has anyone ever sat through it? Because if so, I would love to know the plot.'

'Are you telling me your play is worse?' Faunt raised a doubting eyebrow.

'I'm telling you it's dangerous – or potentially so, anyway. And you're getting off the point, as you so often do.'

'No, I'm not,' Faunt insisted. 'You haven't told me why Scadbury.'

'The Lord Chamberlain believes – and he's probably right – that his Puritan friends won't approve of his having an acting troupe, so he's trying them out outside of London. Knowing Tom Walsingham as I do, I thought of Scadbury.'

'How long have you been here?'

'A day,' Marlowe said. Then, remembering the night before, added, 'but it seems longer.'

'You've spoken to Walsingham?'

'A chat, yes,' Marlowe said. 'And I dined with him and his wife last night.'

'Hmm,' Faunt was wandering down the lawn that sloped to the butts. 'But she's not his wife yet, is she?'

'It appears not.'

'Well, all's well there,' Faunt said. 'She's just a little more brazen than most.'

'Tell me about it.' Marlowe suppressed a shudder.

'I couldn't,' Faunt said. 'Now, you tell me, did the conversation at dinner take on a Northern perspective?'

Marlowe blinked. 'You've lost me there.'

Faunt sighed and came to a decision. 'I can see I'll have to be plain,' he said. 'I see that you working for the Queen's new Spymaster has dimmed your brain a little. In the event of the Queen, God preserve her, dying without issue . . .'

'. . . As she must,' Marlowe cut in.

'Indeed,' Faunt nodded. 'In that eventuality, who is Her Majesty's most likely successor? Her closest relative?'

Light dawned. 'You mean . . .?'

Faunt checked the coast for clarity one more time. 'Precisely,' he said. 'That sad pederast whose tongue is too big for his mouth, His Majesty the King of Scots.'

'So, when you said, "Northern perspective" . . .?'

'The day is coming, Kit,' Faunt murmured, 'when men will have a stark choice. The Queen of England or the King of Scots. But for now, any talk of the latter is strictly banned. And anyone who openly touts for James risks his head, literally.'

'And you suspect Walsingham?' Marlowe was incredulous.

'I suspect everybody,' Faunt said.

'A more loyal man never drew breath,' the playwright went on.

'I hope you're right,' Faunt muttered.

'Nicholas, you worked for the man's cousin, as did I. Tell me, as one projectioner to another, can you seriously doubt Thomas?'

'Kit,' Faunt looked the man in the eyes, 'these are dangerous days. The Privy Council is trying to hold the damned country together, but the Queen is becoming a liability. If only she'd listened to Burghley's advice – well, everybody's advice, really – and married, we'd have heirs to the throne coming out of our arseholes by now and they'd have heirs too. As it is, well, any Johannes Factotum is likely to cast in his lot if he has even the remotest claim to the throne. Heresy though it is to say so, that's exactly how the bloody Tudors got it in the first place.'

There was a long silence.

'Now, I know Tom Walsingham is a friend of yours. And I *could* be wrong – it's rare, but it has happened. All I'm doing is keeping an eye while I'm here. When's the play going on?'

'A week today, we'd hoped,' Marlowe said.

'If I haven't learned all I need to by then, I promise you I'll move on to my next port of call. It's not just Walsingham we're interested in.'

'When you say "we" . . .?' Marlowe raised an eyebrow.

'Burghley,' Faunt said. 'I'm working for Burghley.'

'Master Sledd,' Amyntas Finch said, his hands on his hips. 'May I ask why, if I was not needed in the role of walking gentleman, that *that* gentleman,' he inclined his head towards Faunt, 'is now a walking gentleman?'

Tom Sledd straightened up from counting soldier's helmets for the battle scene, holding three fingers in the air, 'And three makes fifteen,' he said. 'There were a lot of gentlemen there, Amyntas,' he said. 'What's your point?'

'I was just wondering,' the big man said, 'why I am now assistant stage manager and he is a walking gentleman?'

Sledd shrugged. 'He's probably rubbish at carpentry and carrying heavy stuff,' he muttered, 'whereas you are really rather good at both, aren't you?'

Finch grinned. 'Am I?' he said. 'Comes from cutting up beasts, I suppose. Gives you all sorts of strange talents you didn't know you had. If you can carry a carcase, you can certainly carry scenery. It's all in the legs.' He demonstrated with a couple of deep knee bends, breathing loudly out through the nose and in through the mouth.

'It's as good a training as any,' Sledd agreed. All actors were cattle, he had learned that early, so carrying carcases and putting on plays had to have a lot in common. He had been surprised himself to see Nicholas Faunt suddenly part of the company, but he had stopped trying to second guess Faunt and Marlowe years ago. He had simply doffed a metaphorical cap at him and added a completely fake name to the wages manifest. As he had no intention of paying Faunt – he had never found out precisely but was pretty sure that projectioners were, in general, richer than Croesus – it hardly mattered what he put. The accountant would be puzzled one day in the future by Guitruud Clutterbuick, but sufficient unto the day was the evil thereof when it came to paying actors.

'So, you think I might have a future in being an assistant stage manager, Master Sledd?' Finch was relentless. Sledd knew that Philip Henslowe would never part with enough money to provide him with an assistant, but the idea was very seductive. The odd evening off, for example, might be covered by an assistant. Someone to hold the other end of a recalcitrant piece of scenery. Even . . . and here Sledd went off into a happy reverie . . . a day's holiday now and again. He could take the family to the goose fair. He could . . . actually, it had been so long since Tom Sledd had had a day of leisure that he had no idea what he would do. But there were probably many things, if he put his mind to it.

'I'll see what I can do, Amyntas. May I ask *you* a question?' he said, straightening up and stretching his back, his hands on his hips.

'Of course,' Finch said, trying to look intelligent.

'Are you sure you still want to be called Amyntas? I mean . . . it was your stage name, wasn't it?'

Finch was wounded. 'I am still in the stage business, Master Sledd,' he said, peevishly. 'Every person working in the theatre could become a leading man one day. I heard that somewhere.'

'Ah, Right. Well, as long as you're sure.'

'Certain, Master Sledd. I'm not sure I would even answer to George any more, anyway.'

'Then Amyntas it is,' Sledd said. He had heard far worse. For example, what kind of name was Ingram Frizer when it was at home?

SIX

'Frizer? Skeres? Are you free for a moment?' Tom Sledd could have kicked himself. Of *course* Frizer and Skeres weren't free. They charged for their time, no matter what they were doing, whether it was their supposedly legitimate business or something far darker about which it was best not to know.

On cue, they glanced at each other and nodded, stepping forward to see what Sledd could possibly want. They were not that happy being out of London for so long. Sometimes, yes, it was not unwelcome, a change of scene, not hiding, of course, just simply being . . . elsewhere briefly. But at the moment, they had a lot of irons in the fire; fish were frying, pies needed their fingers. But they had heard of Scadbury from several acquaintances – Skeres and Frizer had no friends, certainly not each other – and there might be rich pickings to be had. If all else failed, there was always the possibility that they would catch the beautiful and famously loose Mistress Audrey doing what she liked doing best somewhere indiscreet.

'Master Sledd,' Skeres said smoothly. 'In what way may we be of assistance?'

'There's no money in this,' Sledd thought it only fair to point out.

Frizer shrugged. 'We don't always want money, Master Sledd. That's insulting, that is. You've never met a man kinder to old ladies than Nicholas here. Why, I've seen him . . .'

Skeres looked startled at what Frizer might be about to divulge and Sledd held up a hasty hand. 'No insult intended, lads, I assure you,' he said, hastily. 'Only, I have in error omitted to bring any copyists with us. A play as new as this is bound to need alterations and I suggested to Master Marlowe that we may need a few. He was pleased to offer a guinea to anyone who would be able to go and fetch him a couple. From Master Henslowe's team, I mean.'

The conversation had not been quite that simple. Marlowe had walked into Tom's makeshift workroom and asked him where the copyists were lodged, as he had a few insertions that were needed as quickly as they could get their quills sharpened. Sledd blushed to remember the rest.

'What copyists?'

Marlowe had stopped in his tracks as though pole-axed. 'The copyists. The minimum of two copyists. They were on the list.'

Sledd had looked at his friend, wild-eyed. 'What list?'

'The list I gave you.'

'I saw no list!'

'Well, you must have. Because everything and everyone else is here!'

It had been at approximately this point that Sledd had lost his temper and thought not for the first time of taking up a position as something calmer. A privy digger, perhaps. Or something to do with rats. 'Let me tell you why that is,' he had said, through teeth clenched so tightly they hurt. 'Everything and everyone else is here because I am *amazingly good at my job*! What I am not is a fortune teller. Where was this mythical list, then?' He had thrust his jaw out aggressively and struck rather an attitude, which in retrospect he realized made him look rather like the late king in a funny mirror.

Marlowe had stood his ground. It took more than a stage manager having a tantrum to disconcert him. 'I left it on your desk.'

'I don't *have* a desk.' That was another thing which had always rankled and Sledd added it to the pile of things to annoy him.

'Well,' Marlowe had waved a hand, 'you know. That table where you do your plans and things. There. It was perfectly obviously a list and it had "a minimum of two copyists" at the top.'

'I didn't see it,' Sledd had snapped. 'So they aren't here.'

'When will they be?' Marlowe had asked, sweet reason written all over him.

Sledd had deflated like a pricked bladder, which he had also forgotten to pack, probably. 'Tomorrow,' he had grunted.

Marlowe's eyebrow had risen alarmingly.

'Tonight, then.' What was the point? 'Does Henslowe know?'

Marlowe had shaken his head.

'I'll need some money, then,' he had told the playwright. 'They won't come for nothing, you know. Not if Henslowe doesn't know.'

'You forgot them,' Marlowe had pointed out as he made for the door. 'You pay. You can take it out of Mistress Clutterbuick's wages. Like you normally do.'

And so here he was, with Skeres and Frizer, making a deal which might just as well have been with the devil.

Skeres sipped his ale and turned to his fellow walking gentleman. 'I know we'd planned to get back to London from time to time, Ing,' he said, 'but I didn't think it would be this quick.'

'Or this profitable,' Frizer agreed. 'I didn't think he'd go for a guinea each, that's for sure.'

'How much do you think the copyists will want, though?' Skeres was always prone to seeing the fly rather than the ointment.

'Nothing, if we sell it right,' Frizer said. He had never tried, but he could probably have induced the fly to pay him for a nice healing swim. 'A nice holiday in the country.'

Skeres laughed and nudged him. 'Free board and lodge.'

'No Philip Henslowe breathing down their necks.'

'A candle what gives some light.' Skeres was thinking fast now. 'Not that tallow muck he gives them.'

'They'll be paying us,' Frizer said, a light suddenly coming on behind his eyes.

'Now then, Ing,' Skeres said, suddenly serious. 'Don't let's run before we can walk.' He looked thoughtful. 'It *is* an idea though, I grant you.' He glanced out of the window of the Mermaid at what showed of the day through the greasy panes. 'We shouldn't be sitting here all afternoon, though. We have to get those copyists back before midnight or . . .'

'Or?' Frizer was scornful. 'It's Tom Sledd. What's he going to do?'

'It's Kit Marlowe I worry about,' Skeres said. 'There's plenty *he* could do.'

'What's Kit Marlowe?' A head was suddenly between theirs and they both jumped.

'Ha!' Frizer said, trying not to choke on his ale. 'Master Poley. I didn't see you there.'

'Most people don't,' Poley said, slipping into the settle beside him. 'Like I said, what's Kit Marlowe?'

'Oh, nothing, really,' Skeres said. 'We're just running an errand. He's down at Scadbury. Putting on a play for the nobs. You know how it is with him.'

'An errand?' Poley looked askance. 'You two? Running an errand?'

'For money!' Frizer had a reputation to keep.

'Of course.' Poley looked at the two walking gentlemen with a reptilian smile. 'Any ale in that jug?'

'Oh, sorry, Master Poley,' Skeres said, clicking his fingers at the serving girl who mimed counting coins into her hand but went off to get a new jug anyway. Almost every tavern in London and beyond was owed money by Skeres and Frizer, but they usually paid eventually and they were good customers if counted by volume not reliability.

'So, what errand?' Poley was clearly not going to give up.

'He's got this play we're doing . . .' Skeres began.

'We're two noblemen at the court of Edward the Second,' Frizer added. 'With lines and everything. I,' he held his hand to his breast, 'am Sir John of Hainault – on account of how I can do the accent.'

'And I,' said Skeres, in no accent known to man, 'am Rice ap Howell. Look you.'

'Have you gone native, you two?' Poley asked, pouring himself some ale from the newly delivered jug.

'Waddya mean?' Frizer asked, poking Poley in the bicep.

'Do that again, Frizer,' Poley said through clenched teeth, spinning in his seat and reaching for the dagger he kept at his back, 'and it will be the last thing that finger ever does. Or arm, even.'

'Yes, Ing,' Skeres weighed in on the winning side, his

favourite. 'You're always doing that. I'm black and blue some days.'

'Well, I'm sorry, I'm sure,' Frizer said, edging away from Poley as far as the settle would allow. 'So, like I said, we're these two noblemen, with lines and everything. But the play is new. He's still writing bits of it, I reckon, so he needs a couple of copyists.'

'Got all the jargon, I see,' Poley said, sneering.

'Well, we have to blend,' Frizer said. 'No good sticking out like sore thumbs, is it, Nicholas?'

'And,' Skeres' voice held a touch of awe, 'the pay's not bad, either.'

'In fact, you might almost say, the pay's the thing,' Poley said. 'You soon won't need your other little side-lines.'

Skeres and Frizer were outraged. Finally, Skeres found his voice. 'We'll never give those up,' he said. 'It takes a lifetime to learn what we've learned.'

'So,' Poley said. 'Copyists, you say. Do you know where to find them?'

'Oh, yes,' Frizer told him. 'Philip Henslowe has dozens. We'll just . . . persuade . . . a couple of his.'

'Philip Henslowe has dozens of what?' This time the voice came from the doorway. Thomas Kyd lounged there, tall and skinny and as pissed as an owl who has been drinking for three days without stopping.

'Who're you?' Poley said. He liked to know who was talking to him at all times. Being addressed by a couple of yards of pump water in fancy clothes did not sit well with him.

Kyd slouched over to the table and fell, rather than sat, on the bench. 'Is there any ale in that jug?'

With a resigned sigh, Skeres clicked his fingers again and the serving wench stumped off to add a few more scratches to the tally and bring more drink.

'Copyists,' Frizer said. He had never much liked Thomas Kyd. He was a jumped-up little nobody and his play was shit. He had had a line but he had had no idea what it meant.

'What?' Kyd looked up, puzzled.

'Philip Henslowe has dozens of copyists.'

Kyd narrowed his eyes, then regretted it because it made

his head ache. He supported his chin in his hand, not that it helped much. 'Damn copyists to Hell,' he said, as best he could. 'They made a nonsense out of my play, that's what they did. They couldn't follow a line if their lives depended on it.'

'What play was this?' Poley asked.

'*The Schp . . . Schp . . .*'

'*The Spanish Tragedy*.' Frizer filled in the blanks. They hadn't got all day.

'Oh,' Poley said. 'I have heard that it is very good. Nice clear narrative was what I had heard.'

Kyd lifted his head and his eyes shone. 'It *is*,' he cried. 'It *has* got a nice clear narrative. It has, hasn't it, Master Frizer?'

'Clear as . . . clear as day,' Frizer agreed. He was thanking his lucky stars that this idiot was too far gone in drink to remember that it was Skeres and he who had led the discontent about the convoluted nonsense.

'Yes. It *is*.' Kyd was looking happier.

'So, why isn't it being performed?' Poley looked around the table, puzzled.

Kyd leaned forward, resting on his forearms so he could whisper to the three men. His eyes, when closer too, were red-rimmed and more than a little mad. 'That Kit Marlowe,' he spat and the other three leaned back to try and get out of range. 'He's jealous, that's what he is. He made them put his load of nonsense on instead. Mighty line! Ha! That's a good one!' He crashed back onto the bench and nearly went over backwards.

'Steady, Master Kyd,' Poley said. 'You'll hurt yourself.'

With the logic of the intoxicated, Kyd was on him like a cobra. 'How do you know my name?'

'When I heard the name of your play, of course I knew you at once,' Poley said, with a smile which mollified Kyd and scared Skeres and Frizer almost into immobility.

'Of course you did,' Kyd murmured. 'Of course you did.' His head lolled onto his arms and he gave an enormous snore, which made him jump. He looked up, his eyes spinning wildly. 'He threw me out, you know,' he said to the air above their heads.

'Who did?' Poley asked smoothly.

'Him. Marlowe. Threw me out of Hog Lane.' Kyd thrust out his bottom lip truculently. 'Like last night's leftovers. And that maid of his. Annie Wossname. Sh'loved me you know. Much more'n him. She couldn't do enough for me. Made sure the doors were shut so I wasn' in a draught.' He frowned. 'All that sort've thing. Yes.'

His eyelids drooped and his head nodded. The three men on the settle slid quietly one by one off the seat and made for the door. With any luck, he would pay the bill without even realizing. Just as Frizer closed the door quietly behind him, he heard the playwright say to the empty chair, 'It's all his fault. All that bloody Kit Marlowe, with his fire and air. I'll get him, if it's the last thing I do.' This dramatic declaration was followed by a crash as Kyd leaned back again, but this time, with a less fortunate outcome.

'He sounds as if he is in a nasty temper,' Poley remarked as they prepared to go their separate ways.

'Ah, Tom Kyd's no threat to anyone,' Skeres said. 'He's all wind and piss. He just needs to sleep it off. He'll have forgotten all about it by tomorrow.'

'You're probably right,' Poley said. He patted his chest and looked around. 'I seem to have lost . . .' he looked at the two walking gentlemen. 'Which of you has had my purse?'

They were horrified. It was certainly true that the odd purse did come their way, but if they knew one thing it was that it was certainly not good for the health to steal from the likes of Robert Poley. They spread innocent arms wide.

'Hmm.' He looked them in the eyes. 'Yes, perhaps you are not that stupid. I must have dropped it inside. I'll go and look under the settle.' He turned to go. 'I hope you find your . . . what did you say they were called?'

'Copyists.'

'That's right. Well, good luck, boys. May you never forget your lines.' And the door swung to and he was gone.

Frizer gave a shudder that went from the top of his head to the soles of his boots. 'Why does he bring me out in goose flesh?' he asked his colleague.

Skeres snorted. 'Because you have a brain in your head,' he said. 'Because he's Robert Poley.'

'I've been thinking, Ned,' Will Shaxsper sat under the eaves in the Old Nursery at Scadbury, a sheaf of papers in one hand and a quill in the other.

'Never a good idea, dear boy.' Alleyn was sprawling on the settle, blowing smoke rings to the panelled ceiling.

'No, I mean, this play of Marlowe's.'

'What about it? Apart from the fact that I don't appear until page three.'

'Well, take this line of mine – "and take me in thine arms," and this one – "Sometime a lovely boy" . . . "naked arms" . . . "to hide those parts which men delight to see" . . .'

'They're your lines, aren't they?' Alleyn queried.

'Yes, they are. And that's what worries me.'

'Worries you how?' Alleyn was still playing with his pipe.

'Well, I'll be frank, Ned,' Shaxsper said. 'It's always been my ambition to make my mark in the theatre – oh, as a playwright, of course. I couldn't hold a candle to you as an actor.'

Alleyn toyed with a lordly answer but in the end simply bowed his head, exhaling a cloud of fragrant smoke.

'And then, after a suitable period being lauded by everybody, perhaps go home to Stratford and buy a new place. Hang up my quill and just enjoy life.'

'Swan of Avon, eh?' Alleyn chuckled.

'Exactly.' Shaxsper clicked his fingers. 'Exactly. I couldn't have put it better myself.'

'Well, what's stopping you?'

'This play of Marlowe's for a start,' Shaxsper said. 'I'm playing your minion, Ned. Your ingle. Good God, man, we're in bed together!'

Alleyn stopped blowing smoke and sat bolt upright. 'Don't be ridiculous. Where did you read that?'

'Everywhere.'

'Let me have a look.'

Shaxsper passed the papers to Alleyn.

'What's this?' the tragedian said, riffling through them. 'I haven't got this.'

Shaxsper frowned. 'Well, it's got a few stage directions. Hasn't yours?'

'No,' Alleyn snapped. 'Kit Marlowe knows better than to tell *me* how to play a part. In your case, of course . . . Mother of God!'

'What?'

'This is the elder Mortimer "Great Alexander lov'd Hephaestus, The conquering Hercules for Hylas wept, And for Patroclus stern Achilles droop'd" . . . er . . . "The Roman Tully loved Octavius, Grave Socrates wild Alcibiades". And then, look here. "They kiss"! That's the stage direction. Oh, I know, I've been kissing boys for years, but only when they're supposed to be women. If this gets out . . .'

'. . . which it will,' Shaxsper said. 'Look what happened with Anthony Bacon a few years back in Paris.'

'What happened?' Alleyn usually let current affairs pass him by.

'Bacon took to fondling his pages . . . not pages, of course, but people in hose . . . in full view of the French court.'

'Ah, well, the *French* court.' Alleyn dismissed it. 'That's different.'

'And they hanged John Swan and John Lister in Edinburgh when I was a lad.'

'Did they?' Alleyn frowned. 'For sodomy? Well, I never.'

'I should hope not,' Shaxsper said. 'What can we do, Ned? If we go ahead with this, we'll be, at best, laughing stocks. And at worst, we'll be dead.'

'You're right.' Alleyn had reached a decision. 'We'll go and see Marlowe.'

'They're classical allusions, Ned,' Marlowe said. He didn't welcome being wakened at this hour of the night and at the first knock on his door, his dagger was in his hand and his back was to the wall.

'What are?' Alleyn wanted answers and he wasn't getting any.

'The bit you just quoted. Alexander, Hephaestus, Hercules, Hylas and the rest. They're ancient history.'

'Unlike you,' Shaxsper said, grown mighty with the

country's greatest tragedian at his back, 'Alleyn and I are not university wits. We don't have the benefit of a Classical education. I'd go so far as to say that my knowledge of history is severely limited.'

'Glad to hear you say it, Will,' Marlowe smiled. 'A man has to know his limitations.'

'We won't do it, Kit,' Alleyn folded his arms. 'The kind of thing you are writing about is against the law in this great country of ours. It's a hanging offence.'

'Nicholas Udall got away with it,' Marlowe reminded them, 'so did Matthew Heaton . . . a priest, by the way. The law is an ass in such matters. Anyway, it's faithful to history. Edward the Second and Piers Gaveston. Read your Holinshed.'

'So you won't change it?'

'Not a line.' It was Marlowe's turn to fold his arms. 'Mighty or otherwise.'

The four horsemen rode south east out of London with the wind at their backs. The brothers Roger and Peter Dalston were not natural riders. For too long they had been cabined and confined in cloisters in Lincoln's Inn and, more recently, at a warehouse run by Philip Henslowe. There were times when they never saw the light of day, still less rode the open roads of Gloriana's England.

Ingram Frizer and Nicholas Skeres were altogether more travelled, albeit often at speeds slightly ahead of the law or in between spitting out refuse flung at them at the cart's tail by outraged honest citizens.

'Well,' Skeres answered Roger Dalston's question, 'it's a new play by Christopher Marlowe. It's about this Welshman, Rice ap Howell . . .' He paused for effect. 'Moi.'

'Actually,' Frizer couldn't help but butt in, 'it's one of Kit's most brilliant creations. Centres on Sir John of Hainault. Naturally, I play the part.'

The Dalstons looked at each other. What they loved was words and the way the ink flowed on vellum. Actors they could take or leave.

They left the old pilgrim's way at Deptford where the masts of the Queen's ships swayed in the wind and the cormorants dipped in the brackish water. Kent was not much the garden of England as they trotted towards the North Downs. They passed wagons rumbling northwards in the early morning, drovers taking their cattle to slaughter in the stews of Smithfield. It didn't feel like Christmas at all.

'It doesn't feel like Christmas,' Thomas Walsingham sat in his chair, his dog on one boot, his lady on the other. Audrey lifted her jewelled head from his lap.

'There's a play toward, Thomas,' she said brightly. 'It'll be marvellous. And, because of who has written it, some *very* important people are going to be here.'

'Oh, I know, I know,' Walsingham smiled down at her, 'but from the snippets of rehearsal I've caught, it's not going to be very jolly. More of a tragedy than a comedy. And I *do* like a laugh.'

'Well, then,' she bounced to her feet and sat on his knee, tracing her fingers round the fringe of his beard, 'why don't we have a Christmas to remember? A Lord of Misrule, devil-dancing, hobby-horses, the whole nonsense?'

'I'm not sure Baines would approve,' Walsingham raised an eyebrow.

'Baines is an old killjoy,' she pouted. 'Look, darling,' she turned his face to hers, 'He's your chaplain and a damned hedge-priest. Who the Hell cares what he thinks? Tell me,' she stroked his thigh, 'will you be my Lord of Misrule?'

He looked at her, then burst out laughing.

'Only of course,' she said, placing her fingers on his lips, 'if your Yule log is big enough.'

'Roger and Peter Dalston, Master Marlowe,' the brothers bowed. 'We've heard so much about you.'

'If it's from Henslowe, it's not true,' Marlowe chuckled. 'Thank you, gentlemen, for coming. And I'm sorry to spoil your Christmas. Rush job, I'm afraid. *The Troublesome Reign of Edward the Second*.'

'Oh, yes,' Peter nodded sagely, 'Fell foul of his barons, didn't he?'

'They were different days,' Marlowe said.

'Oh, I don't know,' Roger smiled. 'History has a habit of repeating itself in my experience.'

Marlowe shook their hands again. 'It's your experience I need, boys,' he said, 'and your speed with a quill. Now, the El Dorado question – can you read my handwriting?'

'What are you writing there?'

Roger Dalston nearly dropped his quill. It was cold in the library at Scadbury but the copyist hadn't noticed the frost on the window panes or his breath snaking out on the air. That was because of the play he was copying out. Roger Dalston was a clever man; his brother Peter merely a fast writer. What he saw unfolding in the pages before him filled him with horror. It may have been about a king long dead, but it had echoes of the world that Dalston knew today, parallels that ran straight to Hell.

'Who are you?' he asked. The man wore the robes of a priest but that meant little these days.

'I am Richard Baines, Thomas Walsingham's chaplain.'

'Roger Dalston, Master Baines.' The copyist rose and bowed.

'I didn't ask your name, menial; I asked what you were writing.'

'*The Troublesome Reign and Lamentable Death of Edward the Second,* sir,' he said. 'Christopher Marlowe's new play.'

Baines held out his hand. 'Everything written under this roof must be passed by me first. Master Walsingham's orders.'

'But . . . Master Marlowe . . .'

'. . . is an irrelevance. Have you finished?'

'Not quite. Another scene.'

Baines sat down. 'Then I'll wait.'

The candle guttered in the cold of dawn. It would be Christmas in two days' time but Advent held no interest for the vicar of Chislehurst who was also chaplain to Thomas Walsingham. Baines had snatched the copied play from Dalston and had read it, from the first page to the last. During it, his eyes had widened from time to time. He had taken out the rosary he kept in his secret drawer and had crossed himself in the horror of what he read. At last, he reached the last page – 'Sweet father, here unto thy murdered ghost I offer up this wicked traitor's head; And let these tears, distilling from mine eyes, Be witness of my grief and innocency.'

Slowly, his scowl softened, turning to a smile. He took up a quill and parchment, dabbing in the inkwell. What had Audrey Walsingham said? Write it down? Well, he would. And he would enclose it with this damnable play. And he found himself mouthing Marlowe's words again – 'I offer up this wicked traitor's head.'

SEVEN

The snow came to Scadbury that Monday, blanketing the drawbridge and the gables, settling silently on the turrets and battlements, tumbling from a leaden sky. Soon after dawn, it stopped and all the world was white.

The Lord Chamberlain's Men had a play to perform and not all of them were happy with its content, but Mistress Walsingham was insistent that the Christmas festivities must come first, so Tom Sledd's ingenuity was yet again put to the test. By mid-morning, with a lot of noise and many competing egos, the procession was ready for the road, complete with hobby-horses, fire-breathing dragons and a great deal of ale.

It had to be said that Thomas Walsingham looked every inch the Lord of Misrule, even if the role was wrong for him. The humblest peasant from the estate should have played the part, for at this time of the year the world was turned upside-down and the meek inherited the earth. Thomas Walsingham, amongst his immediate family, was indeed a very humble man, but when it came to worldly goods, he could have bought and sold the rest of the procession ten times over. Audrey had insisted he take the role, however, and so Lord of Misrule he was.

A scarlet mask hid his face and a plume of white feathers covered his hair and trailed down his back. His venetians were ribboned and his hose cross-gartered, but all of it paled into insignificance compared with his cod-piece, a massive silver horn that jutted from his groin and, if truth were told, was rather heavy and gave him a peculiar gait. The bells on his toes jingled as he danced through the snow and the music struck up.

The Rose's band hadn't expected this but they were troupers and stepped as lively as the snow would let them, slipping and sliding over the drawbridge as terrified ducks squawked and flapped, joining the moorhens in their collective flight to safety. The drums thudded and thundered and the shawms and kits echoed around the outer courtyard. The local crowd gathered on the avenue's verge had come prepared, with good Kentish ale and warm bread, much of it from Scadbury's own kitchens. What finery they had, they wore, with ribbons and scarves across their shoulders and hanging from their sleeves. The whole of the county seemed to be there.

Frizer and Skeres rode hobby-horses side by side, flicking the wooden animals' tails and rearing their heads.

'Better than a play, this,' Frizer said, smiling and waving to the crowd. 'Looks like everyone's in it, though.'

'Bit like the Spanish Tragedy in a way. Bet we won't make as much as we did last year, though,' Skeres said.

'Oh, the Inns of Court do,' Frizer remembered. 'Yes, that was a good one.'

'Well, it was until the Lord Mayor got all hoity-toity.'

'Miserable old fart,' Frizer sneered, executing a leap and a twirl for a particularly pretty girl in the crowd, 'What *was* his problem? It's only a bit of fun.'

'That sergeant died, though, didn't he?' Skeres couldn't quite remember the details. He *had* downed a few.

'Eventually, yes,' Frizer's eye caught that of another girl in the waving crowd and bowed his horse's head low, making her giggle and blush. 'Aye, aye,' he winked at her and nudged Skeres. 'You may have to bugger off to the stables tonight, Nick.'

'We're in the stables already, Ing,' Skeres reminded him. 'As behoofs.' He reared his horse. 'Get it? Behoofs?'

'That's a good one, Nick,' Frizer said, straight-faced. 'Quick. Tell it to Master Marlowe. He'll put that into *Edward the Second* – it could do with a few laughs.'

Master Marlowe, his face covered with black damask, was walking with Nicholas Faunt halfway back. Mercifully, the musicians were forward and to the rear, so neither man felt they had to caper nimbly; walking in time would do.

'Any minute now,' Faunt murmured, 'I'm going to realize how utterly stupid and pointless all this is.' He glanced at Marlowe. 'And you look ridiculous.'

'Where's your sense of history?' Marlowe smiled. 'This is Saturnalia, the Roman winter solstice.'

Faunt clicked his fingers and threw his head back, 'And here's me thinking we're celebrating the birth of our Lord Jesus Christ.'

'You old Puritan,' Marlowe chuckled.

'Talking of Puritans . . .' Faunt pointed ahead to where the church of St Nicholas stood grey and silent under its snow-clad roof. At the lych-gate, arms folded and feet planted apart, stood Richard Baines. The look on his face said that he was not a happy man. A curate stood beside him, gnawing his lip with nerves.

The column came to a halt, Skeres and Frizer colliding with each other and sending other revellers tumbling like a row of ninepins. The last ten minutes had been pointless. Both their caps were empty, though they had been holding them out to the crowd for most of the time. No, technically, that wasn't true. Frizer had a rotten apple in his. The Lord of Misrule, his lady beside him in a riot of feathers and lace, her lovely face hidden behind a hawk's beak, was waving frantically for the band to stop playing.

'I,' Walsingham began the time-honoured ceremony, 'am the Lord of Misrule, the Abbot of Unreason, the Master of Merry Disports.'

'Are you?' Baines sneered, looking him up and down. Walsingham blinked. That wasn't in the script.

'We are come,' the master of Scadbury went on regardless, 'to honour the season and make merry.'

Baines stood head to head with him. 'You are come to desecrate this house of God, like devils incarnate,' he said. 'I cannot . . .' and he pulled his curate to him, linking his arm in his, a human chain of just two links, '*we* cannot, in all conscience, let you pass.'

Walsingham took off the mask, with some difficulty it had to be said and closed to the priest, blowing a recalcitrant feather from his mouth. 'Richard,' he smiled. 'Look. It's me. Thomas.'

'What's the matter with him?' Audrey called, irritated by the delay.

Walsingham half turned and patted the air as if to calm

everything down. He turned back to Baines. 'It's just a bit of fun, Richard,' he said. 'Chance for my people to let their hair down for once. You know how hard they work all year round.'

'I know how hard the Lord works,' Baines said, 'to keep this Ungodly rabble from His house.'

Walsingham turned again to Audrey. The woman snarled, tore off her hawk mask and trudged through the snow to confront Baines. 'What *is* going on?'

'Richard's having a bit of a turn,' Walsingham whispered in her ear.

Audrey looked over his shoulder at the glowering priest. She swept past the Lord of Misrule and all but pressed her nose against Baines's. 'Can I remind you,' she hissed, 'that you are my husband's chaplain?'

'He's not your husband,' Baines hissed back, 'and I am also the vicar of Chislehurst.'

'Not for much longer,' she shouted. 'Archbishop Whitgift, as you know, is a *very* good friend.' She caught sight of the curate. 'What are *you* looking at?' she snapped.

'Nothing, my lady,' the lad jabbered, unable to look the mistress of Scadbury in the eye.

'Are you seriously denying us entry to your miserable churchyard?' Audrey asked Baines.

'I will not have the souls of the dead ridiculed by this tomfoolery,' the chaplain said. 'Tomorrow is Christmas Eve. All these people should be preparing for the coming of the Lord. It could be the day after next, you know.'

'And I,' Marlowe murmured to Faunt, 'could be the next Pope.'

'This is better than a play, this is,' Frizer nudged Skeres, wrestling as he was to control his horse. 'A bord says Mistress Wossname lands the vicar one.'

Skeres looked the man – and horse – up and down. 'You haven't got a bord.'

'A groat, then,' Frizer was infinitely adaptable. 'I've got a groat.'

Walsingham tried the softly, softly approach. 'Look, Richard, we've had these little processions for years. Old Reverend Carmichael never objected.'

'Old Reverend Carmichael was a half-wit,' Baines observed. 'Not a tooth in his head nor a thought in it, either. The Lord's day is coming, Thomas. And some of us must stand ready.'

Thomas Walsingham was a man of his times and a man of his class. Masks and costumes were all very well, but, essentially, Baines was right. What the procession was doing was mocking God. And that was not Walsingham's way. He turned his back on Baines and marched through the crowd, putting his scarlet mask back on. 'Back to the house, everybody,' he shouted, lurching a little as someone knocked him painfully in the codpiece. 'Music! Ho!' And the band struck up.

'This isn't over,' Audrey hissed at Baines, but the chaplain stared right through her.

The drums thundered once more and the crowd cheered. The company of the Lord of Misrule was on the road again.

The fire crackled in the great hearth in the hall at Scadbury. Audrey Walsingham smiled as she looked around at her guests, the great and good of the surrounding countryside as well as some of Thomas's more illustrious contacts at Whitehall. Christmas was always a difficult time to assure a hostess of a good turnout and indeed, she had lost some of the bigger names she would have liked to see under her roof. Her rather unusual arrangement with Thomas was not known to everybody and of those who knew, some had shunned them from the moment she hung her first garment in the press in their chamber; the others had taken no notice whatsoever. But she didn't care. She was Audrey Walsingham in every sense apart from strict legality and if she wasn't always loyal to Thomas, well, that was her business. She chose her men with care and only dallied with those with far more to lose than she had herself. She looked across the room to where Kit Marlowe sat, beautiful in his festive clothes, fresh cheeked and bright-eyed from the outdoor revels and she forced a smile. Even she could not get it right every time and revenge was a dish best served cold.

She felt a nudge in her ribs. 'Aud,' Thomas's voice husked in her ear, 'you're staring, dear. Try not to do that. It's common.' It wasn't often that he reminded her of her relatively humble birth but every now and again, especially when he had taken a cup or two of wine and then a cup or two more, he would bring it up. In private, she would lambast him until he was sorry he had spoken. In public, she was as soft and compliant as any man could wish.

'I beg your pardon, my lord,' she said, bowing her head. 'I was not staring. I was resting my eyes by letting them wander. At whom was I staring? I must go and apologize at once.'

Thomas clapped her on the back. A sure sign he had taken too much wine; he started to treat her as one of the fellows up in Whitehall, all slaps and buffets and bonhomie. 'No need for that, Aud, old girl.'

She winced. When he started old girling her, it usually meant she would be troubled by his inexpert pawing next.

'Just saying. Don't want to embarrass the guests.' He leaned over and almost buried his masked head in her décolletage. She backed away.

'Thomas! Please! Not in front of everyone.' She smiled around over his head and got some sympathetic glances from the women nearby. All men are beasts, they seemed to say. She could have told some of them in great detail just *how* beastly their men were, given half a chance.

'Sorry,' he muttered, straightening up. 'Bit dizzy.' He pulled at his codpiece, trying to settle it more comfortably. 'Bit hot, tell you the truth. Can I take this thing off now?'

'No, you certainly cannot!' Audrey Walsingham kept her chatelaine voice to a minimum with Thomas. He needed careful handling, at least until she was safely married to him and truly Mistress of Scadbury, not merely his mistress. 'You are the Lord of Misrule. How would it look if you suddenly appeared in your normal clothes. Look, everyone else is wearing their costumes still.'

He turned his monstrous plumed head from side to side, trying to focus through the eye holes which were set rather too far apart. True, everyone else was covered in ribbons and they did look very colourful. But their masks were just over part of their faces and no one that he could see was carrying a monstrous protuberance like he was. It was pulling on parts he didn't like being pulled on and the straps had worked their way between his buttocks in a way that was becoming rather intrusive. He would be walking funny for days, he knew, and he had some serious meetings with serious people planned in the next couple of days. He tried to think of how to explain his lurching gait and nothing repeatable would come to mind. But he was a man still in love and he turned to his lady and fixed her with first one eye and then the next. 'All right, Aud,' he said, his voice reverberating in his mask. 'If you insist.'

'I do,' she said, planting a kiss on the mask above where his cheek might well have been. 'It's just for the rest of the evening and then,' she flicked his silver codpiece with a polished nail, 'we'll see what you've got for little Audrey under here, shall we?'

It was Thomas's turn to wince now. The only way he was even tolerably comfortable was to think chaste thoughts; anything else caused terrible chafing. He bowed as best he could and wandered away.

The crowd was indeed the biggest Scadbury had ever seen. Before Audrey had entered his life, Thomas Walsingham had entertained little and then only a few close friends. He did have his cousin, Francis, and his family down from time to time, but even then they scarcely reached double figures. But now, the entire countryside had been emptied as everyone, not just the great and good but the tenants on the estate, the servants of guests and of the house and of course, last but not least, the Lord Chamberlain's Men, were crammed into the room.

The banquet was not of the usual sort. There was no room for everyone to sit down and so the food had been set up on buffets along the walls, made up of trestle tables from all over the estate, spread with linen and strewn with streamers and paper flowers. Candles burned in all the sconces and some of the guests had already learned that naked flames and twirling feathers did not mix; the smell of burning wafted over the company, vying with the smell of food.

Audrey Walsingham did not like to stint. She had not left her father's house to live in sin with Thomas in order to do without. So she had ordered plates and tureens, napkins and finger bowls and so much food that two grocers in Chislehurst had bought new houses on the proceeds. The trestles groaned with roast meats and vegetables, candied fruits and jellies, loaves of bread still warm from the Scadbury ovens and pots of new butter. At one end, barrels of ale were supported on great beams and jugs of wine stood on trestles in front of them. Every cup and goblet in the house had been commandeered and under the trestle were boxes lined with straw with yet more, newly brought in by carrier that morning. The bills when they came would make Thomas Walsingham's eyes pop, but it was worth it, just to show the neighbourhood and in particular Christopher Marlowe, the cobbler's son from Canterbury, how Audrey Walsingham lived.

The cobbler's son from Canterbury was more comfortable in his costume than his host and also not anything like as far in his cups. Marlowe liked a drink as much as the next man, depending on who the next man might be, but he had made it a policy since his first days in Cambridge to always be the soberest man in the room. It was safer that way. But he could walk the walk and talk the talk and few people would have guessed, looking at his lop-sided smile and his tousled hair that he was anything other than inebriated. Around him were either people as skilled as he in the art of looking drunk or people who were, actually, very drunk indeed. Some were cradling goblets against their chests, oblivious to the ale seeping into their doublets, plastering down the feathers and ribbons so they would never be the same again. Others could hold it better and were still standing, hunks of bread and meat in one hand, a drinking cup in the other, making conversation which was at the moment sparkling and witty but which in the cold, clear light of dawn would come back to them with every banal or, worse, insulting or downright slanderous, syllable hideously intact.

Most of the faces he didn't know and nearly all the faces were now visible, the masks pushed up on foreheads or abandoned entirely. But he could see all of his number, for the most part the worst for drink, clustered in little cliques all over the room, talking shop, as actors always will, drunk or sober. There was Ned Alleyn standing at the wine trestle, one arm extended in a dramatic pose, a goose leg held aloft as though it were a dagger. The other arm, predictably, was draped over the shoulder of a serving girl from one of the nearby great houses, decked just for today in a revealing dress of scarlet lawn, with flowing ribbons for sleeves.

Tom Sledd, eating a fastidiously sliced piece of roast beef wrapped in a hunk of bread and accompanied by some pickled onions, was poking Amyntas Finch in the chest with a didactic finger and telling him something that seemed very important. Finch was looking puzzled and Marlowe smiled to see it. This was Tom Sledd at his drunkest, very earnest and sincere but talking absolute rubbish. The room was too noisy to hear, but the playwright knew that the stage manager was using words which were undoubtedly English, but which had never been heard in that order before and never would be again. He saluted Finch with a lazy hand when the big man caught his eye, a puzzled look on his face. This didn't happen often, but if he was to be Sledd's assistant, he needed to practice understanding gibberish when he heard it.

Frizer and Skeres, predictably, had kept their hobby-horses and were completely in character, whinnying and caracoling around the room to the intense annoyance of everyone. Experience had taught them that people didn't watch their purses much when they were wearing funny clothes; there seemed no rhyme nor reason to it, but their fat pickings at such festivities could not be argued with. Everyone smiled when they were near, the women patting the horses' necks and pretending to give them sugar lumps while their husbands were made lighter by the next week's housekeeping. Life was good.

The non-acting fraternity were, by and large, in one corner of the room, looking as awkward as they felt. Although they spent their days with actors, it was somewhat of a belief system with them that they were not theatrical. They looked on actors in much the same way that doctors looked upon their patients; as a necessary evil, one they couldn't live without. Marlowe could see the dark head of one of the Dalston brothers, but in the press of people and the smoky light from the candles could not tell which. In fact, he admitted to himself, he was hard-pressed to tell them apart anyway, until one of them spoke, in which case he could tell; Roger was the clever one and should go far, as long as he didn't keep his stupider younger brother clinging to his coat-tail, holding him back. The copyist had let his hair down insofar as he had ribbons from his shoulders and, if the tape around the back of his head was any guide, a mask on his face. Otherwise, he looked as normal – slightly hunched over and with his head down.

Marlowe scanned the crowd looking for Shaxsper. He was normally so easy to find, with his domed head glowing in any light but there was no sign of him. When feeling mellow, Marlowe might think that he was sitting miserably in his lodging, missing Mistress Shaxsper and all the little Shaxspers, but common sense told him that he was probably assuaging his homesickness in the bed of some maidservant or another, having worn out his welcome with all the seamstresses in the Rose's company. Then he looked again – there was no mistaking that enormous brow, even when topped, as it was, by a bright orange wig. But true to form, he did indeed have a maidservant about his person – as always, not quite as pretty or enthusiastic as the one Ned Alleyn had annexed, but he was, after all, only second on the playbill.

Nicholas Faunt slid onto the bench which Marlowe was occupying, nudging him along with his elbow to make room. 'Nice evening,' he said, in his usual flat, inflexionless voice. Nicholas Faunt gave nothing away, not even in a greeting.

'As they go,' Marlowe conceded. He could match banality for banality any day of the week.

'Are we playing the drunk tonight?' Faunt asked. He could do either, drunk or sober.

'Mildly intoxicated, I think,' Marlowe said. 'There are enough falling down drunks here already without us faking it.'

'True.' Faunt crossed his eyes and turned his head to scan the room. There seemed to be nothing amiss. There was some action over to his left, where some of the estate lads were having what they would no doubt have called fun lifting a huge Yule log and dropping it on each other's feet. 'That's a bit odd,' Faunt remarked, pointing.

'Yes,' Marlowe said, with a smile. 'I did ask about that. It's a game, apparently, though how anyone knows who the winner is and when is anybody's guess.'

'Last man standing, I suppose,' Faunt said, laconically.

A noise as of cats being castrated with blunt scissors suddenly issued from the far end of the room.

'Time to go,' Marlowe said, hauling himself to his feet, not forgetting to sway a little. 'I smell folk dancing.'

'Holy Mother of God,' Faunt murmured and stood up, following the poet out of the room by a small door half hidden behind the buffet. 'Where are we going?'

'Somewhere quieter,' Marlowe promised him. 'I've been to these things before. It starts with folk dancing and ends with some God-forsaken game like Hoodman Blind or Hide and Seek. Unless I miss my guess, there'll be a quiet game of Gleek or Ruff going on somewhere and if we keep our heads down, we won't be bothered again tonight.'

'I don't care what people say about you, Kit . . .' Faunt began.

'Happily, neither do I,' Marlowe butted in.

'. . . but you do know how to make yourself at home.'

'It's where I hang my hat,' Marlowe observed. He pushed open a door and put his head around it. 'Here it is,' he said over his shoulder to Faunt. 'Have you any small change? It's a penny a point most nights.'

And, like thieves in the night, the two projectioners slid round the door and closed it softly behind them.

In the great hall, things were hotting up and not just because people kept being set alight by candles. The local louts had given up on their game of Dun is in the Mire, having realized, like Marlowe, that there was no way of deciding the winner. After a few desultory goes at some folk dancing and having come to the conclusion that no one but old Gammer Gosworthy knew all the steps and she hadn't walked unaided since 1576, a game of Hide and Seek was suggested and Amyntas Finch was chosen as the seeker. It was an easy choice, as he was clearly not a man who could easily hide and it was considered by the company to be unfair on him to ask him to try.

In an extraordinarily short time, the great hall was empty, all bar Finch and Gammer Gosworthy, who was half asleep and muttering the steps of John Come Kiss Me to herself. Finch had been mildly outraged when Audrey Walsingham had asked him whether he knew how to count to one thousand – the number needed to give everyone a chance to hide – and had smiled at her kind consideration that he might like to walk three times around the manor house instead. But stuck here with a mad old granny, chewing her gums and chuckling lasciviously to himself, he decided to split the difference and at three hundred he stole out of the hall and set off widdershins around the building.

Marlowe lifted his head from examining his cards and listened carefully. 'Here we go, boys,' he muttered to his companions. 'Time to bar the door. If that's not the sound of distant Hide and Seek, I'm a Dutchman.'

James Lewknor, who was losing heavily, was of the opinion that the game should be declared null and void, but a glance from Faunt changed his mind and he went across and barred the door, peeping out first. Coming back to the table, he announced that Marlowe was right, that the house was full of scurrying people, all intent on a hiding place.

'How did you know, Master Marlowe?' he asked, impressed.

'He's a spy,' Faunt said, pushing another penny into the centre of the table.

'You do like your joke, master,' a farmer from the edge of the estate said with a chuckle. 'Ain't no such thing, as everyone knows.'

'No, indeed there isn't,' Marlowe said. 'Excuse my friend. He does like a laugh.'

The men around the table looked at Faunt. If ever there was a face which had never cracked a smile, this was surely it. They bent again to their cards, aware that the air had taken on a sudden chill.

Not everyone was concentrating on finding a good place to hide. Alleyn and Shaxsper, with other ideas on their mind, were heading off across the stable yard to their cosy billet in the hayloft, swept and appointed with comfortable beds for their use. Alleyn's little maidservant was leading the way, pulling him anxiously across the cobbles. He was beginning to wonder whether perhaps he wasn't a little old for this game these days. Shaxsper's girl, on the other hand, was suddenly not so keen. The wig had been convincing only in dim candlelight and the help of a few goblets of cheap wine. Now it was slung rakishly over one eye in the light of the courtyard torches, she was not so sure that this actor was all that much of a catch. But then she remembered what her old mother had always told her about men from Lunnon and especially those in the theatre being as rich as someone called Greaseus and she shrugged and caught up his hasty steps with a hop and a skip. The worst it could be was fun and at the best she might get a nice lining to her purse.

Tom Sledd had beaten them to it and he was lying on his palliasse groaning when they stumped up the stairs with their prizes.

'Sledd,' Alleyn said. 'Get out. I want some privacy.'

Tom Sledd was not in the mood for ego. 'If you want me to move, Ned,' he muttered, 'you'll have to be in the mood for cleaning up sick. Because you'll have to if I have to so much as roll over.'

Alleyn looked down at him and made a decision.

'Well, keep your eyes closed, then,' he said, truculently.

'No problem there,' Sledd said. On more than one count, that was currently a given.

'And stop your ears.'

'Pardon?' Sledd said and fell asleep, snoring loudly.

The servant girl was looking around her. 'It's not very romantic, Ned, is it?' she said. This was worse than her room in the attics of the main house.

'Romantic?' Alleyn was puzzled. Here she was, with the doyen of the acting profession and she wanted romance?

'Well. Straw palliasses? We have wool over in the house.'

'Mine is wool,' he said, affronted. 'I am after all the Leading Man.' He struck his customary pose.

She kicked it with a slippered toe, wet and muddy from the yard. 'Well . . . all right then.' She slipped her arms out of her gown with the speed of long practice and Alleyn squared up for a lunge. Just before he made contact with two of the most glorious breasts he had seen since daybreak, a scream cut through the night. The girl started back and gathered up her clothes to hide herself. Tom Sledd sat up in bed as if on strings and then fell back, groaning. Shaxsper, still trying to inveigle the girl of his choice up the ladder swore like a sailor and ran for the door.

'What the Hell was that?' he asked the night in general.

All over the great house, windows were being thrown open and people were shouting and yelling unintelligibly.

Alleyn hung his head down through the trapdoor. 'Can you see what it is, Will?' he asked.

'No, nothing,' Shaxsper said. 'Get your venetians tied, Ned, and help me go and look.'

Alleyn adjusted his voice to outrage, Level Three and boomed back at him. 'I am fully clothed, Master Shaxsper. I would thank you to remember I am a married man.' This pronouncement was followed by the sound of a slap and a weak chuckle from Tom Sledd. Alleyn slid down the ladder like a rat leaving a sinking ship and the two actors ran across the yard back to the house.

EIGHT

In the house, all was chaos. The card players had let themselves out of their room and were standing at the bottom of the stairs, controlling the crowd. Marlowe and Faunt had a natural authority and apart from the very drunk, most people were listening to them. The steward of the house had assembled his staff to one side and was marshalling them as he thought fit, the women back to the kitchen where there would be safety in numbers, and the men in serried ranks, ready for anything that could be dealt with by a wooden staff or two and a dirty look.

'Did anyone here scream?' Faunt asked. The crowd all looked at each other, shrugging and shaking their heads.

'Where did it come from?' Marlowe asked. 'Was it upstairs? Down? Inside? Out?'

A statuesque woman wearing a startling mask of Medusa pushed up onto her piled-up curls stepped forward. 'It was down there,' she pointed down a passageway to her left.

'No,' a burly man with a tiger's face hanging below his chin said. 'It was definitely upstairs.'

Audrey Walsingham pushed her way to the front. 'Sound travels very oddly in this house,' she said. 'It comes from having been built over many years, with additions and demolitions which most people have forgotten now. There are even secret passages, or so we have been told. No one can remember quite where they were any more. So we all need to keep quiet and see if the scream comes again.'

Everyone breathed as quietly as they could. Marlowe was relieved to see Alleyn at the back of the crowd; his first thought, as ever, was whether he could have been responsible, as he so often was. He looked around for Tom Sledd and couldn't see him anywhere. Catching sight of Shaxsper, he mouthed the stage manager's name at him with a quizzical raise of an eyebrow. Shaxsper mimed sleeping and throwing up with beautiful economy of movement and Marlowe thought not for the first time what a shame it was he ever had to speak; the man's body was far better at getting things across than ever his mouth was.

Just as the crowd at the bottom of the sweeping stair were beginning to get restive, the scream came again, but this time followed by words. 'Help!' the voice cried. 'Help! He's dead! Oh, God, he's dead!'

This time it was clear where the sound had come from and the woman with the Medusa head had been right all along. The crowd split immediately into those who wouldn't go near a cry like that if their lives depended on it and those who would rush towards any crisis, in the hope of gore and horror.

As the thirty or so thrill-seekers ran down the passage hell for leather, a door about halfway down opened and Amyntas Finch stepped into their path. It was only with extreme presence of mind that he was able to step back and prevent himself from being trampled.

'Well, this isn't much fun,' he said, shaking newly-fallen flakes of snow from his hair. 'You might have waited until I had tried to find at least one person.'

'Don't worry, Amyntas,' Marlowe said, bringing up the rear of the mob. 'It's nothing personal. I think something must have happened down here – there's been screaming. Didn't you hear it from outside?'

The big man shrugged. 'No. The wind's getting up again. I couldn't hear a thing.'

Another scream, much louder than the first, split the air and made everyone's ears ring. 'Thomas!' a woman screeched. 'Thomas! They've killed him!'

Marlowe was running through the crowd before the voice died away, pushing his way through until he came to a boot-room, damp and cold, lit only by borrowed light from the passage. Slumped in a corner was the Lord of Misrule, his scarlet face turned up to the ceiling, his white feathers trailing in his blood. His enormous codpiece sagged sadly to one side, its weight too much for the dead body which wore it. Kneeling at the man's side, Audrey Walsingham was bent over in grief. Her costume was wet with blood at the knees and her hair was hanging loose over her face. She was still screaming, but quietly, as though she were grieving from very far away, perhaps on a distant star where dead love goes.

Faunt stepped carefully around the pooling blood and gently lifted her to her feet. He put an arm around her shoulders and turned her from the body, sitting her on a simple bench along one wall. He was murmuring to her and her screams and sobs began to subside. Marlowe lit a stub of candle from one of the sconces in the passage and then turned to the people at his back and pushed and cajoled until they were the other side of the door. He approached the body as carefully as Faunt had done. That the man was dead could not be in doubt. Not only was his head at a rakish angle to the body where he had hit the wall with terrific force and slid down it, leaving a smear of horror behind him, but the pool of blood in which he lay must be almost all a human body could hold.

Leaving Faunt to comfort Audrey Walsingham and keep her back turned to the sight of her dead love – because, in spite of what he knew, Marlowe was convinced she did love Thomas – he eased the mask off the dead man's head.

'Oh.' Marlowe was usually more in control than to let out any kind of exclamation, but he had been dreading the sight of his dead friend's face. But it wasn't Thomas Walsingham under the scarlet mask. It was Roger Dalston.

It was dawn before the chaos had calmed. James Lewknor apologized to the gentry there but he would have to take their names before they left, numbed and cold in their waiting carriages. The others he knew, the family retainers and the people of the estate, men and women who had served the Walsinghams all their lives, wet nurses who had fed little Thomas, pall-bearers who had carried his father to the vaults of St Nicholas. One by one, they paid their respects to the Master and Mistress of Scadbury and wished them, almost as an afterthought, a merry Christmas.

As a cold dawn crept over the turrets of Scadbury, three men sat in the brown parlour around the ashes of a fire. Padraig was with them, but the dog who might have been the eyes and ears of the Night Watch, was too old to see or smell and he lay on the straw floor, snoring.

'Bad business,' Walsingham said, 'but I'm glad you two are here.'

Marlowe asked the question first but it was in Faunt's mind too. 'Is there anyone, Thomas, who would want to see you dead?'

'That's a devil of a question, Kit,' Walsingham frowned. 'Oh, I may have crossed the odd farmer occasionally, inadvertently annoyed a merchant or two, but . . . murder? No, no.'

Faunt had a subject he needed to broach. 'You know, Thomas, that both of us served your late cousin?'

'Of course,' Walsingham nodded, 'and that he was the Queen's spymaster and you two are projectioners. That's why I'm glad you're here.'

'You never . . .?' Faunt began.

'Got involved in the spying game?' Walsingham chuckled. 'God, no; I don't have the brains for it. I don't really see what Audrey sees in me. I was behind the Arras when intelligence was being doled out.'

The answer 'owning half of Kent' was on Marlowe's lips, but, true to his calling, no sound came out.

'What actually happened to him?' Walsingham asked. 'This Roger Dalston, I mean.'

Marlowe and Faunt had viewed the body, albeit by candlelight. They had laid it on a trestle table in one of the brewhouses, stripped the dead man of his Lord of Misrule costume and had locked the door as they left. Only Marlowe had a key and it lay inside his doublet, in the slit in the cloth alongside the stiletto dagger he had taken to wearing these days as well as the obvious one at his back.

'His neck was broken,' Marlowe said. 'Somebody rammed his head against the wall. The blow shattered his skull and dislocated his spine. I doubt he knew what hit him.'

'Would it take someone exceptionally powerful to do that?' Walsingham asked.

'Not necessarily,' Faunt said. 'If he was pushed from the top of the little flight of steps just behind him, the weight of his own body would have done it. It could even have been a woman.'

'I was less than honest a moment ago,' Marlowe said, 'when I asked you who might want you dead, Thomas.'

'What do you mean?'

'I mean that Faunt and I noticed something odd about the costume Dalston was found in.'

'My costume?' Walsingham was confused.

'The leggings,' Faunt said. 'They were not cross-gartered.'

'So?'

'So,' Marlowe said, 'the hose were put on inside out.'

'The man dressed in the dark,' Walsingham said. 'We've all done it.'

'But why would a play copyist from London put on the costume at all?' Faunt asked. 'And how did he get it?'

'We believe,' Marlowe said, 'that Dalston was dressed in the costume by somebody else, *after* he was dead. The blood from his head merely kept draining out after the mask had been put on.'

'But why . . .?' None of this was making sense to Walsingham.

'When did you see the costume last?' Faunt asked.

'When Audrey and I . . . retired.'

'Retired?' Marlowe took him up on it. 'But Mistress Walsingham was up when the screams were heard. She was organizing the staff. Fully dressed, mask and all.'

'Yes.' Walsingham was blushing a little. 'I don't mean *retired*, as in went to sleep. I mean *retired,* as in went to bed, if you take my meaning.'

The projectioners did.

'When I heard the screams, the room was in darkness and Audrey had gone. I fumbled around for my costume and couldn't find it. I . . . Oh, my God!' A look of horror crossed Walsingham's face.

'What?' Faunt asked.

'Whoever killed Dalston was in our private chambers, watching, waiting. He must have stolen the costume then.'

'Yes,' Marlowe nodded, glancing at Faunt and thinking what *he* was thinking. 'Yes, that must be it.' He stood up suddenly.

'Gentlemen,' he said, 'you must forgive me. I have a grieving brother to talk to.'

Peter Dalston was sitting in the library, scratching furiously with his quill, the feather in his hand darting and bobbing above the page. He didn't look up when Marlowe came in. He didn't look up when Marlowe sat down.

'Master Dalston,' the playwright said softly, 'please accept our condolences. I have a brother, albeit years younger than me. I can't imagine . . .'

'I am very busy, Master Marlowe,' the copyist's voice was firm, if brittle, a nerve jumping in his jaw.

'I can see that,' Marlowe said, 'But there's no great urgency . . .'

'It's the only way I can cope,' Dalston said, snappily. He looked at Marlowe for the first time. 'My brother, sir, was the dearest thing in the world to me. I have no wife, no children. No family at all.' He looked down at the scribbled pages, the curling parchment, the inkwell. 'All I have is this. My work. Your work.'

Marlowe leaned back in his chair. 'I must ask you about your brother,' he said, 'to try and make sense of this.'

Reluctantly, Dalston put down the quill, letting it rest for a moment on the few lines from the younger Mortimer. 'What do you want to know?' he asked.

'Did he have enemies?'

'Enemies?' Dalston would have laughed if his world was not drowned in tears. 'Roger was the sweetest man,' he said. He sniffed, recalling who knew what memories. 'He was the thinker of the family. We were both articled to Lincoln's Inn, but Roger was far cleverer than I. He'd have gone to the bar, for sure.'

'How did you end up in the theatre?' Marlowe asked, though perhaps 'in the theatre' wasn't quite the right phrase.

'We met Master Henslowe on a matter of law,' Dalston said. 'Business in the City. He persuaded us that creativity was a finer way of making a living than the law.' He looked almost embarrassed. 'And it paid better.'

'So, there was no-one Roger might have crossed? No-one who bore him a grudge?'

'No-one.' Dalston was sure.

'When was the last time you saw him?' Marlowe was trying to piece together the last moments of a man's life; it wasn't easy.

'Before the feast,' the copyist said. 'Roger and I are not very social people, Master Marlowe. We copy plays for people who dress up but we don't do it ourselves. Out of respect for Master Walsingham, we took part in the procession, but we draw the line at hide and seek.'

'Very wise,' Marlowe said.

'Roger had become very keen on your play, though.'

'He had? I'm flattered.'

'That's the kind of man he was,' Dalston went on. 'He could have been called to the bar. He could . . . saving your presence . . . have become a playwright.'

Marlowe laughed. 'There's nothing magic about it,' he said, 'a little imagination controlled by iambic pentameter.'

'He was trying to summon up the courage to talk to you about it.'

'He was?' Marlowe chuckled. 'Am I so unapproachable?'

Dalston was straight-faced. 'You are a great man, sir,' he said. 'Roger called you the greatest playwright in the world.'

Marlowe laughed again. 'Possibly Canterbury,' he said. 'Let's go no further than that.'

'Everybody thinks so,' Dalston told him, 'but I think Roger found *this* play disturbing.'

'Disturbing?' Marlowe frowned. 'Why?'

'He didn't say exactly,' the copyist took up his quill again, 'but he spoke to everybody about it, asking them what they thought.'

'Everybody?' Marlowe asked.

'The Lord Chamberlain's Men, even – and I thought him bold for this – Master Thomas himself.'

There was a pause, the silence filled by more scratching of the quill.

'Master Marlowe,' Dalston looked up again, 'May I see my brother? I haven't had the chance to say a proper goodbye.'

'Of course,' Marlowe said softly. He stood up. 'Come,

Master Dalston. The Mortimers will keep.' And he led the man away.

'Changed your mind, Master Marlowe?' Audrey Walsingham had abandoned her costume of the previous day and was wearing a simple gown of purple velvet. Although he had never even seen her, Marlowe knew that this was the colour of the Queen.

'In what respect, Mistress?' Marlowe asked. The pair faced each other in the brown parlour, Thomas having ridden out with his hounds to clear his head.

She crossed the room and stood close to him. 'There is only one respect,' she said, brushing a delicate finger over the brocade of his doublet.

'Madam,' he said, carefully moving her hand away, 'a man is dead.'

'Indeed,' she spun away from him, crossing the room again and touched one finger on the keys of her virginals. 'Needs tuning,' she said.

Marlowe crossed to her and closed the lid. 'And I need answers.'

'You?' She turned to him. 'You are a playwright and poet, Master Marlowe. What right have you to demand anything from me? What I have I offered to you two nights ago and you refused.'

'Did you kill Roger Dalston?' he asked her flatly.

Her eyes flashed and her hand snaked out to slap his face, but Marlowe was faster and he held it in mid-air.

'It's a simple question, Audrey,' he said, softly, looking into her eyes. 'A mere yes or no would do.'

She pulled her arm away. 'No, then,' she said, arching her neck and standing tall.

'Very well,' Marlowe nodded, trying to read her cold, beautiful face. 'Do you know who did?'

Audrey Walsingham was not the most patient of women, but she had her pride. Part of her wanted to rip this popinjay's eyes from his head and crush them beneath her feet, but that would be beneath her dignity.

'I have no idea how many people were under my roof last

night,' she said. 'Any one of them may have wanted the wretched man dead.'

'And any one of them would want to dress him as your . . . husband?'

'I have no idea,' she said.

'Tell me, Mistress,' he looked hard at her, 'when you and Thomas . . . "retired" as he put it . . .?'

'Made the beast with two backs, you mean?'

'Colourful,' Marlowe nodded, 'and a euphemism for all that.'

'All right,' she smiled. 'Here's another one. Thomas "occupied" me. How's that?'

'Very good,' Marlowe smiled.

'He didn't last long. He never does.'

'Where was this?'

She sighed. This was getting very boring. 'In our bedchamber, Master Marlowe. Would you like to see the sheets?'

'No,' Marlowe said, 'but I'll wager somebody did.'

'What do you mean?'

'When Thomas had finished his "occupation", what happened?'

'He went to sleep. Men will.'

'And you?'

'If you must know, I was not satisfied. I went in search of fulfilment.'

'Went where?'

She wagged a finger at him. 'No, you don't, Christopher Marlowe,' she said. 'You won't catch me like that.'

'While you were with Thomas, did you notice anything?'

'Such as?' Audrey raised an eyebrow.

'Such as someone watching you? Waiting in the shadows?'

'Watching us?' Her eyes widened. 'How delicious!' She closed to him. 'It wasn't you, was it, Kit? Finding out what you missed the other night?'

'No, Madam,' he said. 'It wasn't. But whoever it was stole your husband's costume as soon as you'd gone. What time was that, by the way?'

'I don't know,' she said. 'I'd like to say that in Thomas's arms I lost all track of time, transported as I was to heights of ecstasy . . . except that would be a lie. It was before cock-crow, certainly.'

'Your chamber door was not locked?'

'No,' she said, demurely. 'My chamber door is never locked. Remember that, Kit, if you like.'

He smiled, bowed and left. As he was closing the door, he heard her speak, but was not sure whether it was for his ears or not, so he simply paused a moment and carried on his way.

'I do love Thomas,' Audrey Walsingham said to the empty air. 'I do love him.'

And Marlowe knew it to be true.

'How was she, Ned?' Marlowe had found a loaf of bread from somewhere and was munching it.

'How was who?' the actor asked, reaching across and tearing at the crust.

'The lady of the house.'

Alleyn shrugged. 'Don't know what you're talking about,' he said.

'Ned, Ned,' Marlowe put an arm around the man's shoulder. 'It's me, Kit. You're not usually so reticent about your conquests.'

Alleyn looked from left to right, checking that even in the Great Hall, the walls didn't have ears.

'Well, between you and me,' he murmured, 'conquest doesn't come into it.'

'How so?'

'The lady of the house was panting for it. I had been softening up that serving girl and it was all going nicely, when suddenly, Mistress Audrey was by my side and . . . well, being friendly. I was a bit shocked, if I'm honest with you.' Alleyn arranged his features into those of a man more sinned against than sinning. It wasn't hugely successful; he could have done with some make-up around the eyes. 'Anyway, why do you want to know? Interested yourself?'

'No,' Marlowe said.

'No, of course not,' Alleyn sneered. 'Well, I felt a bit guilty, of course, what with her being our hostess, so to speak.'

'Did you?' If he did, it would be for the first time.

'No, not really. And she goes like a mare on heat, Kit. I could barely keep up. I was glad that scream came later just before I had to perform with the girl. I think I may have made a bit of a fool of myself there, if I had been called upon to step forward, so to speak.' Alleyn's voice died away. Even he, wrapped in an ego as big as the great outdoors, could see that being glad that there was a murder just so that his lack of priapic splendour would not be noticed, was a little in bad taste.

'What time was her . . . approach?' Never had so many euphemisms been used in so short a time.

'God, I don't know. I never time myself in such matters.'

'Quite. Quite.'

'But as best I recall, we slipped away into some kind of kitchen area – it was damned cold, I can tell you that. Smelled of cheese.'

'The dairy?'

'Is that what it's called? I have no idea. Mistress Alleyn sees to all that side of things. Anyway, we went in there, she had her dress over her head in seconds and was on me like a cobra. Then afterwards, she was back in her dress and out the door before I could recover my . . .' Alleyn paused, stuck for the right word.

'Wits?' Marlowe asked, flatly.

'Breath, I was going to say. Breath. I didn't know women could do that. Not that it's any of my business when it's all over, of course. I don't really notice. But I do remember being surprised; I would have thought a woman like Audrey would have maids and the whole process would take hours.'

'Then what?'

'Then what what?'

'What did you do after she had dressed and left?'

'Well, I recovered my . . .'

'Wits.'

'Breath and went back out to join the party. Someone suggested Hide and Seek and Will and I and . . .'

This time, Marlowe didn't fill in the gap.

'Will and I went out to the stables. Tom Sledd was there, drunk as a pig and before anything could happen, there was a scream.'

'At least that rules both you and, I suppose, Mistress Walsingham out as murderers . . . Unless, of course, you're lying through your teeth. Again.'

Marlowe and Faunt sat opposite each other in the brown parlour, Padraig curled up around Marlowe's feet, assuming him to be the more acceptable face of espionage. That was fine by Faunt; he'd never met a dog he hadn't instinctively wanted to kick.

'So, Nicholas,' the playwright was lighting his pipe, 'where are we?'

'I was hoping you'd tell me,' Faunt said, sipping his Rhenish, thoughtfully provided by Thomas Walsingham.

'All right.' Marlowe cleared his throat and focussed. 'Roger Dalston, copyist, ex-clerk of Lincoln's Inn, is found dead in the boot room shortly before dawn today. He has clearly been murdered, neck broken, skull smashed.'

'Who found him?' Faunt was helping to retrace the man's steps.

'Dorcas, a maid of all work.'

'Who was doing all her work in said boot room.'

'Exactly.'

'What did she do?' Faunt asked the question rhetorically; many people in Scadbury still had the sound ringing in their ears.

'Which brought the whole house running,'

'Yes. Many were playing hide and seek. Some were asleep, either in their beds, someone else's or simply slumped in a corner somewhere,' Marlowe said. 'There were people all over the place – guests, servants . . .'

'The Lord Chamberlain's Men,' Faunt threw in.

'Especially the Lord Chamberlain's Men,' Marlowe nodded. 'You and I have talked to them all now. We can pinpoint where they were and who can vouch for whom. Somehow, I can't see anyone from Scadbury or the neighbourhood being involved in this. Dalston was a Londoner and nobody knew him.'

'Was the brother forthcoming?' Faunt asked.

'A simple soul,' Marlowe said. 'He broke down when he

saw Roger's body but after that opened up quite a bit. I get the impression that the deceased wasn't nearly as dim as Peter. He was clever, ambitious, an over-reacher, perhaps.'

Faunt looked at Marlowe over his cup. 'The most dangerous type,' he murmured.

Marlowe ignored him. 'He seemed very interested in *Edward the Second*,' he said.

'The king or the play?'

'Perhaps both. He was asking the boys about the play; all the Lord Chamberlain's men.'

Faunt snorted. 'And how did that go?' he asked.

'I should imagine that Skeres and Frizer will have built their parts up. I know Alleyn and Shaxsper aren't happy with it.'

'Not as other courtiers, eh?' Faunt raised an eyebrow.

'They were different time, Nicholas,' Marlowe said, defending his take on things.

'The law's no different,' Faunt said. 'I had occasion to report a sodomite only last year. They hanged him.'

'They'll hang us all given half a chance,' Marlowe said.

Faunt chuckled darkly. 'Careful, Kit,' he said. 'That kind of defeatist talk sounds almost treasonable.'

'Of course,' Marlowe was watching the smoke curl upwards from his pipe, eddying in the updraught of the chimney, 'there may be more to it.'

'In what way?' Faunt asked.

'What if . . . and this is only a guess at this stage . . . what if Roger Dalston isn't the only victim? What if John Foxe died by the same hand?'

'And Moll,' Faunt reminded the playwright.

'Moll died because she could identify Foxe's killer. She was an afterthought. Grieves me to say it though it does, she was just an example of a killer's tidying up. Foxe was about to star in a play by Kit Marlowe. Dalston was copying out the same play.'

'But so was brother Peter,' Faunt pointed out, 'and as of this hour he still seems to have breath in his body. And anyway, when Foxe met his maker, did he know he was to play in *Edward the Second*? Wasn't it still all about the *Spanish Tragedy* back then?'

'Er . . . not exactly,' Marlowe said. 'I told him. Asked if he could keep a secret at the auditions. I thought it only fair.'

'They don't kill people for acting,' Faunt said. 'Although perhaps they should and perhaps it's only a matter of time. No, if the two are linked, it must be something else.'

Marlowe let a moment pass, sucking the pipeclay thoughtfully. 'How are you progressing with Thomas Walsingham?' he asked.

Faunt looked at him. 'Now, Kit,' he said, 'you know I cannot divulge. Affairs of state and all that.'

Marlowe sighed. 'So,' he said, 'back to Dalston. Alleyn, Shaxsper, Sledd, Frizer, Skeres, Finch, Dalston, you, me, Johannes Factotum, all have alibis.'

'Watertight?' Faunt asked.

'Probably not,' Marlowe said. 'Least of all the object of your current obsession – the Walsinghams. He was fast asleep, or so his wife would have us believe.'

'Upright member of society,' Faunt nodded solemnly. 'Land owner. Benefactor. All round good egg.'

'Suspected by Nicholas Faunt,' Marlowe reminded him, 'projectioner of Whitehall.'

'She; Audrey.' Faunt changed direction.

'Ah, the dark lady,' Marlowe smiled.

'Of course,' Faunt said. 'There is one person we haven't considered. One person whose whereabouts are still a mystery on the night in question.

'Who?' Marlowe was all ears.

'The Reverend Baines.'

'Gone mad from what we saw at the lych-gate.'

'True,' Faunt nodded, 'but is that merely Nor' by Nor'west?'

'Point taken. It's late, Nicholas,' Marlowe said, knocking out his pipe and standing up. 'I'll take my leave.'

'Good night, Kit,' Faunt said. 'Oh, and by the way, Merry Christmas, Kit Marlowe.'

'And to you, Nicholas Faunt.'

NINE

The palace of Whitehall lay under a thick carpet of snow. Even the buskins of the Queen's guard were silent as they patrolled the parapets, the glow of their fires making magical lights on the crystals that sparkled like silver.

If there was poetry on such a night, sharpened by frost and lit by the moon, it was lost on the four men who sat huddled in the upstairs chambers of Lord Burghley. He had left his long-suffering mule at the gate now that the meadows of Westminster merged with the white cloak of the Strand and had hurried indoors to his fire and his Rhenish. His second son stood beside him until the others arrived and then he too sat down. The Queen's imp didn't need to be reminded how all men – and most women – loomed over him. In a chair, the world seemed more equitable; furniture was a great leveller.

Howard of Effingham had arrived next, his admiral's cloak soaked because he had ridden from Deptford through the night and it was still snowing along the river. He gratefully accepted Burghley's mulled wine and cradled the cup in his hands until the feeling returned to his fingers, his boots steaming in the heat of the fire.

Last to arrive was Henry Carey. The first Baron Hunsdon was the reason they were all there and the others didn't appreciate being kept waiting by him. Greetings were exchanged, hands shaken and the business of the inner circle of Her Majesty's Privy Council began.

'Right, gentlemen. What have we?' Burghley opened the proceedings.

'Essex wants to join us,' Hunsdon scowled.

Burghley shot a glance at his son. 'I'm sure he does,' he said.

'The Queen'll never allow it,' Howard said, leaning over to the table set before the fire and refilling his cup.

'Her Majesty blows with the wind, Charles,' Burghley said. 'And Essex is a smooth operator.'

'Never trust a man,' Hunsdon growled, 'whose beard is a different colour from his hair.'

'Point taken,' Burghley said, 'but the Queen's growing fond of him again after that debacle in Rouen. I suppose we'll have to let him in.'

'Perhaps he can hold the horses,' Effingham smirked and the others laughed.

'Robert,' Burghley turned to his son, 'what news of Ireland?'

'Tyrconnell's plotting with the Spaniards,' the spymaster said.

'There's a surprise,' Hunsdon muttered.

'I have a man on it,' Cecil said. That was good enough for the others. The Queen's imp knew his business.

'This fellow Penry . . .' Hunsdon brought it up; someone had to and it might as well be him.

'Who?' Effingham asked. 'Have I missed something?'

'Puritan,' Burghley said. 'One of the elect. He's been publishing religious rubbish for months now.'

'We'll have to close him down,' Cecil suggested.

'Almost certainly,' Burghley nodded. 'But we have to tread warily there, for obvious reasons. Hunsdon, where are we on the Scadbury business?'

Hunsdon shifted in his sear. He reached to his left and pulled up a letter satchel stuffed with papers. 'I take it you all have this?' he said. 'Marlowe's play?'

There were mutters all round.

'Filth,' snorted Effingham. 'Pure filth. What's Tilney doing? Is he Master of the Revels or isn't he?'

'Tilney hasn't seen it,' Hunsdon said. 'No one has but us. Marlowe intends to put it on at Scadbury in . . . where are we now? I always lose track at Christmas. A week.'

'What's Walsingham's take on it all?' Effingham asked. 'A eulogy to sodomy under his own roof? It's outrageous!'

'You're missing the point, Charles,' Burghley said. 'The bigger picture, so to speak. The play is about an attack on the royal person. I don't need to tell you what could happen if members of the public see this.'

'They'll draw parallels,' Cecil said, making sure that even Effingham understood. 'They'll make comparisons with today.'

'I've been invited to the play,' Hunsdon said. 'They *are* my troupe, after all.'

'I suggest we all go,' Burghley said. 'Robert, you know Marlowe best. Where is he going with this?'

'He's one of my best projectioners,' the spymaster said. 'Did stalwart work for Francis Walsingham too.'

'And now he's hiding with his cousin at Scadbury,' Effingham scoffed. 'Cowardly shit. It'll do him no good.'

'There are elements abroad,' Cecil said, looking at each man in turn, 'and by abroad, I mean here, in England, that are champing at the bit to overthrow the Queen.'

There were cries of 'No!' and 'Shame!' but they all knew it was true.

'John Penry is one. Essex may be another – he'll take some watching. But there may yet be others, connected perhaps with Scadbury.'

'Walsingham?' Effingham wanted to know.

'Not that simple, my lord.' Cecil shook his head and closed his lips. The Queen's imp was good at silences.

'There's something else,' Hunsdon said. 'We've all got copies of Marlowe's play thanks to the miracle of my very own printing press, but I believe only I have this.' He pulled more paper from his satchel, this time only a single sheet. 'It's from a man called Richard Baines.'

It didn't matter how often he watched it happen, Christopher Marlowe never tired of watching Tom Sledd create wonders. True, it was always preceded by a few days of head-scratching and moaning, cries of 'Impossible!' and 'It can't be done!' and then, suddenly, it *was* possible and it *could* be done. And here he was, at Scadbury, watching the Great Hall becoming transformed into another place, a place from another time.

Thomas Walsingham, with his customary generosity, had lent carpenters and their assistants wood from his store. Audrey had raided her linen presses and a keen eye would have been able to see where her best sheets now formed rich hangings, with the addition of some judicious dyes. Tapestries from bedchambers were folded and stitched to make couches and beds fit for a king and his ingle. Trestles, chairs, all were called into service and soon all was ready.

'Kit,' Tom called across the Hall, wiping a sawdust begrimed hand across his forehead. 'Do you want to come and walk the stage?'

Marlowe stood up and walked down the aisle left down the middle of the rows of seats at the back. Space had been left at the front for the groundlings, as was the custom, but they would be sitting cross-legged in neat rows like their betters behind them; no room for roistering and vegetable throwing here. Marlowe just hoped the cast could cope with an audience who were quiet until the end of a Scene, at which point they would politely clap. He had heard Thomas Walsingham haranguing his staff on just that subject only that morning, so he knew it would be so.

As he got nearer to the stage, the magic started to dim. Brush-strokes became visible. Gigantic, frantically applied stitches were clearly seen to be keeping rich furnishings together. The gilding became so much thin gold paint. But even so, it would do – a country audience was not a discerning one and candlelight could hide a multitude of sins.

Marlowe hopped up onto the stage and bounced a couple of times. There was nothing worse than a squeaking stage at a dramatic moment. But this seemed firm enough.

'I didn't need to make it very high, Kit,' Tom said, watching him. 'So I just put some beams down and then laid planks. It will make it easier to dismantle afterwards.' He chuckled. 'Do you remember when we did *Faustus* in . . . ooh, when was it?'

Marlowe smiled. 'Long ago, Tom, when we and the world were young.'

Sledd slapped his arm. 'Come on, Kit, we're neither of us thirty yet and as for the world, it's young enough, surely. I haven't noticed it showing its age, anyway.'

'No more do we, Tom, no more do we. But don't you find all these plays tend to run together in your mind? Just one season after another, winter, spring, summer, fall and then another winter.'

Tom Sledd loved his family more than he could say. And then, a very close second, he loved Kit Marlowe. He didn't like to see him introspective, particularly with what was already proving to be a difficult play to put on. He had had lines of people waiting with their pages, wanting to be sure that they wouldn't be thrown into gaol or worse for what they would be saying on stage. Shaxsper and Alleyn could be seen at any odd moment, heads together, muttering and looking over their shoulders. All plays had a resident shade. This one's shade was the colour of death and bore a scythe over its shoulder. Before he could say anything, while he sought the right words, Marlowe was himself again, his eyes flashing fire and his curls standing up around his head in an angelic aureole.

'Why so miserable, Tom?' he said, as though it was his friend who had been talking like a lost soul. 'We have a play to put on. I had a line in my head, you know, that I really wanted to use but can't quite get it in. I had written it to try and make that gibberish of Kyd's a bit better and I do love it. But try as I might, I can't make it fit. Perhaps if I play around with it a bit . . .'

'What was it, Kit?' Shaxsper was suddenly at his elbow. 'Perhaps I can help.'

Marlowe laughed and put his arm over Shaxsper's shoulder. 'Perhaps you can, Will,' he said, 'but it won't be easy. It goes – or I should say, it went – "The play's the thing, wherein we'll catch the conscience of the king." See – it worked really well for *Tragedy* but there's nowhere in *Edward*.'

'There is a king in it,' Alleyn's orotund vowels rolled around the half-dressed stage.

'There is indeed, Ned,' Marlowe agreed. 'But no play to catch his conscience.' He gave himself a shake. 'I seem dogged by lines at the moment. I have never had such perfect recall of anything I have written as I have of *Edward*. So,' and he gave Alleyn a playful punch on the arm, 'make sure you don't fluff your lines, Ned. Because I'll be listening, don't forget.'

'Ha!' Alleyn cried as though in pain.

'Sorry, Ned.' Marlowe was contrite. 'Did I hurt you?'

Alleyn saw Shaxsper's eyes, wide with panic. 'Er . . . perhaps a little. Gout. I do believe, a little gout.'

Marlowe looked concerned. 'In your arm, Ned? Is that not a little unusual? You must take care of yourself. You're an important man, as you well know.' The playwright turned to Sledd and the two actors slunk away.

'He knows,' Shaxsper hissed. 'He knows, by Christ.'

'How can he know?' Alleyn whispered. 'We haven't written anything down, we haven't told anyone else a thing. By the time he discovers it, it will be too late. There is only one performance.'

Sledd and Marlowe were walking the stage, making sure there was room for all the moves, the battle and the blood.

'What is the matter with those two?' Marlowe asked, jerking his head in the direction of Shaxsper and Alleyn.

Sledd gave them a fleeting glance. 'I really don't know,' he said. 'They are like cats on hot bricks every night, muttering and flinging themselves about like someone with St Vitus' Dance. You'd think Alleyn would be exhausted, the way he goes on; it's like a bawdy house up there till well gone midnight. Then he and Shaxsper whisper away until dawn for all I know. If it wasn't for the serving wenches, I would wonder if they weren't taking their parts a bit too seriously.'

Marlowe smiled. 'The day Alleyn takes any part seriously, is the day I hang up my quill, Tom,' he said. 'Now, are you *sure* this bed will take the weight?'

Alleyn and Shaxsper crept out of the Great Hall by a side door.

Shaxsper shook his head again. 'It's no good, Ned,' he said. 'He knows.'

Richard Baines had never heard confession in the church of St Nicholas. That was because, to all intents and purposes, he was an Anglican priest and Papist claptrap like that had been swept away, along with wall paintings and relics and the blood and the body of Christ.

He knelt in his secret chapel, barely large enough for him to kneel in. It was hidden behind the rood screen and the door could be locked from the inside as well as the out. Only Richard Baines had a key and it never left his person. Even when he was in bed with Audrey Walsingham, it dangled around his neck.

'What's this, Richard?' she had asked him once as she stroked his chest and nuzzled her head into his shoulder.

'The key to my soul,' he had told her and she found the answer poetic enough in a pathetic sort of way and took her stroking down lower. Thomas had been away.

He crossed himself in the little chapel and reached up to kiss the crucifix. He had known it would be like this. A Papist in an Anglican land was worse than a leper. They had told him so at the seminary, the scorpion's nest as the Puritans called it, at Douai. 'Trust to your God and your vows' they had told him. But that was before he had met Audrey Walsingham and before he had lost the soul whose key he carried. 'The body and blood of Christ,' he muttered, '*Hoc est corpus*'.

He heard a sound beyond the door, beyond the screen. That damned snivelling curate. He waited until the footsteps died away, then he clicked the lock and stepped into the light of the chancel. He relocked the door and pulled the heavy curtain across it, tucking the key under his robes. All traces of the Papacy had gone and he stood in his severe, whitewashed church, looking every inch the severe, whitewashed Puritan.

'Parkin!' he called to the curate.

The young man jumped, his heart in his mouth. He had no idea the vicar was there.

'Master Baines,' the lad skipped over to him.

Baines held the boy's narrow shoulders and looked him in the eye. 'How old are you?'

'Nineteen summers, Master Baines.'

'From Oxford, yes?'

'Merton College, Master Baines.'

'Well,' Baines smiled, 'we can't have everything in this life, can we? Tell me, Parkin,' he turned the lad around, 'what do you see there? Over the door?'

The curate squinted. The light was fading in the late afternoon and that part of the chancel was particularly dark.

'Er . . . the royal arms, Master Baines,' he said. 'Her Majesty's device.'

'And what does it say underneath, Parkin?' Baines asked. 'The motto?'

'*Semper Eadem*,' the boy said, growing ever more uneasy at the vicar's questions.

Baines still had one arm around the curate's neck and he leaned towards him, whispering in his ear. 'And what does it mean?' he asked.

Parkin swallowed hard. He had been speaking and writing Latin for years now, at Merton and before that at the King's School, Warwick. Surely, he wasn't *still* being tested.

'Always the same,' he whispered back, half-expecting to feel the kiss of a flail across his buttocks if he'd got it wrong.

'Always the same,' Baines nodded, 'but it doesn't have to be, does it?' he asked.

'I . . . I don't follow, Master Baines.' Parkin was trying, as gently as he could, to pull away, but the priest of St Nicholas was having none of it.

'Just imagine,' Baines said, 'for all your life – and nearly all of mine, come to that – that Jezebel has ruled England.'

Parkin almost gasped. Jezebel? That was the Queen. And that was what Papists called her.

'See it in your mind's eye, lad,' Baines said. 'The lions and lilies vanish in the light of God's glory, transformed into the lions and castles of Aragon and Asturias, Castile and Leon. The pomegranate in place of the rose, the Fleece instead of the Garter.'

Parkin was no expert at heraldry, but he knew that Richard Baines was staring up, not at the arms of Elizabeth but of Philip of Spain. There was a strange light in the vicar's eyes and his lips were moving with no sound.

'She's old, boy,' Baines said suddenly, 'the Queen. Old and decaying and corrupt. God has cast her out. And when she goes, finally, writhing and screaming into the fires of Hell, *then* we'll strike. Me and my followers.' He gripped the boy's shoulders again, swinging him back to face him. 'We must be ready, Parkin, for that great day, must we not?'

'Um . . . yes,' Parkin blurted out, his bladder suddenly unsure of itself. 'Yes, sir. Of course.'

'Of course,' Baines smiled. He patted the boy on the cheek,

then placed his hand on his head and forced him to kneel. His right hand came out, on the third finger, a ring that Parkin had never seen before. Baines's left hand was pulling the curate's head towards him, waiting until the boy's lips touched the gilt of the ring before he relaxed the pressure and let the boy stand up.

'Now,' Baines said, as though he were a different man, 'lock the church, would you? God's house should be open always, but these are dangerous times. And there are men under Thomas Walsingham's roof we would do well to watch. Good night to you, Parkin.'

Henry Parkin had never really meant to become a churchman. When he was a boy at school in Warwick he had had plans to become a household name. This was the time of the self-made man, when any jack could become a master. Parkin wanted to be part of all that. He wasn't sure at that point quite how he would achieve it, but he was sure he would be famous one day. To find himself now as a curate to a madman in a church in the middle of nowhere was something which filled him with a mixture of sorrow and blind terror. He had known that Richard Baines and he could never be friends from the moment they met. He had known that Baines was a little off-kilter when judged against the men who had trained him to be a member of the clergy. But that he was as mad as this – how could he possibly have guessed that?

After Baines had swept out on a flurry of cassock and a faint whiff of incense, Parkin sat a while. The church was simple, just how he liked it. He had been told by parishioners, the older ones, the ones who remembered other times than these, that under the whitewash there were beautiful paintings, of the saints in heaven and Christ in majesty. In general, Parkin disapproved of that kind of thing but a part of him that craved beauty and ornament wished they were still there. Then, as he went through the church blowing out candles and preparing it for its night of slumber, well deserved after all the Christmas services, he could have looked up and sought comfort from the gentle face of his Redeemer. As it was, all he could do was scuttle down the nave like a rodent with a fox on its trail.

Outside, the cold air calmed him. There was frost in the air and no sign yet of spring. His grandmother, back in his village of Honiley, deep in the Warwickshire fields, had always said that she could smell spring on the day after the midwinter solstice. His mother had told him that the old lady was a little touched in the head, but even so, he always lifted his nose in the air to smell the spring as soon as Christmas was over. But all he could smell tonight was his own rank sweat, pooled cold and clammy under his arms and down his back after his encounter with Richard Baines. Men like Baines always got their comeuppance. The trick here would be to make sure he didn't get his as well, by mere proximity. He gave himself a shake. He must tell someone and he must tell someone now.

As he entered the big house through the back door as was his habit, he stopped to think for a moment. It was no good going in to see Master Walsingham with a half-baked reiteration of what had gone on with Baines. The man was after all the chaplain to the house and was more likely to be believed than he was. He would lose his position. His parents would be so disappointed. Then he shrugged and knocked on Lewknor's door. Disappointment and a living son was probably better than pride and a pile of ashes to bury.

The steward opened the door and smiled. Like most people in the house he had a soft spot for the curate, saddled with Richard Baines day and night. 'Master Henry,' he said, opening his door wide. 'How can I help you?'

'I need to see Master Walsingham, urgently, Master Lewknor, if that is possible,' he said, not going in.

'I don't know whether . . . why don't you go to the brown parlour? That's where I saw him last.' People didn't stand on ceremony at Scadbury.

'Is that all right?' Parkin was humble, as always. 'I don't want to bother him, but . . . well, I do need to see him.'

'He'll be happy to see you, I'm sure,' the steward said. 'If he's not there, come back and we'll see if we can find him for you.'

Parkin trotted along the passageway and up a small flight of stairs. If it wasn't for Richard Baines, Scadbury would be a good place to live. He let his mind wander, pictured himself as the vicar of Chislehurst, growing old in the living, a brood of children and a comfortable wife under the roof of a nice country benefice. He reached the door of the brown parlour and tapped, listening with his ear against the thick planks.

It was hard to tell, but he thought he heard someone call 'Enter' so he did. Sitting in front of a roaring fire, Padraig's head in her lap, sat Audrey Walsingham. Her head was turned to see who was knocking and Parkin thought he had never seen her looking more beautiful.

'I'm sorry, Mistress Walsingham,' he stammered, 'I was looking for . . .' now, here was a difficulty. He had heard the rumours, but he had no option but to say 'your husband', which he knew could not be true.

She laughed and patted the seat of the padded couch beside her. 'He's out checking on the hounds,' she said, pleasantly. 'He'll be hours once he starts talking to the kennel master. Come and tell me all about it; you look worried.'

Parkin had heard veiled comments about how Mistress Walsingham ate men for breakfast but he had not really quite understood the allusion. The fire did look very inviting though and he missed his dogs at home, so Padraig was also a draw. As if pulled on wires, he went in and sat down.

'Now, then, Master . . . Parkin, isn't it? Henry, if I remember correctly?'

Parkin was delighted and amazed. That the legendary beauty who ruled Scadbury and its master should know his name was beyond his wildest dreams. He tore his eyes away from her face and looked down at his fingers, lacing and unlacing in his lap.

'Mistress Walsingham,' he said, keeping his eyes down, 'I have just had a disturbing incident with Master Baines in the church.'

'Really?' Audrey Walsingham was genuinely surprised. Her thoughts were always focussed on when she could get the next man into bed and she thought she was a good judge of people in that respect. Richard had always seemed so . . . enthusiastic. 'Do you mean he . . . well, did he touch you?'

Parkin's eyes flew up to meet hers. 'No,' he said, quickly, 'No, nothing like that.' He had heard the rumours about his superior and Mistress Walsingham and although he largely dismissed them, he was a great believer in no smoke without fire. 'Much worse. He . . .' suddenly, what had happened in the church seemed less clear; could he have imagined it? He shook himself. He must do what he had come here to do, whatever the consequences. 'He . . . seemed to be telling me that he was planning the overthrow of the Queen.'

Audrey Walsingham's eyebrows all but disappeared into her hair. 'Richard?' she said. 'Really, Master Parkin, I think you must have misunderstood.'

Henry Parkin was young. He was inexperienced. But he also knew that in this room, though he lagged behind in cunning, he was streets ahead when it came to basic intelligence. 'I am sorry to argue with you, Mistress Walsingham,' he said, firmly. 'But it is hard to mistake someone calling the Queen a Jezebel for something else. He spoke of Spain. He spoke of the Queen writhing in the fires of Hell.' He leaned forward. 'Mistress Walsingham; he's mad. For certain, he's mad.'

'Richard can have quite strong views,' Audrey Walsingham said. 'Sometimes he gets carried away, perhaps. I still think you misunderstood. I will speak to him. And meanwhile – I would prefer you not to speak of this to anyone else, Henry. Can you promise me that, please?'

'But . . .'

'Henry?'

Parkin was not sure how this interview had gone. He had told his tale and so it was off his chest, but . . . would anything be done? Would Baines be allowed to stay and plot his overthrow of the Queen? Indeed, was he even plotting the overthrow of the Queen or was he simply madder than a hare in March? He stood up and Audrey extended her hand. He bent over it and could scarcely suppress a shudder, as he remembered Baines's hand thrust out for him to venerate his ring. He looked up and found her eyes boring into him.

'*Henry?*'

He took a deep breath. 'Yes, Mistress Walsingham,' he said. 'I promise.'

'Good. Please close the door as you leave.'

And that, Henry knew, was simply that.

* * *

Frizer and Skeres were lolling on Scadbury's battlements during their break from rehearsals the next morning. Had this been the Rose, there would have been a gaggle of Winchester Geese on hand to warm their cockles and an inn within a walking gentleman's distance which offered cheap ale to those of the thespian persuasion. There would even had been an old bear to torment. As it was, although Scadbury was elegant and spacious and the stables warm and comfortable, the place generally lacked the cosmopolitan atmosphere of London's finest theatres and the pair were reduced to sharing a pipe.

'Hello,' Skeres, with his height advantage, could see the road beyond the bend.

'What?' Frizer's view was momentarily lost in smoke.

'Carriages,' Skeres said. 'Two of 'em. And . . .' he was frowning, trying to focus over the distance, 'I count twelve outriders.'

Frizer strained himself to catch the view. His partner-in-crime was right. The gallopers were actually trotting, helmets gleaming in the weak winter sun and cloaks snapping behind them in the wind. The noise was of creaking wheels, jingling bits and clattering hoofs and it came to them clearly on the cold air.

'It's the Queen!' Frizer shouted, dropping his pipe when he clapped his hands together.

'Don't talk nonsense,' Skeres scowled. 'Look at that banner. See the motto – *Sero sed Sero*? That's Burghley, that is.'

'What's that mean, then?'

'I dunno. Have to ask Marlowe – he's supposed to be the scholar. I only know it 'cos I once came into possession of a little trinket belonging to Lord Burghley.'

'You never told me that,' Frizer said.

'You never asked,' Skeres countered. 'No, he was giving them away to the poor cripples of Her Majesty's navy soon after the Armada.'

'You were never in the navy, Nick,' Frizer felt he had to point out.

'You know that,' Skeres acknowledged, 'and I know that. Thankfully, Lord Burghley didn't. He shook my hand – which may have been when the trinket became mine – and said

"Thank you, my man, for what you've done for England." Well, it's no more than the truth, is it? Good God, I didn't know they were *all* coming.'

The two men slipped down from the crenellations and crossed to the other side of the wall. The outriders clattered beneath them over the drawbridge, followed by the carriages. Thomas and Audrey Walsingham were hurrying out of the house to welcome the arrivals.

'There's Burghley,' Skeres muttered out of the corner of his mouth. 'The ancient one. White beard.'

'I know,' Frizer said, proving how in touch he was with current affairs. 'Who's the midget? His jester?'

'His little boy,' Skeres said, 'and I mean that. They say Robert Cecil is a total bastard – not in the bloodline sense of course, just in his attitude.'

There was much bobbing, bowing and handshaking, doffing of caps and, in Audrey's case, curtseying.

'There he is,' Skeres nudged Frizer, 'our master himself – the Lord Chamberlain.'

'Makes you proud, don't it?' Frizer smiled. 'Gives you a sort of warm glow.'

'Well,' Skeres was more pragmatic, 'if it ever came to him paying us anything it would.'

'Who's the fourth bloke?' Frizer wanted to know.

'Ah, he was there too, when I received the undying gratitude from his Lordship for my inestimable services in destroying the Armada. He's Howard of bloody Effingham, the Lord Admiral.'

'Coo.' Frizer was impressed. 'Say what you like about Kit Marlowe, he knows some powerful people. And they've all come to see his play.'

'You're right, Ing,' Skeres nodded. 'That's a third of the Privy Council of this great country of ours, right there, down in the courtyard.'

'If the devil cast his net, eh?' Frizer chuckled.

'You've got that right,' Skeres said.

TEN

Kit Marlowe, playwright and poet, was the only version of the man at Scadbury that night. Audrey Walsingham might have wished to add 'lover' to that category, but even if he had been so inclined, there would have been no room for that. He had written plays before, of course, and had seen them performed to great acclaim. He was welcome in almost all of the great houses of England and enjoyed a level of comfort in his private dwelling that his family at home in Canterbury could only dream of. He had friends and if they didn't outnumber his enemies, this didn't bother him. He could number among them aristocracy, the Bishop of Winchester's Geese, pickpockets, dons, serving men and women, actors, stage managers (just one of those) and a bear. He thought himself a lucky man indeed.

But for now, he sat alone, in the furthest corner of the back row of seats in the Great Hall of Scadbury. The ingenuity of Amyntas Finch had provided a modest rake to the seating, so that even those at the back, filling the row beside him, had as good a view as those at the front. Chosen servants and tenants were already in place in the space between where the seats ended and the stage began. Henry Carey made sure that his own manservant sat directly in front of him; he didn't want the Hunsdon shins to come into unplanned contact with the general hoi polloi.

Tom Sledd had done wonders. Bearing in mind that the whole thing would have disappeared by morning, Marlowe felt that some kind of faerieland had been concocted there in the Great Hall, to tell a tale of love, loss and politics. He sighed when he thought that it would be the politics which most people would remember longest. Though as the love and loss were from a rather unusual angle, to say the least, perhaps that would also stick in their minds. It was good that Alleyn and Shaxsper seemed to have put their stupid prejudices behind them; he knew that the beauty of his words would see the thing through.

The ramshackle band which had accompanied the procession of the Lord of Misrule had been rehearsed and rehearsed almost to the point of madness by a musical youth from the Rose. He was no actor, though he longed to be, but his perfect pitch was not something that Tom Sledd was willing to do without, so he usually got a part, in this particular play, a monk, so he could surreptitiously conduct using his wide sleeves as camouflage. They struck up now and several maids ran to and fro, extinguishing candles at the back of the room and lighting those at the front, to illuminate the stage.

Shaxsper, his bliss complete that he had an entrance long before Alleyn, walked onto the stage, a letter in his hand. Marlowe tutted a little because the Stratford oaf had still not lost the habit of walking like some kind of barnyard fowl, strutting with straight legs and nodding his head in time. Sledd had done his best with the wig, but it was almost a whole size too small and tended to look a little like a basket upended. But still. The beauty of the words would soon make men forget that Shaxsper looked like something got up to frighten crows, rather than the beautiful boy who entranced a king.

Having strutted to the front, Shaxsper brandished his letter and in a remarkably clear voice and just a hint remaining of his unfortunate accent, he began. 'My father is deceas'd. Come, Gaveston. And share the kingdom with thy dearest friend.'

'Look up, look up,' muttered Marlowe. 'Let them know you're reading that bit and the next is all you.'

Shaxsper looked up and smiled winsomely.

Marlowe winced a little, but it was not too bad. He reminded himself that this was not London. He could cast the part properly for London.

'Ah, words that make me surfeit with delight!' Shaxsper said, his eyes on far horizons. 'What greater bliss can hap to Gaveston than live and be the favourite of a king! My liege, I come!'

Marlowe's head snapped up. My liege? What in Hell's name was the idiot thinking? Forget your lines, by all means.

Make them up if all else fails but . . . my liege? What second-rate playwright had Shaxsper been reading to come up with a word like that? But Gaveston was now pacing back and forth.

'My knee shall bow to none but to the king. As for the multitude, that are but sparks, rak'd up in embers of their poverty – *Tanti* – I'll fawn first on the wind, that glanceth at my lips, and flieth away.'

Marlowe was now sitting upright and looking wildly from left to right. By his quick reckoning, the fool had missed out at least a dozen lines. Mighty lines! His lines! He leaned out as far as he dare and saw the little precocious lad who held the pages look desperately at the stage and thumb through what he held in his lap. This was somewhat of a relief, because it at least proved that he, the writer of the words being mangled down there, was not, as he had begun to think, as mad as a tree. Someone else had noticed too. There would be Hell to pay when he got his hands round the Warwickshire idiot's throat, but for now, Finch's ingenuity had him trapped, because the seats were balanced on single beams and there was no way out once everyone was seated.

The three poor men had entered and Gaveston had got rid of them, using more or less the words Marlowe had written. The next speech was one which had kept him up for more than one fevered night, scouring his books for the right references, writing back and forth to Michael Johns, who had forgotten more than most men ever knew and who had loved Marlowe from the day they met. This speech had Johns embedded in every line and if Shaxsper changed a single word, he would . . .

'These are not men for me,' Shaxsper declaimed, holding out one arm in unconscious parody of Alleyn, 'I must have wanton poets, pleasant wits, musicians, that with touching of a string may draw the pliant king which way I please.'

Marlowe flopped back in his seat and made the whole row judder. The farmer sitting next to him turned in fury. He was having to sit through this arrant nonsense because his wife had pretensions to be a lady. If he was pitched off backwards and broke his back, that would just put the final touch to the evening from Hell and he wasn't having any. Marlowe shrugged apologetically and sat still. Shaxsper seemed to have found his feet, so it might all yet go well.

'Music and poetry is his delight,' Shaxsper told his audience, 'Therefore I'll have Italian masks by night, sweet speeches, comedies, and pleasing shows and in the day, when he shall walk abroad, like sylvan nymphs my servants shall be clad.'

Marlowe frowned, but pages, servants, it was an easy mistake to make.

'My men, like satyrs grazing on the lawns, shall with their goat-feet dance the antic hay. Sometime a lovely girl in Dian's shape, with hair that gilds the water as it glides, crownets of pearl about her naked arms and in her sportful hands an olive-tree, to hide those parts which men delight to see, shall bathe her in a spring.'

The farmer nudged Marlowe and chuckled. 'I like a bit of dirty talk in a play. That Master Marlowe, he knows how to tickle a fellow's fancy.' He turned to his wife and nudged her too. 'You'll be ready for a good siring tonight, Mistress, nor I'm mistaken.'

But Master Marlowe had turned his face to the wall, and, in the corner, in the dark, made plans for revenge.

The rest of the play ground on, with Alleyn and Shaxsper taking out anything that might bear reference to the actual relationship between the king and Gaveston. Alleyn even fondled a few faux-female rumps as the court whirled and gavotted through their moves. Marlowe could only grind his teeth in impotent rage, made worse by the fact that the audience seemed, by and large, to be enjoying themselves. The farmer, in particular, was turning out to be a bit of a handful and Marlowe could only assume that at home, he had little cause for bawdy enjoyment. His wife, red cheeked and phlegmatic by his side, made that assumption likely to be accurate.

As soon as the interval was announced, with another flurry of shawms and tabors, Marlowe was on his feet, balancing precariously on the beam, bouncing with annoyance as the farmer and his wife waited patiently for others to sidle along and make their way to the brown parlour, where refreshments had been laid out.

Marlowe tried to remain calm and listened to the conversations of others, trapped like him at the far end of lower rows.

'I'm puzzled,' said a languid voice at his knee level.

'Are you, dear?' a disinterested female voice said. 'What about?'

'Well, as I remember it,' the first voice said, 'and I am sure I am right, the king and Gaveston weren't just jolly good friends.'

'Oh, really, dear. Did they not like each other then?'

'Umm . . .'

Marlowe glanced down and saw what was clearly an educated man, with finely etched features and a keen eye, standing beside a young thing who could have been his daughter. Marlowe checked his unworthy thoughts. Perhaps she *was* his daughter. But 'dear'? Possibly not.

The older man leaned forward to speak in the girl's ear, but Marlowe's hearing was keen and he caught every word. 'They were . . . well, they were very friendly.'

'They seemed friendly, dear, yes,' the flat voice answered. 'They chat a lot, don't they? I must say I couldn't follow it all.'

'No.' The man was getting testy now. 'I mean *really* friendly.' He bent his head more and now even Marlowe's bat-like ears couldn't hear his words but their meaning was clear enough from the girl's reaction.

She turned her face up to the man's, her cheeks a furious red, her mouth a horrified 'O'. She narrowed her eyes and when she spoke it was with a tight voice which betokened trouble when she got him home. 'If you *ever* use that language in front of me again, you loathsome creature,' she spat, 'that will be the end of this marriage in anything but name. I *blush* that you even know of such things.' She looked him up and down with contempt. 'Though it explains a lot which had been puzzling me.'

Marlowe raised a sympathetic eyebrow as he met the man's startled glance. He had expected his play to ruffle some feathers and indeed it had; it was just that the ruffling and the feathers were not what he had foreseen.

*   *   *

In the room behind the stage which had been given over to costumes and waiting areas, everything was preternaturally quiet. Usually, at this point on an opening night, there would be back-slapping and excitement, with the boys playing the women getting up to all kinds of tricks just to let off steam. If a silent room could become even more silent, this one did as Marlowe entered, bringing a blast of cold air into the stuff atmosphere.

He stood just inside the door and waited for someone to speak. Though he was without the flaming sword, he looked for all the world like Gabriel guarding the gate of Eden. It was certain that no one was going to pass until Marlowe was good and ready.

'Well, Kit,' it was, of course, Tom Sledd who broke the silence. 'It seems to be going well. Only hearing good things from the audience.' He tried a merry laugh but it died in his throat, a thought unborn.

'Really?' Marlowe's lips were tight and his face was pale. 'So far what I have heard is a farmer threatening his wife with a good seeing to and a wife who thinks her husband has a dirty mind because he was wondering if all his history teaching in the past has been wrong.' He scanned the room and found Alleyn, trying to look nonchalant in a dark corner. '*Has* his history teaching all been wrong, Ned?'

Alleyn looked up as though aware of Marlowe's presence for the first time. 'Hmm? Oh, Kit. Didn't see you there. Sorry, what was the question?'

'People seem to be confused, Ned. Any of them out there who has ever heard of Gaveston and the king seem to think that their relationship was a little closer than you and Shaxsper have been portraying it. Can this be right?'

Alleyn smiled hopefully, looking around the room but no one would meet his eye.

'Well, can it, Ned?' Marlowe's voice rose to a roar and even in the buffet room the length of the Great Hall away, people turned their heads.

Alleyn looked desperately for Shaxsper. This had, after all, been all his idea. But he was nowhere to be seen. 'I . . . well, that is *we* . . .' An idea dawned deep at the back of Alleyn's brain. It was a rare event, but he grasped the opportunity with both hands. 'We didn't want to upset the ladies.' That was it. He had no details or corroborating evidence, but it seemed like a good enough excuse to him and he was an acknowledged champion when it came to making up excuses.

'You didn't want to upset the ladies.' Marlowe spoke low and slow and with every word advanced a step into the room. Faunt, who knew all of Marlowe's moves, stepped forward too, watching for the hand in the small of the back. It wasn't that he cared whether Alleyn lived or died – in fact, if he had a preference, it would be for died – but in the middle of a play with a front row like they had tonight, would not be a good time.

Alleyn's hands fluttered. 'Well, there are a lot of ladies in the audience.' He pointed at Marlowe, never a good idea. 'You yourself have just mentioned two. But mainly,' and his expression became saintly, with eyes upturned, 'we were thinking of our hostess. Mistress Audrey Walsingham is a lady of refined character who would be upset by such insinuations.' He smiled and ducked his head. As far as he was concerned, that was the whole matter disposed of neatly and tied in a bow. He looked up after a minute and gave a small scream. Silently, as certain as death, Marlowe had crossed the room on soundless feet and was inches from him, a dagger in his hand.

'I assume you mean the same Mistress Audrey Walsingham who you described to me as going like a mare on heat?' Marlowe asked, reasonably. Queen Isabella sniggered and was immediately quelled by a smack round the head from Tom Sledd.

'That doesn't sound like me,' Alleyn whined. 'I would never be so disrespectful as to speak that way about a lady.'

This time everyone sniggered and Marlowe let the laughter die down before he spoke. First, he sheathed his dagger and then stepped back. 'Alleyn,' he said, 'you and Shaxsper, because I know you were involved, Will, so you can come out now.' He turned and waited until Shaxsper, wig even more askew, emerged from a pile of cloaks discarded from Act I, Scene II. 'You and Shaxsper have interfered with my play and made it into a pointless laughing stock. You have Edward the

Second, possibly the most notorious homosexual this country has yet produced, patting the arses of courtiers – female only of course – and playing rough games with all and sundry with hardly a glance at Gaveston, who in actuality filled his nights and days with longing. It seems a little hard on poor old Piers, come to think of it, that he met a hideous death because he occasionally played a round or two of stoolball with the king.'

The boys in the cast were so near to laughing they almost burst, but knew it may be the last noise they ever made, so managed to keep silent.

'Will, come round where I can see you. Perhaps you will be able to explain why you did what you did.'

Shaxsper made his way through the crowd which parted for him as though he were a leper.

'Yes, Kit,' he said. 'I can explain.'

'Excellent. Can you make a start, because we need to get on with this travesty, I suppose?'

'Well . . .' despite his pretensions to being a playwright, Shaxsper's brain was not of the quickest and it was even more than usually devoid of ideas as the man stood in front of possibly the angriest person he had ever seen. The Warwickshire man said the first thing that came into his head and it was by no means his finest hour. 'It was all his idea,' he said, pointing with a trembling finger at Alleyn.

The actor leapt up with more agility than he ever showed on stage. 'Me?' he thundered. '*Me?* It was you, you jumped-up popinjay. You didn't want to ruin your reputation, as if you even have one! *I*,' and he thumped his chest with abandon and nearly winded himself, '*I* am the greatest actor of the age and, if I may say so, probably the greatest lover also. No one would believe that *I* could be anything other than a red-blooded man.' He paused for breath. All that emphasis had taken it out of him rather. 'Whereas *you*, you bald-headed, spindle-shanked apology, who has ever heard of *you*? Or ever will, come to that.'

He turned his back on Shaxsper and turned to Marlowe, who was, when all was said and done, his bread and butter. 'Master Marlowe,' this time his voice was low and honeyed, 'I can only apologize for any damage this oaf has done you.

The rest of the play shall be as written, word for word. I give you my solemn promise.'

'Are you insane?' Shaxsper snapped. 'Apart from anything else, everyone thinks that the king and Gaveston are just boon companions at best so if they start spooning and kissing like a couple of girls, don't you think the audience might be a bit confused, to say the least.'

'Audiences don't notice what's in front of them,' Alleyn said, shortly. 'Don't you remember that time when we had to replace Dido halfway through and the new actor was six foot if he was an inch and the previous one was only up to his elbow. Nobody noticed a thing.'

Marlowe stepped in. Time was wasting and they needed to work out what to do to rescue what they could. 'Hate to say it though I do,' he said, 'Shaxsper is right. We can't change this particular horse in midstream. Just go on as you would have done and we'll take the consequences.'

Alleyn blinked. He had not expected that. He smiled and extended a hand. 'No hard feelings, Kit?' he said.

Marlowe looked at his hand as if it was smeared with the filthiest mire and then met his eyes. 'Hard feelings, Ned? No, no hard feelings. Just blind hatred and a promise from me – that if I live to be a hundred, you will never, while I live, act on any stage in this whole world again.' He spun on his heel and walked out, into the murmuration that could only be an audience resuming its seats, full of wine and sweetmeats.

There was silence for a moment or two as everyone digested what had happened. Inevitably, it was Skeres who spoke first. 'That went well,' he said.

Outside, the shawms struck up and the cast of *The Troublesome Reign and Lamentable Death of Edward the Second, king of England* lined up, ready for the second half.

Thomas Walsingham had given the brown parlour over to the Privy Council for the duration of their stay at Scadbury. They would not be here for long, and Whitehall was only ten miles away. Even in that time, however, horsemen arrived throughout the night, bringing messages for one or all of them. The government of Queen Elizabeth never slept.

'Well,' Howard was the first to break silence and Padraig raised his head from the straw floor as if to catch his every word, 'I have to say I don't really know what all the fuss was about. I thought the play was rather good.'

'They changed it,' Burghley was pouring himself another claret from Walsingham's bottomless cellar. 'Cleaned it up.'

'Well, good,' Howard nodded. 'Common sense at last.'

'With respect, my lord,' Cecil said, sitting across from the Admiral, 'you're missing the point.'

'Really?' Howard had never liked Burghley's little boy and daily, as he grew ever more powerful and more bumptious, he liked him even less. 'In what way?'

Cecil sighed. How his father had put up with such idiots in council for all these years he couldn't imagine. 'The written version we saw talked of sodomy, unnatural love. However, that's by the way and no theatre crowd would stand for it. What's more important – and what is still there in what we've just seen – is the attack on us.'

'Us?' Hunsdon frowned.

'Specifically,' Burghley weighed in, 'my son and I.'

'The Regnum Cecilianum,' Hunsdon nodded.

'Call it what you will,' Burghley snapped, 'that is precisely the kind of propaganda rubbish that men like Marlowe peddle.'

Howard looked confused and Cecil came to his rescue. 'For Edward II read Her Majesty,' he said. 'Consider what happens in the play. Edward is infatuated with Gaveston and heaps on him titles and power.'

'The Regnum Cecilianum,' Hunsdon said again, understanding exactly what was going on.

'It's wider than that,' Cecil said. 'We all of us in this room have had power thrust upon us, by the grace of Her Majesty. Parliament – in the play, the various earls and churchmen offended by Edward and Gaveston – has been ignored.'

'How often,' Burghley said, 'has Her Majesty given Parliament her "answers answerless". She has ignored their requests, granted favours to her favourites.'

'Leicester,' Howard remembered. 'Essex. Ralegh.'

'You, my lord,' Cecil reminded him. 'My Lord Hunsdon, my father and myself.'

'And she let my sailors rot after the Armada,' Howard remembered too, 'dying of gangrene in the ships at Plymouth.'

'I gave them money,' Burghley insisted. 'Food. Medicine.'

Howard leaned forward to look Burghley in the eye. '*You* did, Burghley,' he said. 'Not the Queen.'

'Consider the play again,' Cecil said. 'What do the discontented Lords do? They overthrow Gaveston, striking off his head on some accursed hill. And the king? The king is murdered at Berkeley castle.'

'I was hoping for a poker up his arse,' Howard grinned, but if that was an attempt at levity, it didn't work.

Cecil ignored him. 'What Marlowe is saying is this,' he said. 'The Queen and her government are corrupt. It is the duty of parliament to overthrow both. I cannot conceive of a clearer example of treason.'

'Nor I,' said Hunsdon.

'So Marlowe must die?' Howard wanted confirmation.

'He must be brought to book,' Burghley said. 'In what way, exactly, we must decide. Faunt is here watching him; our man is tidying up the loose ends. But we have to meet this over-reacher Marlowe face to face. His mouth must be stopped.'

He got up and crossed to the door. 'Ho!' he called along the passageway. One of his guards clicked to attention. 'Find Master Marlowe,' Burghley said, 'and bring him here. Now.'

No one rose when Marlowe walked in. Still fuming over the wreckage that Alleyn and Shaxsper had caused to his play, he had not undressed but had spent the last hour pacing his room. Faunt, on his way to the stables, had heard the odd book hit the oak panelling and resigned himself to the fact that for somebody, it was going to be a noisy night; nothing he could say would calm the playwright down.

'You sent for me, my Lords?' Marlowe had not expected, any more than Skeres and Frizer had, all four of the inner sanctum of the Privy Council, yet here they were, looking at him, grim-faced.

'The play, Marlowe,' Burghley, as usual, opened proceedings.

Marlowe waited. Perhaps this was his chance to use the line

that was gnawing at his brain, 'The play's the thing,' he said, 'wherein I'll catch the conscience of the king.'

'You'll catch a great deal more than that, sir,' Burghley snapped. 'It's sedition, pure and simple. Treason against the state.'

'Is it, my Lord?' Marlowe played the ingenue, 'but it all happened over two hundred years ago.'

'Don't trifle with me, sir.' The Lord Treasurer was on his feet. 'I wasn't born yesterday. You knew exactly what you were doing writing this . . . abortion. Your aim was to stir up the populace to revolution.'

'Forgive me, my Lord,' Marlowe said. 'I watched the audience during the performance as I always do. I saw no seething resentment, or flaming brands, no one vowing to tear down the establishment. If revolution was my aim, I failed abysmally.'

'That's because Scadbury isn't London,' Hunsdon said. 'A London mob are more unruly. If they see it enacted on stage, they'll try and act it out themselves – that's how stupid they are.'

'May I remind you, my Lord,' Marlowe said, 'that Scadbury was your idea as much as it was mine. The men you saw performing tonight are your men, sir; the Lord Chamberlain's Men.'

'I hope you don't blame me, Marlowe,' Hunsdon thundered. 'As far as I knew you were going with Kyd's *Spanish Tragedy*.'

'Unworkable, my Lord,' Marlowe shrugged, 'as it turned out.'

'We have your original words, Marlowe,' Burghley said. 'The draft of the play as you wrote it. If you or your players toned it down, that doesn't change the original concept – or the purpose behind it.'

'Where did you get the original?' Marlowe asked. There was no 'my Lord' now.

'That's no concern of yours,' Burghley told him.

'It is very much a concern of mine,' Marlowe said, 'because the man who probably copied it out is dead.'

'What?' Howard blinked. 'Who was that?'

'A copyist named Roger Dalston,' the playwright told him.

'He was found murdered eight nights ago, here at Scadbury, wearing the costume of the Lord of Misrule.'

The Privy Council looked at each other. 'These things happen,' Burghley said with a shrug, as though discussing the weather. 'It is of no consequence.'

Marlowe closed to the man and the other three were out of their seats, even little Robert who barely reached Marlowe's shoulder. 'It was of consequence to his brother,' the playwright growled, 'as it must be to all his family and friends.'

There was a silence and the four stood in a row, their backs to the fire, their faces immobile.

'Marlowe,' Burghley said, 'let this be one final warning to you. Her Majesty's government will not tolerate opposition. What you have done is tantamount to treason. And we hang traitors. This travesty of a play will never be performed again. My men have orders to destroy every copy of it and since it has not been lodged with the Master of the Revels, it will, in fact, cease to exist. We will of course keep our copies to ensure your good behaviour. And be assured, Marlowe, that it is the good service in various matters that you have done Her Majesty that has saved you from the noose. Do I make myself clear?'

'Perfectly, my Lord.' Marlowe was calm again.

'One more thing,' Cecil stopped the man in mid-bow. 'Your contract with me is hereby terminated. Rogue agents I can do without. I hope the theatre offers a living wage, Marlowe, because you won't receive another penny from Her Majesty's government.'

'Pieces of silver, Sir Robert,' Marlowe said and he saw himself out.

It had been a long time since Charles Howard had been in a church as simple and unadorned as St Nicholas in Chislehurst. It was late by the time he arrived, leaving his rapier at the door and following the glow of the candlelight from the altar.

A young priest sat there, staring wistfully it seemed to Effingham at the royal arms over the side door.

'Long to reign over us,' the Admiral said.

Henry Parkin leapt to his feet. His encounter with Baines, followed by his encounter with Audrey Walsingham, had shredded his nerves. He had not been to see Marlowe's play and he had no idea who this man with the high ruff and elegant grey beard was.

'Sorry if I startled you, vicar,' the man said. 'Couldn't help noticing you noticing the Queen's arms up there. Thank God for her, eh?'

'Indeed, sir,' Parkin bowed, aware that he was in the presence of greatness.

'Howard,' the man held out his hand, 'of Effingham. Lord Admiral.'

'My Lord.' Parkin almost bent himself double again, lower this time.

'Look,' Effingham placed an avuncular arm around the lad's bony shoulders. 'I know you chaps don't hear confession as such any more, but can I talk to you . . . boy to man, as it were?'

'My Lord,' Parkin stumbled. 'I must tell you that I am not the priest-in-charge. The Reverend Baines . . .'

'Baines?' Effingham frowned. 'I know that name.' He was still frowning and nothing was helping his memory, least of all the lad who stood like a rabbit in the sights of a fowling piece.

'Er . . . I am Henry Parkin, my Lord,' he said at last. 'The curate.'

'You've taken Holy Orders, though?' Effingham checked.

'Oh, yes, my Lord.'

'Well, that's by the way, really. Do you know Christopher Marlowe, the playwright?'

'I have recently met him, my Lord, yes. He is staying . . . oh, but you must know that.'

Effingham patted the pew next to where he sat. This was the second time in twenty-four hours that someone had done that. Parkin had been afraid to sit next to Audrey Walsingham too, but he screwed his courage to the sticking place and sat down.

'You'll forgive me for this, my boy,' Effingham said, 'but, well, things are happening at the moment that . . . the world is turning upside down. Do you follow?'

'Um . . .'

'You saw Marlowe's play last night?'

'No, sir,' Parkin said. 'My calling doesn't allow me to take in the theatre, I'm afraid. Invention of the devil.'

Effingham laughed. 'Yes, so's gunpowder, but what would we do without it, eh? Be crossing ourselves like Papists and speaking Spanish by now, I have no doubt.' He was suddenly serious. 'We . . . that is, my colleagues and I . . . have been pretty beastly to Marlowe, threatening him with . . . well, I think we went too far. Can I tell you about it? Get it off my chest, so to speak. And, young as you are, I'd welcome your views.'

The sun was still struggling over the horizon when the carriages from the stables pulled up outside the great front of Scadbury that Sunday morning, the last of the year. The outriders sat patiently waiting for their betters, their cloaks wrapped around them to try and keep in such warmth as rose from their mounts. All was still; not even a winter robin's song broke the silence and when a horse stamped a hoof or whinnied it sounded like the trump of doom to the men waiting in double rank.

Suddenly, from behind them, there was a clatter that set all the horses jinking, their metal-shod hoofs throwing sparks from the rough gravel in front of the house.

'What in the name of God was that?' the captain of the guard said and all the men were off their horses in a twinkling, facing the source of the noise, swords and daggers in their hands. One, nearest the door, rushed to bar the way; no one must come in or out until the danger was past.

Tom Sledd and Amyntas Finch came around the corner, a beam on one shoulder, another under the other arm. They looked like some strange automaton, joined by the wood but almost a foot apart in height. Because of the difference in the length of their stride, the beam had just crashed to the ground and the tiles in the vine house that stretched the length of the south side of the house would never be quite the same again.

Sledd, leading the way, stopped in his tracks and was nearly bowled over by Finch's continued velocity. The stage manager looked at the row of weapons in front of him and then up to the faces. 'Gentlemen,' he said, when he regained the power of speech.

'Who are you and where are you from?' the captain asked.

'I am Thomas Sledd, of London. This is Amyntas, sometime George, Finch, also of London, I suppose. I never asked. Why do you want to know? All we're doing is taking the stage apart. Master Walsingham is very hospitable, but we don't want to take advantage.'

'We heard a shot,' one of the men said, accusingly.

'No,' Sledd looked puzzled. 'Look, do you mind if we put these down? It's all right for Finch back there, but they're about at the limit of what I can carry.'

The men looked at each other and took a step back. Their officer nodded.

'Right, Amyntas,' Sledd said, over his free shoulder. 'This one first,' he bounced the beam under his arm as best he could, 'then the other, on my count of three. Three.'

The beams crashed to the ground and both men leapt free, to save themselves from a certain broken ankle.

The men sheathed their swords and their daggers. That had definitely been the sound, as near as made no difference.

'Who are you, again?' The officer waved to the man at the door and he stepped back.

'I told you.' Sledd was getting testy. It was cold and he had a stage to remove. 'Sledd and Finch. London.'

'Well . . . about your business, then,' the officer said. 'But wait until my gentlemen have driven away. Wait there and don't move.'

The guards got back on their horses and waited patiently again. With rattling of latches, the great door swung open and Burghley swept out, followed by his son. They climbed into their carriage, which was waiting just outside the porch. It moved off and the next one took its place. Effingham swept out and stepped up onto the step, held steady by a lackey. Hunsdon followed, shivering in the cold and wrapped his cloak more tightly. He looked around him, with some contempt; he would be glad to shake the dust of Scadbury from his boots. The bed had been damp and Effingham's snores, through the wall, were enough to wake the dead. He nodded to the lackey and then saw the two men standing away to the right on a couple of beams. They looked like rather inept acrobats. 'Morning,' he said, with a dip of the head then he sprang into the carriage and it moved off with a crack of the whip.

Tom Sledd turned to Finch as the outriders disappeared around a bend in the avenue. 'That's breeding, that is,' he said. 'He's only met me once, Baron Hunsdon has, at the theatre. But he still takes the time to say good morning.'

Finch shrugged. It was all one to him. Real breeding would have been offering to give a hand with the bloody beams.

ELEVEN

Henry Parkin was sitting in the front pew when the congregation arrived that morning. There were more people than usual; as it was the last Sunday of the year, the infrequent attenders thought it would be ideal to turn up so they could honestly say, if asked, that of course they had attended church in 1592. Recusancy cost money.

A few of the regulars had noticed that the curate was acting a little oddly that morning. The verger had said 'Hello' as was his wont and the organist had nodded to him. They didn't get so much as a nod back. It didn't help that Richard Baines was late. He had been locked away in his little chapel for most of the previous day, wrestling with his conscience. He had been busy scribbling notes, at which he was very good, to the sixty loyal followers who would, as soon as news of the Queen's death came from Placentia or Nonsuch or wherever God should decree she die, reached them, leap to seize her throne. The kingdom of saints would come into its own then. He had been smiling all day at the thought of it.

The organ struck up as Baines hurtled down the aisle, cassock flying. He nodded briefly to Thomas and Audrey Walsingham, blinked at Lewknor and ignored everybody else. There was Parkin, he realized, at the front, sitting alone with nobody behind him. Good. Actually, not good. Why wasn't the man officiating? He should have started the service by now, not be sitting there like one of the congregation.

Baines took a deep breath to clear his head of the wicked thoughts that always entered it when he saw Audrey Walsingham. Try as he might, he could only see her sitting there naked, even when, as today, she was swathed in a fur-lined cape to keep out the cold. The thoughts that swirled in his brain when he saw Thomas were less pleasant; sedition rarely is. He turned, fixing a beatific smile on the congregation and the grin froze on his lips.

'Mother of God!' he shouted and had to clench his fist to stop himself from making the sign of the cross. Now that he was facing Parkin, he could see that the lad was dead, his face drained of blood and his eyes half closed. There was a cake of black blood around his nose and lips and his hands were fixed like claws on the edge of the pew.

There was a scream and Henry Parkin flopped sideways, freed from his upright position by the actions of the sidesman who was sitting behind him.

'He's dead!' somebody shouted. 'The curate's dead!'

Before Baines had a chance to do or say anything, Thomas Walsingham was on his feet, shouting orders, keeping as calm as possible. 'Lewknor,' he muttered to his steward. 'Marlowe and Faunt. Get them here at the double.'

'Seen one of these before, Kit?' Faunt asked. In his hand lay the weapon that had killed Henry Parkin, a murderous iron shaft nearly a foot long that had been rammed through the oak of the pew behind him and right through his scrawny chest.

'I don't believe I have,' Marlowe said.

'It's a marlin spike, common among sailors.'

'Is it now?' Marlowe was looking at the body. Henry Parkin was lying on the floor of the nave. Baines had raved for several minutes that this was God's house and a sacrilege to search a body under that roof, but the Walsinghams steered him away and the congregation vanished, with mutterings and asides, to let Faunt and Marlowe get on with their work.

The body, naked now except for his linen drawers, was unmarked apart for the wound. It was black with dried blood, on back and chest, and the blood had trickled down to pool on the pew seat and soak into the curate's cassock.

'When, would you say?' Faunt asked.

'Last night,' Marlowe said, lifting the lad's right arm. 'The rigor of death is still partly there. I'd say he died before midnight.'

Faunt stood up, weighing the blood-encrusted spike in his hand. He looked along the length of the nave, crouched behind the front pew, sat where the murderer must have sat. He poked the spike through the hole, itself still dark with blood that had streaked out to right and left along the grain. He eased it forward, then slammed hard, his fist hitting the woodwork.

'What do we know about this lad?' he asked Marlowe.

The playwright stood up, leaving the curate staring sightlessly at the vaulted roof. 'As of now, nothing,' he said, 'but that's two murders in nine days, Nicholas. According to Thomas Walsingham, nothing ever happens at Scadbury.'

'Is there a charnel house?' Faunt asked.

'I don't think so,' Marlowe said. 'We'll put him in the dairy, with Dalston. Thank God it's chilly at this time of the year.'

'I understand that Thomas has arranged for Peter to take his brother home for burial and is paying for the funeral,' Faunt said.

'He has. He's a kind man, Thomas Walsingham.'

'Or a murderer,' Faunt said. He was not the sentimental type. 'So I'll start with him. Can you see Baines?'

'In my worst nightmares,' said Marlowe.

'Yes, I hold the advowson,' Thomas Walsingham was grooming his horse. He had people for that, but he liked to keep in touch with his animals. Padraig had ambled out to the stables, about as far as his old legs would carry him these days. 'So I appointed Parkin. Seemed a nice lad. Bit of a mother's boy, perhaps. I can't say I knew him. You'd have to ask Baines.'

And Nicholas Faunt had people for that.

'Thomas Walsingham owns the advowson,' Baines said to Marlowe. He was polishing the church silver. Normally, that would be done by the verger but the poor man was so shocked by the outrage committed in the church that he had gone home to lie down. 'So, he appointed Parkin. I didn't meet him until after the deed was done.'

'You didn't approve the appointment?' Marlowe asked.

'I didn't say that,' Baines snapped. 'Forgive me, Master Marlowe, we're all a little on edge this morning, for obvious reasons. No, it was just that Parkin was a little . . . shall we say, distant. Not one of us.'

'Us?' Marlowe took him up on it.

'Of the Church,' Baines said, spitting apologetically on a chalice and buffing it with a cloth. 'I suspect he probably regretted his calling.'

'Did you object to that?' Marlowe asked.

'It's not unusual in a curate,' Baines sneered. 'They're mostly glorified serving men these days. No backbone.'

'The marlin spike missed Parkin's backbone by an inch,' Marlowe said, 'the ribs too. Whoever killed him knew exactly what he was doing.'

'Marlin spike?' Either Baines was an actor the Rose would die for, or he had no idea what that was.

'The murder weapon. When it comes to the inquest, it'll be the deodand, the earthly value of the thing which commits the crime.'

'I know what a deodand is, Marlowe. *I* went to Cambridge too, you know. A wonder our paths never crossed.'

'Perhaps they did,' Marlowe said. He had forgotten all about the Eagle and Child.

'Perhaps so,' Baines smiled. 'If you're trying to find out who killed my curate,' he said, 'you could do no better than to try Mistress Walsingham.'

'He said what?' Audrey Walsingham put down her crewel work and rammed home her needle with a force which surprised Marlowe.

'That you may be able to help us with our enquiries.'

'Us?' Audrey was as arch as ever this afternoon.

'Faunt and me.'

'Oh, yes,' she smiled. 'You and he are something dark in the Whitehall passageways of power, aren't you? I keep forgetting that. What did Baines mean, do you think? I mean, what were you discussing when he said I could help you?'

'I have no idea,' Marlowe said. 'I was, of course, discussing the death of Henry Parkin and he just told me to see you.' The mistress of Scadbury had not invited him to sit, so he compromised by perching on the arm of a chair in the brown parlour.

'Well, for a start,' she said, taking up the sewing again, 'you know he's mad, don't you? You were there in the Misrule procession. You saw how he stopped Thomas at the lych-gate.'

'I did,' Marlowe said, 'and he was right, by his standards.'

'His standards?' Audrey all but spat. 'He doesn't know the meaning of the word. However . . .' she made a few stitches, dragging out her sentence to give it maximum dramatic value. Marlowe all but applauded; if half the actors at the Rose had her timing, he would be in Heaven. 'The curate did come to see me, as a matter of fact, hours before he died.'

'Really?'

'He wanted Thomas, but Thomas as always, was elsewhere. He told me . . . you might want to sit down properly, Master Marlowe, while I tell you this.'

Marlowe slid down into the chair and sat, all attention.

'He told me the most extraordinary story . . . about Baines, that is.'

The moon crept out from the clouds and lit the moat at Scadbury. The winter days were only just lengthening and there was a chill in the air. But it would take more than a chill to deter old Gammer Gosworthy. She had been walking this way, past the old mill and the butts, on her way to church for the best part of eighty years now and if tonight, her third leg, of polished beech, clacked alongside her, then so be it.

Her dead lay in the churchyard as the Gosworthys had lain for generations. Three of her babies were buried there and her husband, the good-for-almost-nothing. She remembered as if it were yesterday the Sunday of her wedding. She had simpered at the church porch and pretended she was a virgin, with her chestnut hair hanging free and garlanded with ears of corn. And she had gone to confession, always, whoever ruled England and whatever prayer book was the order of the day. She was a young mother when bluff king Hal had broken with Rome, already a grandmother and alone when the Jezebel had set up her evil church. Nothing would stop Gammer Gosworthy from going to confession; as long, of course, as there was a priest to hear it.

Kit Marlowe knew all about the Gammer Gosworthys of

this world. For the last ten years he had rooted out Papists, not because he had any hatred for them, but because they disturbed the peace of the realm and because, well, there were so many reasons why. He watched the old girl as he had watched others. She'd waited until dark and was looking around her to make sure she wasn't being followed. She stopped every now and then, listening for footsteps that were not her own. But she never saw Kit Marlowe and she didn't hear him either.

He crept behind her into the church of St Nicholas where the curate had died only the day before. He saw her bob in front of the altar, then vanish behind the rood screen. He heard the familiar knock on the door, the three raps for the Trinity and the soft intoning of the priest. He pressed himself against the Arras in the chancel and waited.

The old girl had not led a particularly virtuous life but her opportunities for sin were rarer these days and she was not long. Marlowe waited until the clack of her stick died away, then he slid out of the shadows and behind the screen. There was a little door, almost hidden by another Arras and he rapped out the Trinity.

'Forgive me, Father,' he said, 'for I have sinned.'

The door swung open to reveal Richard Baines, in his Papist robes, a rosary in his hands. He took one look at Marlowe and his mouth hung open.

'But then,' said Marlowe, in the awkward silence, 'so have you.'

'And you left him alive?' Faunt was incredulous. 'A Papist *and* a traitor. And you didn't slit his throat right there and then?'

'In the church, Nicholas?' Marlowe chuckled. 'What an appalling suggestion.'

'Unmasking Papists and traitors is what we do for a living, Kit,' Faunt said, 'or had you forgotten?'

'You, maybe,' Marlowe smiled, 'but as Robert Cecil made it crystal clear to me only two days ago, my projectioner days are over. He dispensed with my services. I'm out.'

'So was I, from him,' Faunt said, 'but they can't let us go, believe me. No, it was a huge mistake for Burghley to give his little boy the spymaster job. He just isn't up to it. One of the others'll take you up, you'll see. Hunsdon, Hatton, perhaps even the Queen herself. She loves a pretty face but even if you were ugly as sin, they can't afford to let men like you go.'

'Perhaps it's time, Nicholas,' Marlowe said. 'I've been thinking more about poetry these days. Hero and Leander perhaps. For that I need peace and quiet – here at Scadbury, if Thomas will have me. But first . . .'

'First?'

'First, Nicholas, I have a play to put on.'

'Kit?' Faunt looked alarmed.

'You didn't think that I was going to listen to anything the four horsemen said, did you? Not in the sense of doing what I was told.'

'Is this wise, Marlowe?' Faunt was suddenly serious. 'You could be very much out of your depth.'

'I've swum the Stour, the Cam, the Thames and even the Solent – or at least part of it. What's next? The Styx?'

'Is Baines our man, then?' Faunt asked. 'For the murder of Parkin, I mean?'

'No, Faunt,' Marlowe was serious too. 'But the blade through the back, the clever, neat way it was done. Whoever killed Henry Parkin killed John Foxe too – and it's my guess, Moll and Roger Dalston. The question is why.'

Faunt leaned back in his chair. 'If we have the answer to that,' he said, 'we'll have the "who" in the palms of our hands.'

'Master Walsingham . . .' Marlowe put his head round the door of the brown parlour and saw the master of Scadbury communing with his favourite hound. Padraig's eyes were dim these days, but he knew his master's voice and had his chin on the man's knee as he scratched the top of the scruffy head.

Walsingham turned around, carefully, so as to not disturb the old dog. 'Kit! Come in, come in.'

Marlowe took a seat to one side of the fire. The Yule log from the game of Dun is in the Mire had long gone and a new half-tree was blazing merrily.

'You're very formal,' Walsingham remarked.

Marlowe looked into the flames and smiled. 'I always am when I have a favour to ask,' he said.

Walsingham raised his eyebrows. 'Another? And I thought you had just used my house to put on a play. A play, might I say, that brought a good proportion of the Privy Council through my doors.' He smiled to take the sting out of his words. 'I'm not sure I can afford you, Kit.'

Marlowe could read most men, even those who sought to hide their thoughts, but Thomas Walsingham he could read like the simplest hornbook primer. 'So, you don't want to wait to hear what it is, then?' he said. 'The answer's yes.'

Walsingham frowned. 'Did I say that?' he asked. 'I don't think I said that.'

'Not with your words, no,' Marlowe said with a smile. 'But the rest of you did. I'll ask you anyway. Might I stay on here at Scadbury? I have a poem bubbling in my head and I need to get it down on paper before it boils away and the steam is lost for ever.'

'Kit,' Walsingham said, pushing the dog gently off his knee. He reached for his tobacco pouch and offered it across. 'What sort of poem is it?'

'Just a poem.'

Walsingham was looking down, packing his pipe, but the question hung in the air.

'A love poem, then. I just feel the need to write it down and here . . . I feel that here, the words will flow.'

Walsingham looked serious. He had a face that was made for smiles, but now, he had a look of his cousin about him. 'Are you in love with someone, Kit?' he asked.

Marlowe shook his head. 'No one in particular, Thomas. Words, perhaps. Music a close second. All my friends, some just memories now, sadly. But in love? No.'

'Not Audrey, for instance?' Walsingham was embarrassed now and looked down at his pipe, scowling as if it had offended him.

'Audrey? Good God, no!' As soon as he had spoken, Marlowe realized how that must sound and went on, 'Not that she isn't lovely, Thomas, because she is. But she's your . . .' as always and in common with everyone else, he stuck on the word.

'Exactly!' Walsingham flung out his arm and a burning wad of tobacco fell on Padraig's flank and made the animal yelp. 'Exactly,' he repeated, beating out the small fire. 'It's always the same. "Oh, Master Walsingham, your . . ." No one knows what to call her. And I *have* no call on her. She could go tomorrow and I couldn't stop her.'

'Thomas,' Marlowe said, hurriedly, 'she loves you. If you could have heard her when she thought you were dead, you wouldn't even wonder. She does love you.' He smiled. 'I write poetry. I know these things.'

Walsingham sucked at his pipe, bringing it back to life. 'Pass me that twig, there, off the fire, will you?' he said, to try to change the subject. 'My pipe is going out.'

'There you are, you see,' Marlowe said, not passing him the light. 'You're the same with your pipe as you are with women. Your pipe is burning perfectly well, but you want to relight it. The woman who, may I say, should already be your wife, loves you but you think she doesn't. You have no confidence in yourself, Thomas, that's your trouble.'

'You've changed the subject,' Walsingham observed, watching the smoke rise to the ceiling.

'I don't believe I have. You asked me about Audrey and then . . .'

Walsingham chuckled. 'As always, you have the better of me. But . . . if you aren't in love with Audrey, then who?'

'I told you.' Marlowe spread his arms wide, without setting fire to the dog. 'No one.'

Walsingham shrugged. 'If you say so. But,' and he leaned forward, 'if you want to tell me, it will go with me to the grave.'

'Thomas!' Marlowe used the tone he used to actors. 'I am *not* in love. Now, will you let me stay, or not?'

'Of course you can,' the master of Scadbury laughed. 'With how many people this time, if I may ask? Just so the kitchens know how many carcases to get in.'

'Just me,' Marlowe said. 'The others are packing to leave as we speak. Most of them went a day or so ago. Didn't you notice?'

Walsingham looked around him. 'I did think it had gone a

bit quiet,' he said. 'Home for Twelfth Night, eh? London is very festive at Twelfth Night. I used to enjoy that more than Christmas, when I was a boy.'

'Let's go up for the night,' Marlowe offered, without too much enthusiasm. 'Tom Kyd is gone from Hog Lane, now. I have plenty of room for guests.'

'That's a kind offer, Kit. And any other time, I would take you up on it. But . . .' he leaned over and beckoned Marlowe nearer, 'between you and me, Audrey has been a lot more . . .' he cast his eyes up to the ceiling and fought to find the right word, '. . . come-to-ish of the last few nights. She hasn't always been, I must say. Perhaps,' and he smoothed his moustache and beard ruminatively, 'perhaps she has come to enjoy the pleasures of the marriage bed, if I can use that phrase in this context. I think before that she was . . . well, afraid of my rampant manhood.'

Marlowe, rarely stuck for words, was stuck, for the second time in one conversation. To make time to think, he knocked out his pipe on the hearth and cleaned it with a twig before stowing it in his bosom. 'She probably is,' he said at last. Then, smiling up at his friend, who sat, glowing with love and pride. 'That will be it. Well done, Thomas, for schooling her at last.' He stood up, brushing threads of tobacco from his front, 'I must be away to see off the last of the Lord Chamberlain's Men. And then, if you don't mind, I will retire to my chamber and make a start on my poem.'

'Does it have a title, yet?' Walsingham asked, courteously seeing his guest to the door.

'*Hero and Leander*.'

'Ah.' Walsingham looked askance.

'Hero is a woman. A very beautiful woman.'

'Ah.' This time the single sound was full of relief. Walsingham sometimes wished he had listened to his tutor more carefully.

'Well . . .'

Here it comes, thought Marlowe.

'Don't put me in it, will you?'

'Surely, Master Walsingham,' the door was now open and the politeness of the public domain pertained, 'you must be Leander. Who else?'

And, leaving his host preening just a little, Marlowe went out to say goodbye for the moment to Sledd and his remaining crew.

The one remaining wagon of the Lord Chamberlain's Men was in the stable yard, the horses steaming already in the cold January air. Tom Sledd was directing operations but it was Amyntas Finch who was the real power behind the throne, rearranging here, hefting boxes there and the luggage was tucked as tightly and accurately as any dry-stone wall.

Marlowe watched, impressed. 'He's good at this,' he said to Sledd, who was counting things off as they emerged and were packed.

'He's the best I've seen,' Sledd conceded. 'He's got more onto this wagon than I would have thought possible. And it's packed solid; we won't be wasting half the journey picking bits up off the road.'

'So . . . you like having an Assistant?' Marlowe asked, nudging the stage manager.

'Hmm . . . yes, you were right. I knew you were right from the start. But will *Henslowe* think you're right, that's the trouble, isn't it? That's always the trouble.' He mimed counting money. 'That's all he thinks about.'

'I'll have a word, Tom. Meanwhile, he isn't happy that I have sacked Alleyn. Shaxsper he is delirious about. Alleyn, though . . . we may have to negotiate on that one.'

'Whose idea was it, do you think?' Sledd asked.

'Don't you know?'

Sledd's eyes almost popped out of his head. 'Of *course* I don't know. I was as surprised as you when they started spouting that gibberish!'

'If I were ever to go within a mile of either of them without killing them where they stood, I would doff my cap, Tom, to be truthful. They did all of that and clandestinely. Did anyone else know?'

'No. I gave everyone a bonus in their wages to say thank you. They didn't turn a hair. Even the humblest monk went on as though it were as written.'

'A bonus?' Marlowe frowned. 'Not out of your own money?'

Sledd laughed. 'What own money would that be, then? No, it came out of the purses of Masters Alleyn and Shaxsper, who got no wage at all. And of course of Mistress Guitruud Clutterbuick, who kindly told me he had no need of it. Which was just as well, as I had no intention of paying him.'

'That's a good point. Have you seen Master Faunt today?'

'He rode off at dawn. As usual, he said nothing and I chose not to ask.'

'Always the best plan, Thomas, when dealing with Nicholas Faunt.' Marlowe had no idea how to find the man, but knew that, if the occasion arose, he would come to call.

Amyntas Finch came to the head of the horses and coughed. ''Scuse me, gents,' he said, 'all done as far as I can see.'

Sledd went on tiptoe to look into the wagon. 'Then, let's be off, Amyntas. If you'd like to get the stragglers.'

'Stragglers?' Marlowe asked. 'Is there any room for people back there?' It seemed unlikely.

'Watch this,' Sledd said proudly. If he had hatched Finch himself he could not have been prouder.

Finch appeared around the side of the house with a couple of lads and a seamstress, along with two walking gentlemen, predictably Frizer and Skeres.

''Morning,' Frizer said and hopped up into the wagon. Finch helped up the girl and the lads clambered aboard, hauling Skeres up behind them.

'Skeres had a heavy night,' Sledd said, by way of explanation. 'Now, watch.' He clicked his fingers. 'Haul away,' he shouted.

The five Rose people all grabbed a rope and pulled and, slowly but surely, a tarpaulin appeared from along the side of the wagon, pulling spars with it to keep it up as a roof. When it was completely over, they tied the ropes onto cleats on the opposite side and took seats formed of boxes carefully stowed.

'Look at this, Master Marlowe,' one of the lads called. 'We've got tables for our bit of dinner and everything.'

'Master Finch done it,' the other told him and they snuggled down in their cloaks for what was going to be a very comfortable journey.

'Amyntas,' Marlowe said as the big man climbed onto the

driver's seat, making the whole wagon lurch and sway. 'You are incredible. A real asset to the Rose.'

The man blushed. 'Thank you, Master Marlowe,' he said. 'I try to do a good job, whatever it may be.'

'Well, you've found your niche here, and no mistake,' Marlowe said, giving a friendly slap to a thigh like a ham. 'I'll make sure Henslowe takes him on,' Marlowe said in an aside to Tom. 'The man's a genius.'

'It would be nice to have some help,' Sledd said wistfully, but he wasn't holding his breath. Henslowe didn't pay for genius, in his experience.

'I'll see you soon. I need to get my poem started and then I'll be up to talk to Henslowe.'

'Oh, a new poem.' Sledd looked pleased for his friend. He didn't get enough time for his own work and he was, after all, the country's best poet. 'What's it called?'

'*Hero and Leander*.' Marlowe sighed; he knew what was coming.

Sledd laughed. 'I bet that will get a few people worked up,' he said. 'It's not everybody knows these days that Hero is a girl's name as well.' And with that, he clicked his tongue and his wagon moved off, creaking under Finch's weight.

Marlowe waved as they disappeared down the avenue. He smiled as he turned back into the house. That Tom Sledd could still surprise him after all this time was one of life's most wonderful blessings. But now, he had a poem to write.

TWELVE

Breakfast was usually Christopher Marlowe's favourite meal. For one thing, it was the only meal he could be sure of getting, before the day crept in and changed all his careful plans. But also, it was the simplest and it took him back whenever he sat down to it to his undergraduate days in Cambridge, when life was simple and the days seemed to stretch sunny and endless to the horizon. There must have been cold, grey days like the one he was embarking on now, but he simply didn't remember any. Whatever the weather, they had all begun like this, with some fresh, warm bread with new butter, a pitcher of milk and some porridge, with honey if he was lucky, and today he was. Also, he noted with approval, the porridge was not lumpy and had no dubious black flecks in it, leftovers from burnings of long ago. As far as he could recall, the porridge pot at Corpus Christi had never been washed out. Any remaining clumps from the day before were simply stirred in. An undergraduate with a mathematical bent had calculated that in every bowlful, there was at least one spoonful that was older than the Master.

Breakfast at Scadbury was rather more genteel than breakfast at Corpus Christi. For one thing, there were no yelling scholars, no bread flew through the air and the honey was in a glass bowl and had come from the estate's very own bees. There were apples and other fruit in season. The porridge was not only lump- and fleck-free but was served in individual tureens with a choice of honey, confiture and an item of the cook's own devising which both Walsingham's had advised their guest to avoid; they believed it contained figs but beyond that it was hard to say. But that aside, everything was lovely.

'I shall miss all this,' Marlowe said, as he finally put down his knife, defeated. There came a point when even the most accommodating stomach can take no more.

Thomas Walsingham stopped in mid-bite. 'Miss? Why?'

'Are you leaving us, Kit?' Audrey Walsingham had not repeated her night-time depredations but there was still a predatory gleam in her eye that said that, possibly, with a following wind, tonight might be the night.

'I don't want to,' he said, wiping his mouth with the smoothest, most perfectly ironed napkin he had ever used. 'But time marches on and I must go up to London to see Philip Henslowe about putting on my *Edward*.'

Walsingham's eyes widened. 'Which one?' he asked.

'Well, *mine* of course,' Marlowe said, a little nettled but not surprised. 'Anyway, the miscreation of Alleyn and Shaxsper no longer exists; it was only ever really in their heads and some hurried notes. The notes are burned and as for the heads – one has hidden itself in darkest Warwickshire and the other is probably still sobbing on the bosom of Mistress Alleyn, the only one which will house him now he is no longer famous.'

'Will . . . umm, will Master Henslowe put it on?' Walsingham ventured.

'Oh, come along, Thomas,' Audrey said, poking him with her knife and then muttering apologies when he bridled and rubbed his arm. 'Sorry, was that too hard? There, there. No, but really, Thomas. Audiences are men of the world these days, women of the world too. We all know such things go on and those of us who listened to our tutors . . .' she and Marlowe both turned to stare at him '. . . know that Edward and Gaveston were lovers.'

Walsingham looked around wildly in case servants were in earshot. '*Audrey*!' he hissed. 'Not so loud!'

'Well, they were,' she said, taking a savage bite out of a hard-boiled egg, making her husband wince. 'You can't change history just by not talking about it. Can you, Kit?'

'Indeed not, mistress,' Marlowe said, with a bow. 'We must face it head on.'

'Unlike the king and Gaveston,' Audrey said, straight-faced and even Thomas had to smile.

'Isn't she wonderful, Kit?' he said, patting her hand. 'She has as fine a mind as the next man.'

'Finer,' she said, folding her napkin and getting up, 'depending on the man one is next to. You must excuse me,' she said, pushing back her chair, 'cooks to advise, maids to sack, you know, the cares of a lady of a fine house.' She dropped a kiss on the top of Thomas's head. 'Don't leave without saying goodbye, will you, Master Marlowe?'

'I will make sure I don't,' he said, with a bob of the head.

When she had gone, the master of Scadbury sat back with a sigh. 'She's a handful, Kit, I can't deny it,' he said, 'but I would be nothing without her.'

'Take my advice,' Marlowe said, 'marry the woman, Thomas. Together, the sky will be the limit.'

'And apart?'

Marlowe looked at him sadly. 'Don't talk of being apart, Thomas. We lose more friends than we make in any given year. Keep those you love close. Once they close the door behind them, who knows when they will knock on it again.'

Walsingham grabbed his sleeve as he went towards the door. 'Don't go, Kit,' he said. 'Don't put the play on. I have a bad feeling about it. My skin is crawling.'

Marlowe pulled his sleeve free and patted his friend on the shoulder. 'Perhaps you should bathe Padraig,' he said. 'That's the way to get rid of fleas.' And in two strides, he was gone.

'Kit!' Henslowe was effusive, but wary. He was usually glad to see his golden goose, but he had heard many variations on the play at Scadbury and, being Philip Henslowe, had extracted the worst bits from each one and made them even worse in the retelling. 'It's good to see you back.' He rubbed his hands together. 'Thomas tells me you have been writing down at Scadbury. Good. Good.' He paused expectantly. 'So, what is the new play called?'

'I'm sorry,' Marlowe said, taking an unproffered chair in Henslowe's crowded room. 'Did Tom tell you that I was writing a play?'

'Well, not exactly but . . . well, what else would you be writing?' Henslowe gave vent to a nervous laugh; he had a tendency to it when he could feel bad news coming.

'I have been writing a poem. Still am, if it comes to that.'

Henslowe rolled his eyes. If he had his time all over again he would have nothing whatsoever to do with writers. How long could it take to write a poem, for the love of God? People wrote poems on the walls of the Rose all the time, often in the time it took them to empty their bladders. 'Interesting,' he said, trying to make the word sound convincing. 'What's it about? It could be expanded, perhaps. Into a play.'

'Not everything is a play, Philip,' Marlowe said. 'It is a tale of doomed love.'

Henslowe looked closely at Marlowe. Come to think of it, he did look a little peaky. 'You look peaky, Kit,' he said. 'You didn't catch anything nasty down in the country, did you?' Mistress Henslowe often dreamed aloud, with relevant nudging and shouting, of a country retreat, away from the stink of London, but Henslowe couldn't breathe clean air, as he told her frequently. 'Love, for instance?'

'No, Master Henslowe,' Marlowe was getting testy. 'I am not in love. Nor,' he pre-empted the obvious question, 'did I catch anything else loosely connected with love. I have had the idea of the poem in my head for a long while, and Master Walsingham was kind enough to give me a room in which to work and board and lodgings. All I have to do is dedicate it to him when it's published. That's all he asks.' He looked penetratingly at Henslowe, who did not miss the barb.

'Well,' he said, 'I am very sorry indeed if I work you hard, Kit. But you must admit, you do live well. And don't think I don't know that you have money from other sources. Does Master Walsingham know how much you are paid, what with one thing and another? I would wager he wouldn't be so free with his patronage if he knew.'

'We don't discuss money,' Marlowe said, loftily.

'No more do I,' Henslowe said, stung. 'It's vulgar. However, one must have it. So, a play . . .'

'I am here to discuss *Edward the Second,*' Marlowe said.

Henslowe was on his feet, hands in the air as though to ward off something evil. 'Oh, no, you don't. You don't get me that easily. I've heard of that play. Alleyn is refusing to come back to the Rose because of what you will do to him. Shaxsper *is* back . . .'

Marlowe was on his feet in an instant.

'. . . but as a reserve walking gentleman, pending reinstatement.

What they did was wrong, Kit, but it was with the best intentions.'

'Not getting into trouble, you mean?' Marlowe said, dismissively. 'They're cowards, both of them. They don't have the courage of my convictions, that's their trouble.'

'They said they didn't change much.' Henslowe tried to arbitrate.

'Only the relationship between the king and Gaveston.' Marlowe could see immediately that he may well have spoken in Hebrew. Then an idea which had been only the merest whisper of a thought began to coalesce in his head. 'They wanted a bigger part each, that was their problem,' Marlowe said. He watched Henslowe for a reaction but there was none. 'That's why they tinkered with the words. You can imagine how angry it made me.'

'Hmm.' Henslowe was resting his chin on his hand. 'Go on.'

'So, what I was thinking was, put Burbage in Alleyn's part and Will Kemp in Shaxsper's.'

Henslowe didn't move his hand, but grunted. 'The clown? I thought this was a tragedy.'

'History, to be accurate, but it doesn't end well, that's certain. I just thought that Will Kemp would bring a certain . . . frailty to the role. Eager to please. None too bright. A bit like the man himself, really. Nasty temper when he's had a drink. All he'd need to do is learn the words and spout them. He wouldn't have to act at all.'

Marlowe was still watching Henslowe, who was counting and recounting some copper coins on the desk. Every now and then, he discarded one or bit it to make sure. Finally, he sat up, clapping his hands onto the desk, palms down.

'I worry about Tilney, though,' he said.

'No need!' Marlowe was bright eyed now and well into his story. 'Burghley, Cecil, Hunsdon and Effingham have all seen it.'

'Liked it?' Henslowe cocked an eyebrow.

'*Loved* it. They even followed the words as it was played.'

Henslowe had seen people do that and he always thought them a trifle deranged. 'So they found nothing wrong. Nothing to complain about?'

Marlowe shook his head, his curls bouncing. He looked as innocent as a babe unborn.

'So, there was no talk of sodomy, unnatural vices, things like that?'

Marlowe shook his head again, slightly less emphatically.

Henslowe leaned forward and Marlowe was reminded of the most feared teacher in the King's School when he was a boy. Apart from the fact that the schoolmaster had a head crammed full of ancient languages and more than a smattering of science and Henslowe knew about enough to count money, they were like peas in a pod.

'Last question, Kit,' Henslowe hissed. 'Do you think that I am stupid?'

'By no means,' Marlowe said, cornered. 'No one with an empire like yours could be stupid.'

'Then why – if you will excuse another question – why do you assume I don't have an original version of your play? You had dozens copied – you owe me for the copyists' time, of course, a discount for Roger, naturally – and so how could *you* be stupid enough to assume they were all destroyed but yours? It is this unaccustomed stupidity, Kit, which made me wonder whether you were in love.'

Marlowe looked at Henslowe and a grudging smile crept over his face. 'When will I learn not to try and beat you, Master Henslowe?' he said. 'Thank you for your time. I think probably, it may be time for a repeat of *Faustus*. That one never gets old and I know it is John Dee's favourite. He would enjoy seeing it again, I know.' He got up, narrowly missing a pile of papers near his right foot.

'Repeats?' Henslowe said. 'They're all well and good, but they don't bring in the numbers. I want something new.'

'I don't *have* anything new,' Marlowe said, turning in the doorway. 'You'll have to wait until my poem is finished.'

'I think *The Troublesome Reign and Lamentable Death of Edward the Second, king of England* sounds good for my next production. Bit long for the posters, but it will do.'

Marlowe frowned. 'My version?' he checked.

'Is there another?' Henslowe spread his hands innocently. 'No Alleyn.'

'No Alleyn. Burbage for the king.'

'No Shaxsper.'

'Well . . . he has mouths to feed. Let him have a small part, Kit. Let bygones be bygones. I have a feeling Alleyn was the leader there.'

Marlowe was not sure about that, but conceded the point. 'Kemp for Gaveston, then?'

'If he'll do it.'

'Is Queen Isabella's voice broken?'

'As a shattered hope,' Henslowe said. 'Poor lad. It came on very suddenly, along with spots and whiskers, but he is walking out with one of the seamstresses, so he has got over his disappointment. Happily, he has a brother who has a few years in him yet. Anything else?'

Marlowe could only grin. 'I am . . . overwhelmed, Master Henslowe. Umm . . . you have let Tom keep his assistant, haven't you?'

'Do you think I'm made of money?' Henslowe barked.

'But . . .'

'Don't get your venetians in a bunch. Finch is hired on a pro tem basis, but I like Tom looking less . . .'

'Tired?'

'I was going to say dead,' Henslowe said, 'but tired will do. So, Master Marlowe, what else can I do for you today?'

Marlowe bowed low, sweeping his cape behind him extravagantly. 'Master Henslowe,' he said, 'you have done everything and more.'

'In that case, get out. Time is money. You have a play to cast.'

'Kit! Kit!' Philip Henslowe was beside himself. 'They loved it! They just loved it! I've never seen Burbage better and my idea of Kemp as Gaveston – it worked a treat.'

'Glad you're happy, Philip,' Marlowe smiled.

They had indeed loved it. A new play by Kit Marlowe, the Muse's darling, always brought in the punters, who had no idea of the problems that putting it on created. Shaxsper, who had effectively slaughtered Gaveston at Scadbury, was demoted to the Bishop of Coventry, on account of how he could do the accent. Other players were shuffled around. Amyntas Finch had a walk-on part when he wasn't humping flats for Tom Sledd.

Nicholas Faunt had other things to do, but kept in touch with Marlowe as he was wont to do and as Burghley had ordered. It was mainly through cryptic notes pushed under the door at Hog Lane. When Marlowe was not at home, the maid-servant put them in a pile near the door for him to look at when he got in. As the pile often blew away and was re-assembled at random, the messages were sometimes hard to understand, as when read in any order, they were not immediately clear. The one reading 'Bye egs' Marlowe had rightly attributed to the cook. In the main, they were warning Marlowe to keep his head down and always ended with words to the effect that the writer might as well have saved the ink, because he knew Marlowe would do whatever he pleased. In that at least, they were essentially correct.

The first night had been a riotous success and the audience, gentry and groundlings alike, had demanded that Marlowe appear on stage and take a bow. The second night was full. Nearly three thousand people crammed into the Rose and Frizer and Skeres were sorry they couldn't mingle with the crowd, cutting purses to supplement their meagre wages.

Henslowe may have been beside himself but a slow realization dawned that much more success like this and his players would be demanding more money. Ever a man to spot the fly in the ointment, was Philip Henslowe.

'Marlowe has excelled himself!' read the headline of the *Playbill* which appeared in large numbers, pinned to any bit of wood south of the river and pasted onto walls. *Edward the Second* was the talk of the taverns and fights broke out when drunken men began arguing for and against the king.

It was over a week later that Edmund Tilney, Master of the Queen's Revels, turned up at Henslowe's door. It was early morning and the flag had not yet been raised over the Rose's turret to signal another sell-out performance of the play.

'Master Tilney,' Henslowe bowed and spoke through clenched teeth. Usually a visit from Tilney was like one from the grim reaper, though not half so pleasant. 'What a pleasure.'

'This play, Henslowe.' Tilney had left his horse at the Rose's door, the animal made a little skittish by an old black bear who had snarled at her.

'*Edward the Second,*' Henslowe beamed. 'Marlowe's best yet.'

'But why haven't I seen it?' Tilney asked.

'Er . . . because you haven't been to the Rose recently?' Henslowe suggested. He had no other ideas.

'Don't play silly buggers with me, Henslowe. What I mean is, why hasn't it been lodged in my office? As you know full well, *I* am the official censor in these matters. I am the arbiter. I must know the score from the prologue to epilogue, from soliloquy to the smallest stage direction.'

'Indeed, I do realize that,' Henslowe nodded, quietly draping a curtain over piles of obscene takings from the previous night, 'and lucky we are indeed to have you.'

Tilney's scowl could have turned milk. 'I want a copy and I want it now.'

'Yes, of course,' Henslowe dithered around his little sanctum high in the eaves, shuffling papers, moving playbills, 'Umm . . . I don't seem to have a spare copy,' he grimaced. 'They're all out with the players.'

'Surely, they know their . . . lines by now.' Tilney hated using what he considered stage jargon. The next thing would be that someone, God forbid, would take him for an actor.

'That would be wonderful, Sir Edmund,' Henslowe said, casting his eyes heavenward as though to enjoin the Almighty to help him, 'but you know these actors, they'd forget where they left their arses if they weren't sitting on them.'

The Puritan sucked in his breath.

'Begging your pardon, of course.'

Tilney looked the impresario up and down. 'Yes,' he said, in the tones of a coffin closing, 'delightfully colourful.' And he swept out of the room, setting up an eddy of paperwork which would take hours to settle.

Philip Henslowe knew Edmund Tilney. The pair had been sparring over plays for years and the owner of the Rose knew that the royal censor wasn't going to let things go just like that. He watched the little man bustle his way out onto the wooden O, elbowing Kemp out of the way. The clown followed him for a few paces, taking off the man's walk perfectly, then he swept back to what he was doing just as Tilney turned. The target of the Master of the Revels was Tom Sledd, who was standing centre stage with a copy of the play in his hand as though he knew Tilney had come calling for it. As Henslowe watched from his cobwebbed eyrie, Tilney snatched the papers and darted back across the stage.

Sledd called out something, but Henslowe didn't catch it. Will Kemp toyed with tripping the old curmudgeon up but suddenly remembered that he was Piers Gaveston and thought better of it. Henslowe hurled himself along the perilous gods under the eaves and roared down at Sledd, 'That's coming out of your wages, sonny!'

'I really would have to see it first, my Lord.' Edmund Tilney was at Whitehall, face to face with the Lord Treasurer himself.

'I *have* seen it, Tilney,' Burghley shouted at him, 'and, trust me, it doesn't make pretty viewing.'

'What would you like me to do, my Lord?' Edmund Tilney might have been Master of the Revels but he was outclassed by Burghley.

'Close it down, man. Threaten Henslowe with closure of the Rose if he sticks his neck out.'

'And Marlowe?'

Burghley looked at the man from under his eyebrows. 'Leave Marlowe to me,' he said.

Edmund Tilney had faced unruly mobs before. Every time he closed the theatres, whether because of plague or Puritan objection, some theatre-loving lout would threaten to cave in his face.

But what dismayed Tilney that Wednesday was the sheer size of the crowd. They'd brought their loaves and their cheese, their wine and their ale. The gentry's carriages were lined up along Bankside and boats were bringing yet more playgoers from up-river, where the cognoscenti of Chelsea and Battersea lived. *Edward the Second* was on everybody's lips. There was an electric expectancy in the air.

Up in his eyrie, Philip Henslowe had just heard the bad news. As of now, there was to be no play.

'You cannot be serious,' the impresario said when he could find words at all. There was a humming in his head that tended to get in the way of speech; he just couldn't be hearing this.

'Deadly, Henslowe,' Tilney wasn't going to be rattled by a theatre owner. 'Deadly.'

Henslowe stood up, looming over Tilney as all but Robert Cecil did. 'Well,' he said, levelly, 'you'll have to tell 'em.' He folded his arms. 'Because *I* won't. *And,*' he leaned forward so that their noses almost touched, 'for those who've already paid, no refunds.' And he left the room.

After the words, 'There'll be no play. It's censored,' nobody heard Edmund Tilney say a word. All his Puritan ranting about filth and sodomy and unnatural vice was drowned by a wall of noise.

It was difficult, later, to decide exactly who started it, but Tilney's six men, armed as they were, were quickly overwhelmed. The Master of the Revels himself was hoisted shoulder high, his cap and Colleyweston cloak ripped away and his venetians pulled off. Nor could anyone say later exactly where the apprentices came from, but there they were in numbers, crop-headed and wooden-shoed, laying about them with their clubs.

Tilney crawled out from the scrimmage, battered and bleeding, to be helped away by a couple of Winchester Geese who felt sorry for him. He managed to get himself across the river by nightfall and all that time, the mob had been rampaging up and down Bankside, overturning carriages, stealing horses, fighting running duels with any number of gentlemen who had never backed down from a fight in their lives.

The vicar of St Mary Overy popped out briefly to remind anybody in earshot over the clash of steel, that duelling was illegal in this country and nobody's sword blade should be longer than three feet. He was last seen riding backwards on a donkey, heading east towards Pickleherring Stairs.

Philip Henslowe didn't want the fury of the mob twisting back on him, so he locked the Rose and placed every man he had on duty to protect it. Tom Sledd was there, shoulder to elbow with Amyntas Finch and any number of stage hands, musicians and walking gentlemen. Two who were unaccountably missing were Skeres and Frizer; they were to be found with the mob, looting and smashing glass with the worst of them.

By the time darkness descended, Southwark looked like a battlefield, fires blazing here and there where lanterns had been overturned and candles dropped. Tilney had found a couple of magistrates and the Mayor of London himself had authorized the turning out of the Trained Bands. They wheeled a cannon into position on the southern end of London bridge where the heads of traitors looked wistfully down at them. The flames of the brands the halberdiers carried flickered on their breastplates and helmets and someone rode to Placentia to tell the Queen and to reinforce the ring of steel around her.

Since no one assumed responsibility for restoring order and the inns of Southwark were almost out of ale by this time, it fell to Edmund Tilney to lead the Bands, bustling out across the bridge, one purple eye closed and his head swathed in bandages.

'Where's our play?' shouted somebody in the crowd who recognized him.

'It's not *your* play, pizzle,' Tilney talked tall with two hundred pikemen at his back. 'It is rightly the property of Her Majesty and she has decided . . .'

'You mean *you've* decided,' someone shouted back. That someone was Philip Henslowe, lurking a few rows back now that he was relatively sure that the Rose was safe.

'Take that man's name!' Tilney squawked, unable to make out in the darkness who it was. Nobody moved.

'Put the play on!' somebody else shouted.

'We have a right,' said a cultured voice, clearly a scholar of one of the Inns of Court, 'to watch allegories which throw up examples of the corruption of the present regime.'

'Yeah!' somebody backed him. 'What he said.'

Tilney cleared his throat and held up a hand. 'You will disperse,' he shrilled. 'In two minutes, this culverin beside me,' he walked a few steps away from the gun, 'will fire into the crowd. If you have not dispersed . . .' but he never finished the sentence. There were men in the crowd who knew exactly how long it took to load and fire a culverin. There were men in the crowd who happened to know that the Trained Bands would not level their pikes at their own people. It was all about timing and the mob launched itself, the many-headed monster streaming forward over the bridge. The culverin disappeared in the swarming mass of bodies, about as useful without powder and ball as a dead tree. The gunner himself was swept off his feet, his ramrod snatched by an apprentice as a trophy.

Like a persistent army of ants, the crowd marched across the bridge, pushing the outnumbered Trained Bands backwards, bouncing cudgels off their helmets and batting aside their pikes. There wasn't room between the shops and houses for the Bands to manoeuvre and it was only the arrival of more cannon and cavalry at the northern end of the bridge that brought the mob's attack to a standstill.

'You will disperse!' It was the Mayor himself, sitting stiff-legged on a grey horse at the head of yet more Trained Bands.

'When will we see *Edward the Second*?' the Inns of Court voice called.

'Tilney?' The Mayor looked down at the battered wreck that was the Master of the Revels.

'Tomorrow,' he mumbled through his mouthful of loose teeth. 'No. We'll need at least a day to clear up after this lot. Two days from now.'

'Friday,' called the Mayor, 'at the usual time, two of the clock. You have my word.'

'He gave his word?' Robert Cecil couldn't believe the tale that Edmund Tilney was telling him.

'He did.' Tilney had been re-bandaged, but he hadn't slept and his own mother, assuming he'd ever had one, wouldn't recognize him. 'Rather forward, I thought.'

'So do I,' Cecil frowned. For hours now he'd been receiving snippets of news here at Whitehall and none of it was good. 'What happened then?'

'Eventually the seditious bastards went home,' Tilney told him, 'chanting "Marlowe! Marlowe!"'

'Not only the Muse's darling, then?' Cecil murmured.

'The point is, Robert, we'll have to put the damned play back on. I must say, I was disappointed by the Trained Bands. They're supposed to be . . . well . . . trained.'

'Citizen soldiery,' Cecil mused. 'Not, I can't help thinking, the best way forward.'

'Look,' Tilney whined, 'I'm Master of the Revels, for God's sake. Culture. Art. Poetry. All that stuff. What I am not is a glorified Watchman, still less a commander of the militia. As it is, I've lost two teeth.'

Cecil did his best to look sympathetic, but it didn't come easily to him. 'We'll keep an eye on Master Marlowe,' he said. 'Go home and lie down. You've done enough for one day.'

'And night,' Tilney reminded him and hobbled to the door. Once he'd staggered off along the passageway, Cecil clicked his fingers at a lackey waiting in his outer chamber.

'Sir?'

'Find me Nicholas . . . No, not that. Find me Robert Poley,' Cecil said. 'Tell him I have a little job for him.'

THIRTEEN

'So, what's your take on all this be nice to foreigners, Tom?' Robert Poley was topping up Tom Kyd's cup.

'Be nice to foreigners?' Kyd repeated, trying to focus. 'How d'you mean?'

'Well, you can't have missed them, surely? Various placards in and around the City extolling our European neighbours – and just as many denouncing them. I just wondered where you stood.'

Kyd shrugged. 'Hadn't really thought about it,' he said, missing the cup's rim entirely the first time.

'Really?' Poley sat upright in the snug at the Angel, looking Kyd squarely in the face. 'What with the *Spanish Tragedy* and all, I'd have thought you'd have been sympathetic – to the foreigners, I mean.'

'Well, I . . .'

'I must say, some of the phrases I've read recently – on shop fronts and people's walls at that – have shocked me to the core.'

'Like what?' Kyd was having to choose his consonants carefully now.

'Oh, I don't know . . . er . . . "beastly brutes the Belgians" . . . um . . . "fraudulent father Frenchmen", "faint-hearted Flemings". Outrageous!'

'Very well.' Kyd was largely unmoved. 'Live and let live, I say. Oh, I know the Spaniards want to invade us and everything, but you've got to allow even a Spaniard some leeway.'

'Indubitably,' Poley smiled, freshening Kyd's drink but not his own. 'Live and let live indeed. Of course, you know who's behind all this, don't you? The anti-foreign comments?'

'No.' Kyd hoped that he was shaking his head.

'Marlowe,' Poley said.

Kyd visibly rocked in his chair. 'No!'

'As I live and breathe,' Poley said, sipping his wine.

'Marlowe?' Kyd snarled. 'That bastard!'

'Oh, you mustn't take it personally, Tom. That's why he dumped the *Spanish Tragedy* and put that historical tripe of his on in its place. Nothing wrong with the *Tragedy*, nothing at all. Except that it's Spanish. And Portuguese, of course. And Kit Marlowe can't abide foreigners.'

'Really? I never knew. He might have said.'

'That's well known,' Poley nodded. 'Ever since his Canterbury days. Fell foul, or so they say, of the Flemish weavers there. I mean, we all believe in England, but he takes things too far.'

'Dumped the *Spanish Tragedy*' was the only part that Tom Kyd had really heard.

Poley sighed and shook his head. 'Tragedy indeed,' he said.

Kyd staggered to his feet, holding onto the table with one hand and trying to grab the dagger hilt at his back with the other. 'I'll kill him!' he yelled. Even in a place as rough as the Angel, he got some strange looks.

'No, no,' Poley sat him down gently. 'No, I've seen Marlowe in action, Tom. Saving your presence, you wouldn't stand a chance. No, there are more subtle ways. Tell me, what's the *Spanish Tragedy* about?'

Kyd frowned. How long had Poley got? 'Well . . .' he began.

'In a nutshell, Tom,' Poley said quickly. In answer to Kyd's unspoken question, he did not have all night.

'Er . . . revenge, I s'pose.'

'Exactly. A dish best served cold, is it not?'

Kyd tried to nod.

'So . . .' Poley leaned closer to him. 'Why don't we beat Marlowe at his own game? Print a few handbills of our own. Making it *look* as though Marlowe wrote them? That will give the powers that be an excuse to arrest him. Throw him in the Bridewell. What do you say?'

'Well, I . . . I can't just write . . . I mean, I've had a few, y'know.'

Poley patted his arm. 'Even poets of your calibre have off nights, Tom. I'll tell you what – would it be presumptuous of me to dictate a few lines? You can write it down. Then, tomorrow, or the next day, it'll be your turn to dictate to me. How does that sound?'

Kyd thought for a moment. It actually sounded rather odd, but any chance for revenge against Marlowe. 'Good,' he said. 'Oh,' a sudden thought crossed his mind, 'I haven't got . . .'

'Quill, ink and parchment?' Poley smiled. 'Luckily, I have all three.' For some reason, Kyd found this hysterically funny.

'Now,' said Poley, when Kyd had quietened down a little, 'write this down. Ready?'

Kyd steadied his hand to find the inkwell. 'Ready,' he said and wrote down Poley's words.

'"Your Machiavellian Merchant spoils the state."'

Kyd looked up, eyes wide. 'That's so *good*,' he said. 'Machiavellian. That's what they called Kit at Corpus Christi, you know. Machiavel.' He shook his head, overcome by the wondrous serendipity.

'Hmm,' beamed Poley. 'Go on. "Your usury doth leave us all for dead. Your artifex and craftsmen makes out fate. And . . ."' he pointed, 'a capital A, there, Thomas. It's a new line.'

'Oh, sorry.' Kyd bent close like a child at his lessons and made the small a into an A.

'"And like the Jews you eat me up as bread."'

'*Jew of Malta*!' Kyd had a couple of goes at clicking his fingers and gave up. 'Very good. Very good.'

'I tell you what, Thomas, I will pause when it's a new line. Then you know how to write it. Would that work for you?'

Kyd nodded, waiting eagerly. If a pointer could hold a quill, Kyd would have been its image.

'"Since words nor threats nor any other thing,"' Kyd was in the swing of things now. '"Can make you to avoid this certain ill, We'll cut your throats, in your temples praying, Nor Paris massacre so much blood did spill . . ."'

'*The Massacre at Paris!* Brilliant. Is that it?'

'For now,' Poley told him. 'How shall we sign it?'

'How about . . .?' Kyd was excited. 'Kit Marlowe?'

Poley smiled. 'A little *too* obvious, Tom, don't you think? What about . . . Tamburlaine?'

'His most brilliant creation!' Kyd shouted. 'The scourge of God!'

'The scourge of God, indeed,' Poley said.

'Tamburlaine it is,' Kyd said and signed the parchment with a flourish.

Kit Marlowe looked out of the window in his room at Scadbury. The apple orchards would be in bloom soon now that spring was almost here and he could see the fat buds on the tips of the branches. Finches fossicked here and there for insects hiding in the folds of the pale green. He smiled to himself as he remembered his Cambridge days, closeted in the Court with Parker and Bromerick and the others, with their close-cropped hair and their grey fustian robes. He glanced down at the black velvet he wore now, the silk shirt, the leather-laced venetians. Where was Christopher Marley, the cobbler's son? The scrawny lad who held pots at the Star while grown men got drunk around him? The timid scholar, leaping over puddles in the Dark Entry on his way to school? How long ago was all that? It was yesterday as the calendar of his twenty-nine summers showed.

He took up the quill again. The lines of Paulinus were dull. Clever Latin to be sure, but they lacked the sparkle of today. 'Home when he came,' he wrote, 'he seemed not to be there, But, like exiled air thrust from his sphere, Set in a foreign place . . .' He stretched and got up. In the knot garden below his window, Audrey Walsingham was walking alone, her cloak trailing in the fresh-mown grass and Padraig staggering along behind her. The old dog looked quietly triumphant; another winter beaten, another spring welcomed. What, his panting mouth seemed to say, can vanquish him now?

'Thus near the bed,' Marlowe took up the quill again, 'she blushing stood upright, And from her countenance behold you might, A kind of twilight break, which through her hair, As from an orient cloud, glimps'd here and there; And round about the chamber this false morn, Brought forth the day before the day was born.'

He threw down the quill. Murders hung around him like shadows, whispering in the dark. John Foxe lay flat on his bed, his face grinning up at him. Moll was smiling too, but her smile was the gaping gash in her throat. Roger Dalston wasn't laughing at all, but his mask was, the scarlet death mask of the Lord of Misrule. And last, but by no means least, Henry Parkin sat upright in his pew, faithful to his God until the end. They all of them cried vengeance in Kit Marlowe's head and he knew he would have to leave *Hero and Leander* to another day.

Tom Kyd woke up with a start. The pounding in his head was the result of too much Rhenish at the Fox and Grapes, but the pounding on his door was of a different cadence. It was urgent. It was loud. It was terrifying.

He stumbled out of bed in the half light and realized it was not yet dawn. He had no time to fumble for a candle and he slid the bolt. The door crashed back and big men barged into the room, armed to the teeth and wearing the livery of the Queen.

'Thomas Kyd?' their leader barked, thick lips in a black beard.

'What's all this about?' Kyd asked.

The man grabbed him by the throat, squeezing under his jaw until he thought he would be sick. 'Are you Thomas Kyd?'

'Yes,' he wheezed as best he could.

'Turn it over,' the man barked to the others. While they proceeded to overturn Kyd's bed, Kyd's press, Kyd's life, the bearded man spun the playwright round and tied his hands behind his back.

'Papers,' another man said, having emptied a drawer.

'Bring them,' the bearded man ordered and they bundled Kyd out of the door.

At first he didn't know where he was. The room was pitch black with no chink of light and he knew he was lying in straw, which rustled under his body. Apart from the chafing to his wrists that the ropes had caused, he felt no pain. It was cold here, however, and he sensed that he was deep below ground, in some Hell made even grimmer by man.

The sliding of a bolt made him jump and a shaft of light burst into the room. This was a cell, with a door and no windows. Two guards hauled him to his feet and dragged him out, stumbling up stone steps to a low vaulted room with iron-barred windows high in the walls.

On a chair facing him sat a portly man with a Puritan collar and a kind face. He smiled at him.

'Are you Thomas Kyd?' the man asked.

'I am,' Kyd replied. The last time he had evaded the question, an oaf nearly broke his neck.

'I am William Waad,' the man said, 'Governor of Her Majesty's Tower.'

Kyd blinked and swallowed. Hours ago he was a drunken playwright bemoaning his lot in life. Now he stood at Peter's gate, but the devil was talking to him. Waad held up a sheet of paper. 'Do you recognize this?' he asked.

Kyd's eyes had not refocussed after the darkness yet and it took him a while. 'No,' he lied.

'No?' Waad looked concerned and confused all in one expression. In reality, he was neither. 'What about this?' He held up another sheet.

'Ah,' Kyd almost smiled. This was his. This was real. 'That's the opening page of my play,' he said. '*The Spanish Tragedy*.'

'*The Spanish Tragedy*, yes,' Waad said, 'yes indeed. Very good, I'm sure, but you see, I'm a little confused by all this. You say this,' he held up the *Tragedy*, 'is yours but this,' he held up the other sheet, 'isn't and yet,' he held the two pages together, side by side, 'the handwriting is identical.'

'I . . . er . . . I cannot explain that,' Kyd said.

'Oh, I'm sure you can,' Waad said as though to a small child. 'For everything there is a reason.'

Kyd said nothing. He stared straight ahead, beyond Waad to the cold, grey stones of the wall at the man's back.

Waad stood up. 'Let me show you something,' he said, smiling gently and taking Kyd by the arm. He led him across the flag-stoned floor and up some steps to another level. Kyd stood transfixed. Around him were machines, contraptions of wood and iron, with wheels and cranks and levers.

'You wrote *The Spanish Tragedy*, Master Kyd,' Waad said. 'Tell me, does strappado appear in the play?'

Kyd didn't know what Waad was talking about. He didn't want to know; but Waad had other ideas. 'These little straps,' he pointed to where they dangled from their roof-high supports, 'you tie them around your wrists – or your thumbs – and you haul a person up, off the ground. His own weight does the damage, tears ligaments, dislocates joints. The pain is excruciating.'

Kyd shuddered and swallowed hard.

'Oh, just a little something we borrowed from the Inquisition,' Waad said. 'Ah, now, this,' he led Kyd to a large wheel bolted to the floor. 'This is home grown. Skeffington's Gyves. Want to know how it works?'

'No!' Kyd shouted. 'No, I don't! What kind of butcher are you?'

'Me?' Waad was affronted. 'Oh, my dear fellow, no. I've frightened you and I am so sorry. No, I am not a torturer. We have a man for that. His name is Richard Topcliffe. Come, I'll introduce you.'

'No!' Kyd ran screaming across the room but there was no way out.

'Calm yourself, Master Kyd,' Waad said, softly. 'Not even Master Topcliffe can touch you without the express permission of Her Majesty. Do you think us barbarians? Tell me, Master Kyd, have you had the pleasure of meeting Her Majesty?'

'No.' Kyd's voice was barely audible. 'No, I haven't.'

'You'd like her,' Waad said. 'Still a beauty after all these years. Gloriana. She makes our sun rise, Master Kyd – be in no doubt about that. Would she give her consent to use torture on such as you?' He shook his head and sighed. 'She'd fight it, by God. She'd fight it with every breath in her body, but in the end, for the safety of the realm, the survival of the state . . . Well, she *is* Harry's daughter.'

'Safety of the realm?' Kyd jabbered. 'Survival of the state? In the name of God, what have I done?'

Waad produced another sheet of paper, this time from the purse at his hip. 'Have you seen this before?' he asked.

Kyd squinted at it. It was difficult to read in the dim light, but then, his eyes were full of tears anyway. 'What is it?'

'It's an Arian blasphemy, Master Kyd. A treatise – or part of one – that casts doubt on the divinity of our Lord. It claims that Christ was just a carpenter, the son of Joseph and not the son of God.'

'Where did you get that?' Kyd said, his lip trembling.

'It was found among your papers,' Waad told him, 'when the guards collected you.'

'That's not mine!' Kyd shrieked.

'Oh, really, Master Kyd,' Waad chuckled.

'It's Marlowe's. We shared lodgings in Hog Lane. His rubbish must have got mixed up with mine. You have to believe me!'

'Marlowe?' Waad raised an eyebrow. 'Christopher Marlowe?'

'Yes. Yes, that's him.'

'And the paper I showed you a moment ago, the one signed Tamburlaine, the one in your handwriting . . .?'

'Marlowe,' Kyd shouted. 'Marlowe made me write it.'

Waad chuckled again. 'Marlowe,' he said.

'What did I say about bad pennies?' Marlowe said. He had been walking by the moat at Scadbury, the lily pads wide and glossy under the bright sky. He had seen Nicholas Faunt cantering over the hill towards him. The projectioner reined in and swung out of the saddle.

'Kit, this isn't a social call and I haven't time for niceties. There's a warrant out for your arrest.'

Marlowe laughed. 'Well, that's been a long time coming,' he said.

'Didn't you get my notes?' Faunt was not his usual cool self.

'Indeed,' Marlowe nodded. 'But I didn't understand any of them. You might as well have given them to Thomas Phelippes or John Dee. They were just about as magical.'

'Well then,' Faunt said, glancing over his shoulder. 'No matter. And time for plain speaking. A flunkey called Henry Maunder is on his way here now. He's a reasonable type but he has his orders. Don't make trouble, Kit. Go with him and keep your counsel.'

'What counsel?' Marlowe asked. Faunt was still talking in riddles.

'I wasn't sent here to watch Tom Walsingham,' the projectioner said. 'That was a blind. I was sent by Burghley to watch you.'

'Me?'

'And, if necessary, kill you.'

Marlowe's mouth hung open.

'I know, I know,' Faunt waved his hand. 'We're none of us indispensable and it's just as likely that Cecil would give you the order to kill me. That's our world, Kit Marlowe; we can't change it.'

There was a noise of dogs barking up at the house. 'They're here, Kit,' Faunt said. He grabbed the man's shoulder and held him fast. 'There's something you should know,' he said.

'What?' Marlowe wasn't going anywhere.

'The men we work for, the Privy Council inner circle – Burghley, Cecil, Hunsdon, Howard . . .'

'What about them?'

'They're all atheists, Kit, like you. They believe their soul dies with their bodies. You said it yourself, didn't you? Moses was just a conjuror. Christ was just a man. There is no God.'

'I've made no secret of my views,' Marlowe told him.

'No, but they have. Can you imagine what would happen if this got out? Blasphemy is a burning offence, Kit; we all know that. The four most powerful men in the land would go to the fire. The Queen's government would collapse. No Lord Treasurer. No Spymaster. No Lord High Admiral.'

'These are just titles, Nicholas,' Marlowe said. 'They can be replaced.'

'Not quickly enough,' Faunt said. 'A rudderless ship of state. The queen couldn't hold things together. We'd have Spain on our doorstep again, backed by the Irish. There'd be a Puritan witch-hunt of the likes we can't imagine.'

There were horsemen on the hill. Faunt saw them. Marlowe saw them. The projectioner swung into the saddle, holding his horse's rein. 'They'll insist you report to them every day,' Faunt said. 'Maunder will call them the Star Chamber but it'll be the four horsemen; no one else. Give me . . . give me five days. Then get yourself to Deptford, a ship called the *Cormorant* – its captain owes me a favour. It'll take you to Scotland, to the court of King James. You'll be safe there.' Faunt looked into the man's eyes. 'And may the God you don't believe in keep you safe, Kit Marlowe.'

And he was gone, galloping away along the moat's edge back into the morning.

The gallopers fanned out beyond Scadbury's outer gate. The *Semper Eadem* fluttered from the pole of the second rider who swerved in to join the first. They had seen the horseman gallop away to the east and there was no point in chasing him. Their target was Christopher Marlowe and he wasn't going anywhere.

The riders pulled up at the bottom of the hill, their horses tossing their heads and pawing the ground. The animals had been ridden hard from Whitehall and their flanks were flecked with foam.

'Christopher Marlowe,' the riders' leader said, 'I am Henry Maunder, Her Majesty's Messenger.'

'Master Maunder,' Marlowe nodded. The man didn't deserve a bow.

'I have a warrant for your arrest,' Maunder told him.

Marlowe held out his hand and took the scroll. He tore the Queen's seal from the ribbon and read it. 'There are no charges here,' he said, 'without charges, this is meaningless.'

'I have my orders, sir,' Maunder said. 'You are to come with us.'

'Where to?' Marlowe asked.

'You don't need to know,' a truculent guard broke in and Maunder put up a warning hand.

'No need for rudeness. As Master Marlowe so rightly says, there are no specific charges. People want to talk to you, Master Marlowe. That's all.'

Marlowe looked at him for a long time, a stare which would make most men quail but which Henry Maunder took like a man.

'So, where?' Marlowe said.

'The Star Chamber.'

The Court of the Star Chamber lay buried in the bowels of Whitehall. It had been set up by the first of the Tudors as a secret court and it had a reputation of getting its business done. There were no juries. There were no independent judges. Just the cold, unreasoning face of Tudor law. And justice? Justice had no place in the Star Chamber.

Henry Maunder had not left Marlowe's side since Scadbury. He had waited while the playwright packed his bags, saddled his horse and said goodbye to Thomas Walsingham.

'I'll be back, Thomas,' Marlowe had said, 'there's a poem half-finished in my rooms. I want to add the next verses before too much ink has dried.'

'It won't be touched, Kit,' Walsingham had promised. 'You have my word.'

Of Audrey Walsingham there was no sign and in a way, Marlowe was glad of that. Her haughty face; her cold, hard eyes he could do without.

It was afternoon before they reached Whitehall, buzzing now with the business of government. Marlowe and Maunder clattered into the outer courtyard above the Thames Stair and left their horses. Guards saluted as the Queen's Messenger passed, hand on his sword hilt, buskins clashing on the cobbles.

'Wait here,' he growled to Marlowe and disappeared through a small door.

Marlowe checked his options. He had walked through two courts, both ringed with crenellated walls and walkways, both bristling with pike-carrying guards. His sword was tied to his saddle-bow, yards away from where he stood now. His dagger was still in the small of his back and the secret stiletto inside his doublet. What either of those could do against a dozen or more pikes was anybody's guess.

Then, Maunder was back. 'This way,' he said and he led the playwright up a spiral staircase lit by a single tall window. This was not a part of the palace that Marlowe knew. When they reached the first floor, the walls were dark with mature oak. There were no portraits, no tapestries, just grim-grained wood. Maunder tapped on the door they came to and it swung wide.

The room was small and cramped with a low vaulted ceiling painted blue and glowing with stars. There was a solitary chair in the centre, bolted to the flag-stoned floor. Facing it, on either side of a vast, empty fireplace, were two chairs, each of them occupied by grimly familiar faces. Marlowe heard the heavy door click shut behind him and heard the hiss of steel as Maunder drew his sword. The messenger stood, legs apart, with the blade-tip on the ground.

'Welcome, Master Marlowe,' it was Burghley who opened the proceedings, 'to the Court of Star Chamber.'

'I'd expected a different judge,' Marlowe said, 'from men who already believe me guilty.'

'Guilty of what?' Hunsdon asked.

Marlowe smiled and sat, uninvited, in the bolted chair. 'You tell me, my Lord. The warrant that your lickspittle here showed me contains no charges.'

'The charges will be decided by the outcome of this session.' Cecil spoke for the first time.

'Nothing like making it up as you go along,' Marlowe said. 'I, after all, have been making a living from doing exactly that for some years now. So far, I see nothing resembling the law of the land.'

'We *are* the law of the land, Marlowe,' Effingham said.

'Clearly,' Marlowe nodded.

'Hunsdon,' Burghley jerked his head in the man's direction.

The baron unfolded parchment and laid it on the table in front of him. '"Marlowe contends",' he read aloud, '"that Moses was a conjuror, that the first beginning of religion was only to keep men in awe."'

'Correct,' Marlowe nodded.

'Did you say that?' Burghley asked.

'No. Richard Baines did, unless I miss my guess.'

'You know Baines has reported on you?' Hunsdon frowned.

'I believe so,' Marlowe said. 'The man is insane.'

'"Marlowe further contends that Christ was a bastard and his mother dishonest."'

'That depends on who was actually Christ's father – the Lord or Joseph of Nazareth, the carpenter.'

'Blasphemy!' Effingham snapped.

'Isn't it, though?' Marlowe smiled.

Hunsdon read on, '"The angel Gabriel was a bord to the Holy Ghost."'

'I don't even know what that means,' Marlowe said.

'"That Christ deserved better to die than Barabbas."'

'I'm more familiar with my own Barabbas,' Marlowe smiled. 'The Jew of Malta.'

'"That St John the Evangelist was bedfellow to Christ . . . that he used him as the sinners of Sodom."'

Marlowe wasn't smiling now. 'I have never said that,' he told them. Marlowe knew he was many things. If they wanted to hang him, burn him, quarter him, press him – there was more than one way to die, after all – they would find something. But he was not going to meet any kind of fate for something he hadn't done.

'According to you, Marlowe,' Burghley snapped, his colour rising, 'You deny the existence of God. You believe that all Protestants are hypocritical arses.'

'Rest assure, my Lord,' Marlowe said, 'I don't include you in that company.'

'Then there's this.' Cecil produced another sheet of scribbled writing. '"Was Marlowe's custom, in table talk or otherwise, to jest at divine scriptures, jibe at prayers and argue with what has been written by prophets and holy men."'

'May I see those letters, my lord?' Marlowe was talking to Burghley.

They were passed across to him and Marlowe smiled. 'This one,' he said, 'Richard Baines' note. The man intends to lead a revolution, gentlemen, once the Queen is dead. He doesn't have the nerve to kill her himself, but he has, just perhaps in his mind, a following of sixty men who will replace all of you once Her Majesty has gone. I don't know why Baines isn't in Bedlam, but if I were you, I'd send Master Topcliffe to see him right away.'

He looked at the second letter and his smile faded. 'This saddens me,' he said. 'It's Tom Kyd's handwriting. And it's got Richard Topcliffe all over it.'

'What do you mean?' Cecil asked.

Marlowe looked at the dwarf. 'You know perfectly well what I mean,' he scowled. 'Tom and I are . . . were . . . friends. But I was cruel enough to ridicule a play of his and he clearly can't forgive me for it. One of you gentlemen would have sent him, I suspect, to the Tower and let Topcliffe or merely Governor Waad loose on him. Tom is essentially a good man, but he's not the bravest. Threaten him with torture and he'll say exactly what you want him to say. I would have said, gentlemen, that none of this – the ravings of a madman and the ramblings of a coward – would stand up for a moment in a court of law, but I suspect that in *this* court of law, it will more than suffice.'

'Master Marlowe,' Burghley said, 'we have not yet decided what to do with you. Clearly your play *Edward the Second* will never be shown to the public again. You, on the other hand, must be made an example of. You are an atheist and a damnable one at that. God knows how many men you've contaminated with your diabolical beliefs. Yet . . . we come again to the fact that you have given the country good service. You will go back to Scadbury, but you will report here every day at the hour of midday until we decide what to do with you. Do I make myself clear?'

'You do, my Lord,' Marlowe rose and bowed, sweeping past Maunder for the door.

When he had gone, the Queen's messenger stayed behind. 'When we arrested him,' he said to Burghley, 'I saw Nicholas Faunt riding away as we arrived.'

'He's laid for. Find him, Maunder. I'll confess, I have a soft spot for Marlowe. But Faunt . . . No. He's outlived his usefulness.'

At the bottom of the stairs, Marlowe turned left instead of right. He'd been doing that all his life. This part of the palace, he suddenly recognized. Cecil's apartments lay up another staircase, topped by twisting chimneys. He still had his two daggers and he had business to finish.

He didn't know how long he waited there, in the shadows of Cecil's inner sanctum, grey, anonymous clerks crept in and out, carrying batches of paper, little boxes and bulging satchels. He kept his back to the wall and an Arras in front of him, until dusk was falling over Whitehall and the Cecils came back. Marlowe waited until they were inside, then he flicked the curtains aside. He saw the younger man go for his knife, but he was no match for Marlowe and the projectioner batted aside the blade with his own and knocked it out of the spymaster's hand.

'I am making the assumption, my Lord,' he said to Burghley, 'that you are unarmed.'

'Francis Walsingham would never have taught you that,' Burghley said. 'You're slipping, Marlowe.'

'What do you want?' Cecil snapped. He rarely went head to head with anyone for obvious reasons and he hated losing.

'To finish our conversation,' Marlowe said. 'There is only one thing I heard in the Star Chamber that rang true.'

'Oh?' Burghley raised an eyebrow. 'And what is that?'

'Baines's contention that I stated that all Protestants are hypocritical arses. He got that right. Especially when it comes to you and your fellow horsemen.'

'Horsemen?' Cecil blinked. Had the man lost his senses?

'The four horsemen of the Apocalypse, Master Cecil,' he said, 'You know, from that book that none of you believe in. Hunsdon on his black horse. Effingham on red horse. That's for pestilence. And last of all, my Lord Burghley, you of the pale horse. You are death itself.'

'Am I, Marlowe?'

'I abandoned God a long time ago,' Marlowe said, 'because he does not exist. Baines is right, even though he doesn't believe it – the Church invented God to protect their own interest, making money out of relics and forcing people to buy their way into Heaven. The Church of England, that madman Martin Luther, they're no better. Bigots and hypocrites all.'

'Keep talking, Marlowe,' Cecil hissed. 'You're signing your own death warrant.'

'*I* am?' Marlowe crossed to the man, the blade tip at the spymaster's throat. 'Hypocrisy doesn't begin to describe you four,' he said. 'You four who deny the Trinity. You see, it doesn't matter if Kit Marlowe doesn't believe in God. He's a playwright and a sodomite. He's sold his soul to Faustus's devil years ago. But what about the Highest in the Land? What if the Lord High Admiral, Baron Hunsdon, the Queen's own spymaster and her Lord Treasurer, what if *they* were atheists too? There is no God but Burghley and Robert Cecil is his son.'

The Cecils looked at each other and Marlowe knew that he was right.

'That's why John Foxe had to die, wasn't it? He was Hunsdon's man and he found out the miserable truth. And in case the murderer, the man *you* sent to silence Foxe, could be identified by the mort Moll, she had to die too. What a tangled web we weave . . . The copyist Dalston came next because he knew I was onto something with *Edward II*. As it happened, that was partially unnecessary – I wrote nothing about your atheism in *Edward* because I didn't know about it then.'

'How do you now?' Cecil asked.

Marlowe smiled. 'There's honour among atheists, my Lord. That secret I shall take to my grave. The curate died because one of you – and I'm guessing Effingham – had an attack of conscience. He was never sure of the Godless path, unlike the rest of us, so he blabbed in his version of the confessional. He shouldn't have. And that only leaves me, gentlemen,' Marlowe said. 'And you know, I can kill you here and now with the merest of flicks of this blade.'

'Why don't you, then?' Burghley dared him. 'Go on, scourge of God, use the knife. Kill us.'

'No, my Lord,' Marlowe said. 'Because I too have a conscience. It's not born of the Bible, or love thy neighbour or turn the other cheek. It's born of justice. And of honour. And all the myriad good things that you and your kind have long ago forgotten.' He spun the dagger in mid-air and slammed it home in the sheath.

'You know where I'll be,' he said, making for the door. 'You'll find me at Scadbury. But I wouldn't be too long about it. I'm too dangerous for you to keep me alive, aren't I?'

Thomas Walsingham was not good at goodbyes. And he knew that having Kit Marlowe in his house was possibly the longest goodbye of his life. He sent Audrey to visit relatives in Wales. He sent most of the servants on extended paid holidays. He, the cook and a couple of maidservants made up the entire complement of the Scadbury household and that was how he liked it. In the evenings, he and his friend had their evening meal in a small anteroom to the brown parlour, on a table big enough for two. They talked of shoes and ships and sealing wax, of cabbages and kings, and why the sea is boiling hot and whether pigs have wings. They didn't talk of death. They didn't talk of God or the lack thereof.

And, within obvious limits, Thomas Walsingham was happy.

FOURTEEN

One morning, as he was preparing for the by-now familiar ride from Scadbury into London, one of the smaller and more insignificant maidservants was waiting for Marlowe on a turn of the stair. She spoke so softly that Marlowe had to bend down to hear her and had to ask her to say it twice.

'Please, sir,' she whispered. 'A gentleman gave me this paper and said I was to give you it this morning, early.' She handed it over, a small package wrapped in oiled silk.

'Thank you,' Marlowe said, and gave the girl a sovereign.

'Please sir, no, sir. The gentleman already give me a sovereign. I only had to come up the stair. It ain't worth two.'

Marlowe unfolded the paper. It simply said 'Cormorant. Tomorrow. Morning tide.' He smiled at the girl and gave her another coin. 'No,' he said. 'It's worth three.'

He ran down the stairs two at a time. He was looking forward to his checking in today. Last things can be sad. But sometimes, they could fill a heart with joy. He had a few sad last things to do today, but he would wait to be sad until the time was right.

Nothing had ever been said, in so many words, about how long he could stay in London each day, but the implication had definitely been that Marlowe was allowed to arrive, sign in and leave, returning to Scadbury with due speed. But after his frosty meeting with the Star Chamber, or such as cared to attend, he headed off for the Rose. The theatre was closed; a combination of lingering plague, the intransigence of the Master of the Revels, now recovered from his injuries but in a towering temper for twenty-three and a half hours of any twenty-four and confusion caused by their lack of playwright had convinced even Philip Henslowe that a few dark weeks might be a good idea. He had put the cast on hold on a fifth of their pay, the seamstresses on hold on one tenth and only Tom Sledd still drew anything like a living wage. But hope sprang eternal and everyone believed that come the proper summer, rather than this rather miserable halfway house of May, that the Rose would live again.

Marlowe reined in and tethered his horse at the bottom of the lane that led to the theatre. Horses disturbed Master Sackerson but not half as much as Master Sackerson disturbed horses. An ostler whom Marlowe had mentioned it to had put it down to the smell. Marlowe thought it was more likely to be the bear's dry sense of humour. Horses, in his experience, tended to prefer slapstick.

He walked up to the wall of the Bear Pit and perched on it, looking over. The Scadbury cook had given him some apples from the store and a few early carrots from the warm beds in the kitchen garden. Marlowe crunched one of these and the noise and scent of fresh, sweet vegetable brought the bear out into the weak sunshine.

'Hello,' Marlowe said, throwing him a carrot which he deftly caught and fielded into his mouth. The poet was glad to see the animal hadn't lost his touch in his winter quiet. 'I have some news.'

The bear looked solemn, which was hard to do with carrot juice matting the fur on his chin.

'Don't tell a soul, but I am taking ship for Scotland tomorrow. I . . . well, I fully intend to be back, of course, but I don't know when. So . . .' It was hard to tell even a bear that you don't expect them to live so long, so Marlowe let the sentence tail off. 'Tom will keep you in apples and I know he'll let you know how I get on. I don't know whether that soft article north of the border will like my plays, but I hope he will. I've heard he has a thing about witches – I have an idea for a play with witches in it. It needs work, but it might be a good idea to break the ice.'

He threw a couple of apples to the bear, who caught one and let the other go. He could find it later and let it be for remembrance when his friend had gone. The animal hadn't taken his eyes off Marlowe's face and he seemed to be learning it for later. The playwright did the same. He had taken his leave of many people he loved in his life, but this was the hardest.

He leaned over the wall as far as he dared and extended a hand to the bear's moth-eaten head.

'Take care,' he said. 'Pray for me, won't you?'

The bear dropped to all fours and went back to his shelter against the wall to eat his apple.

And, hidden behind the big tree that hung over the Pit, Tom Sledd stood, letting the tears run unheeded down his face.

Christopher Marlowe had always been quite satisfied with his life; with some ups and downs, it had not gone badly thus far. He had made more big decisions than possibly the average man of his age had made but most had turned out well, with the occasional turn in the road. He had loved. He had tried not to hate too much, though humankind in general had not always made that easy. And now, he was on his way to set sail on the *Cormorant*, heading north to the court of King James VI. Nicholas Faunt, though not a great lover of Scotland as a place – Faunt had very delicate views on cuisine, for example – had told Marlowe that, for him and at this time, it was the place he should be. He had letters of introduction slipped in between his skin and his shirt, held tight in his beautifully cut doublet. He had a small bag with ink, parchment, quills and a few changes of clothing. In fact, Kit Marlowe was ready for the next adventure. He found that not only was spring now well and truly in the air and trying its hand at being summer, it was also in his step.

Marlowe loved being near water. He had been born within sight of the Stour and had spent most summer afternoons of his childhood swimming in it; often afternoons when he should have been in school. At university, he had spent hours in, on or alongside the Cam. In London, he tried not to be too far from the Thames. And now he could smell the river as he walked down Butts Lane, heading to the Middle Water Gate. It wasn't early by some people's standards, but it clearly was for the folk of Deptford; he hadn't seen a soul since he had left his horse with the ostler and with it strict instructions; it was to be collected by a Master Faunt.

He had checked the tide times and had decided to not go on board the *Cormorant* until the very last moment. He had been warned by the captain, employing various nautical terms he chiefly used to confuse landlubbers, not to miss the tide. His heavy purse had bought him leeway for a day, but that was all. The captain had important goods to deliver and couldn't wait a moment longer than eight o'clock that night. But Marlowe was a fair-minded man and the eight o'clock in the morning it was going to be. But he didn't want to give anyone a chance to let the four horsemen know that he was on board, so everything would be timed to the minute, with nothing to spare.

As he got to the end of Butts Lane, more people were around. Dockers, in their heavy aprons and leather over their shoulders. Fishmongers, going down to the docks to meet the fishing smacks as they came in with their load of North Sea wonders. Fishwives, their wicked curved knives stuffed into their belts, heading off for a day up to their knees in herring. And the natives of Deptford, the same natives that any town has; men of law, opening up their offices. The greengrocer, laying out spring cabbage with almost reverent hands. And . . . Amyntas Finch.

Marlowe was in no doubt that it was Finch. No one else had quite such powerful shoulders and there was something about the tilt of the head that was unmistakeable. Marlowe had a writer's eye for detail, honed on the projectioner's stone, and he never made a mistake.

'Master Finch.'

The man didn't stop, but carried on towards the docks, swinging his left leg just a fraction further than the right, as Finch always did. Marlowe sped up a little and touched the man on the shoulder. He spun round and for a moment, Marlowe wondered if he had made a mistake, because at first glance, this man was *not* Amyntas Finch. The amiable, somewhat stupid features were gone under a mask of intelligence and high alert. This man had eyes like flints, darting this way and that. But that was only for a moment. In the blink of an eye, the bovine features of the assistant stage manager at the Rose were there, looming over Marlowe in their usual benign idiocy.

'Master Marlowe.' The man extended a hand. 'How have you been keeping? We've missed you at the Rose.'

'I've been . . . occupied.' Marlowe kept the man's hand in his. He had never really thought himself a man who needed company, but as he said goodbye to his old life, it was good to have a friendly face to wave to as the dock grew smaller. 'I'm about to go . . . away for a while. Would you like to come and see me off?'

'Er . . . that might be a bit awkward, Master Marlowe,' Finch said, extricating his hand. 'I'm on an errand, you see.'

'An errand for Tom?' Marlowe had no idea what Tom Sledd could want with anything in Deptford.

'Master Henslowe.' Finch pulled a wry face. 'A parcel, he said. From the Low Countries. Well,' Finch became conspiratorial, 'with Master Henslowe, I thought perhaps I shouldn't ask too many questions, if you understand me.'

Marlowe laughed. It was true that Henslowe had many fingers in many pies and a parcel from abroad was perhaps best left alone. 'What time is the ship expected?'

'Oh, any moment now,' Finch said, looking vague.

'Only, it will be high tide in about a quarter of an hour and most ships are here already. Getting ready to leave, if anything. I hope you are not late for Master Henslowe's parcel.'

'It will wait,' Finch said, and sounded less than his amiable self.

Marlowe looked up at the big man walking alongside him. 'I know you are fairly new at the Rose,' he said, 'but you must know that Henslowe doesn't really take any messing.'

'Except from you,' Finch said, a hard edge to his voice.

'Well, yes, I suppose you're right. Except from me. Look, Amyntas, I didn't mean to annoy you. If I have, I apologize.'

'Don't worry, Master Marlowe.' The edge was gone again. It was like walking with identical twins, who swapped sides whenever you weren't looking. 'You haven't annoyed me. The parcel will wait.'

'If you're sure,' Marlowe said. 'But you'll have to excuse me. I don't have many minutes to the tide. The master of the *Cormorant* said he couldn't wait six minutes past the hour and I think it must be almost there,' he said. 'Look,' he pointed between two houses, 'I can see a ship crowding on sail.'

'Quite the sailor, aren't you, Master Marlowe?' Finch said and, grabbing his shoulder, spun him round to throw him against the wall of a house, winding him. Suddenly, all the good burghers of Deptford seemed to have gone about their business and disappeared. Marlowe was alone with what seemed to be a madman. 'But a sailor is only half of it, isn't it? You are also an atheist and a traitor. Marlowe, the scourge of God. And for any one of those, you have to die.'

'Die?' Marlowe still hoped to talk his way out of this, as he had so often before. 'Men greater than me are atheists, after all. I could tell you the names of at least four, right here and now.'

Finch laughed. 'I suppose you are thinking of Lord Burghley, Robert Cecil, Lord Howard of Effingham and Baron Hunsdon. But if they are the only ones you are thinking of, Master Marlowe, then your list is woefully short. I could list so many men that it would take me through this tide and the next. No, you will not be dying because you are an atheist. Nor for any of your other crimes, which are many as you and I both know. But simply because,' Finch shrugged, 'you know too much about too many people. Again, almost too long a list to name, but if we stay with my four gentlemen, then that will serve.'

'The four horsemen of the Apocalypse, perhaps, we could call them,' Marlowe said. 'It appeals to my poet's soul.'

'Your soul will be in Hell soon,' Finch observed, as though commenting on the weather. 'Where it belongs.' He was leaning harder on Marlowe's chest, his arm across just along his collarbones. The playwright could feel his bones begin to bend and he thought he could hear them creak. Soon, they would snap and his life would be over. To die in such a place, at the hands of what appeared to be a madman, seemed to be so futile that it spurred Marlowe into speech, even though he could feel his mind beginning to cloud over.

'But what have I done to *you*?' Marlowe asked, in a breathless grunt.

Finch released the pressure a little. 'What you do to other men you do to me,' he said and leaned in again.

'Please, Amyntas. Just a few more minutes.' Marlowe was pleading for his life. 'Let me find out why. Then I will go willingly to the Devil.'

'The Devil doesn't exist,' Finch said. 'If there is no God, then there is no Devil.' He repeated it as a child would repeat its letters. Finch was not a thinker. He was a doer. And he had been told to do some dreadful things. Sometimes, alone in his bed, George Finch, sometime Amyntas, wondered whether he had made a mistake. That his grandmother may have been right and that his immortal soul might burn in everlasting Hell fire for what he had done on earth. He shook his head and Marlowe saw his weakness.

'I don't believe in God either,' Marlowe said, 'so Hell doesn't frighten me. But I sometimes wonder, what if I'm wrong?'

Finch released the pressure across his chest and grabbed his shoulders, bouncing him against the wall, at first not ungently, then harder until Marlowe's teeth rattled. 'No, it's not wrong to not believe in God. God is *dead*. Grandma is *dead*.'

Abruptly, Finch dropped his victim and the playwright fell to the ground, his head spinning. Finch turned around and around, his hands over his ears, muttering. Marlowe, looking down to minimize the giddiness started to crawl away, but the big man saw the movement and it seemed to bring him to his senses. He put a huge foot on Marlowe's outstretched leg and pressed down. Hard.

Marlowe looked up, squinting. 'If I promise not to tell what I know, Amyntas,' he said gently. 'Would that do?'

'Promise?' Finch gave a bark of laughter. 'What is a promise from a man like you? Master Foxe promised and look what he did. He told and told and told. He probably told *you*.' The foot pressed harder and Marlowe jack-knifed in pain.

'I hardly spoke to John Foxe. I gave him a part in the play. Then more or less straight away, he was dead.'

'Killed by a whore, they say,' Finch said. 'The wages of sin is death.'

'For someone who doesn't believe in God, you know your Bible,' Marlowe remarked.

'I was taught my Bible,' Finch agreed. 'That doesn't have to mean I believe in God.'

Marlowe shrugged as best he could. It was an unusual view but it had some merit.

'No one ever does what they promise, you see,' Finch said. 'Do you remember the one who was killed at Scadbury? Not the vicar one, the other.'

'Roger Dalston?'

'Yes, him. I daresay he broke a promise.'

'You're being very vague, Amyntas,' Marlowe said. 'Look, can I get up? I can't run away, you know. I think my leg is broken.'

Finch pressed again and shook his head. 'I didn't hear it crack,' he said. 'It will just be bruised, I expect. It won't hurt when you're dead.'

'True enough.' Marlowe extended a hand and like a friend in the schoolyard, Finch helped him up. 'What promise did Roger Dalston break?' he asked.

'He gave something to the priest. Something he shouldn't have. He should have given it to *me*. I was supposed to get it.'

'And give it to who?'

'My masters. Master Faunt was meant to do it, but he didn't.'

'So . . . you were working with Master Faunt?'

'Not with,' Finch said, screwing up his face. 'Master Faunt was too tricky. I like to keep things simple.'

Marlowe was on his feet, stretching one leg, then the other, easing his aching ribs. Finch was now leaning on him. Marlowe thought this must be how it felt to be pressed to death. He had always feared hanging and the flames though he had also always suspected he would die by one or the other. He had never thought of pressing. Finch was very imaginative in his ways of hurting and killing people. Master Topcliffe had missed an able assistant when Finch went to work for the horsemen.

'So you killed Dalston.'

Finch shrugged and Marlowe's chest screamed for air. 'He bumped his head.'

'And the vicar?' Marlowe knew the answer.

'Yes and no. I got the one who got the secrets out of the Admiral. But I didn't get the one who stole your play.'

'And the girl?' Marlowe said softly.

Finch moved to put his elbow in under Marlowe's breastbone. This had been going on far too long and anyway, he had missed the tide.

'Girl?'

'The whore who killed Foxe?'

Finch made his first mistake. He chuckled. 'Oh, the girl. She was . . . good. It was a shame she had to . . .'

But his last word would have to be with him and anything waiting for him on the other side. Marlowe's dagger, dragged out of its sheath as he took his last deep breath, was buried in the side of Finch's neck and, with a gasp and a sigh, the assistant stage manager was dead.

Despite the intermittently busy streets, now mercifully quiet, Deptford was not the kind of place where anyone would make much of a dead body lying propped against the wall. The general belief of the locals was that if someone was around who could kill someone without being immediately apprehended, then that person was probably best left well alone. So Marlowe, despite having a limp and a bloodstained sleeve, was able to put some distance between him and what remained of Amyntas Finch. It occurred to Marlowe that neither George, nor Amyntas and probably not even Finch were his real names but as he had no intention of mourning him, it mattered little.

He found himself a low wall in the shelter of a house and sat down to catch his breath. His tide had gone, but Faunt had told him that the master of the *Cormorant* would wait for two more before leaving without him, so there was no need to rush. It was better to present himself for his passage without looking like something dragged through a hedge backwards, so he would need to look for an inn or similar hospitable place to clean up and have a rest. His leg hurt like the Devil but it was getting easier as he used it more. What he would look like under his clothes was anybody's guess. He was thinking he would be black and blue and that Finch would have left his mark on him everywhere. He leaned against the bricks and turned his face to the warming sun.

'Kit Marlowe?' A voice he knew broke into his near-sleep. He opened one eye and there, looking down at him with some concern was Ingram Frizer. This meant that close behind would be Nicholas Skeres and as Marlowe moved his head a little to the right, he saw that this was so. Skeres was also looking worried. Marlowe wondered whether he really looked as bad as all that and decided that he must; unless there was money to be made, these two were not usually solicitous.

'You look like shit,' Skeres observed.

Marlowe looked ruefully at the men. So, his suspicions were correct; he really wasn't looking in a fit state to travel. 'I had . . . some trouble,' he said.

'That bloke down the road a way, was it?' Frizer said, not overly concerned. 'Hole in his neck. Looked a lot like that big bloke helps Tom Sledd.'

'Is,' Marlowe said.

'Is what?'

'Is the big bloke that helps . . . helped . . . Tom. He tried to kill me.'

The two walking gentlemen were shocked. 'Surely not just because you sacked him from the play?' Skeres said.

'No,' Marlowe said. 'That was water under the bridge. No, he tried to kill me because . . . Look, boys, I don't expect you're just wandering around here for no reason. It's a story too long for the side of the road. Some other time, perhaps.'

Skeres and Frizer sat down companionably one on either side of Marlowe.

'You do look like shit, you know,' Frizer said, confirming Skeres's opinion. 'So unless you're heading back to Scadbury to get cleaned up, you should stick with us.'

'What makes you think I am at Scadbury?' Marlowe had not really made a big thing of where he was living. He knew the theatre was essentially one big rumour mill, but was often surprised by its efficiency.

Frizer and Skeres leaned forward so they could look at each other round him. They shrugged.

'Everybody knows, I suppose,' Skeres said. 'I don't think anybody was really bothered, no offence.'

'I meantersay,' Frizer offered. 'If you're not writing anything, well . . .'

'There's not much for you to do, is there?'

Marlowe laughed and sucked in his breath as his ribs screamed in protest. He had become so used to being someone watched by what seemed like the whole world that it was hard to believe that anyone at all was totally oblivious to where he was and what he was doing. It was a relief in so many ways – perhaps when he got to Scotland he would lay low for a while, perhaps find himself a little cottage somewhere halfway up a hillside, a mountain, even – he believed they had those in Scotland – and just dream a few years away.

'I'm glad no one missed me,' he said.

Frizer gave a coarse laugh. 'Oh, folks missed you,' he said. 'All the Geese for a start. The seamstresses. That woman with the one eye, you know the one.' He mimed someone so disfavoured that no one who had met her could surely forget her. 'The one that brings cake on first nights. Her.'

Marlowe looked from one to the other. There was no need for them to be quite so blunt.

Then the walking gentlemen burst out laughing. 'Don't be daft,' Skeres chortled. 'Everybody's walking around like a wet week without you. Talking about when you're coming back and what not.'

'When *are* you coming back?' Frizer poked Marlowe in the side in his familiar gesture and the poet yelled in pain. Was there an inch that Finch had not pummelled almost to death?

The men were on their feet, looking down in distress at Marlowe as he sat bent double, breathing hard. 'You can't stay here,' Skeres said. 'And you can't ride nowhere, neither. Come with us. We know this woman, Eleanor Bull, she's called. Nice woman. A bit homely, but very pleasant. Keeps an Ordinary, don't make too much about it, but she serves a nice bit of dinner, lets gentlemen she reckons use a few rooms to play cards, tables, things of that nature. Come with us. Eleanor'll let you have a room to tidy up. She'll clean your clothes for you. Do a bit of mending. Ever such a nice woman, Eleanor Bull is. You'll like her.'

While he was talking, the walking gentleman got Marlowe under the arms and lifted him to his feet. Their years of getting gentlemen drunk enough to not notice when they lifted their purses had made them adept at helping the incapable to walk. Marlowe didn't object when they walked him smartly down the road a way and in through a low doorway along Deptford Strand.

A woman bustled up to them, her apron gathered up into her hands, flour on her arms. 'Oh, Master Frizer,' she flustered, 'Master Skeres. I don't know whether I'm ready for guests today. I was just doing a bit of baking.'

Frizer threw a friendly arm around her shoulder and gave her a casual squeeze. 'El,' he said, familiarly, 'just to oblige a friend. Master Marlowe here was set upon in the street and isn't feeling well. He could do with a rest until . . .' he looked enquiringly at Marlowe, '. . . how long have you got, Master Marlowe?'

'Until eight o'clock tonight,' Marlowe said, 'no longer. I should be away before that, really.'

'Well, until this evening, let's say,' Frizer said. He gave the woman another squeeze. 'Go on, El.'

The woman shrugged him off. 'Remember your place, Master Frizer,' she said, loftily. 'I've got relatives in high places, don't you forget.'

Skeres mimed a rope hanging him by pulling on his collar and crossing his eyes. 'I've got relatives in high places too, El,' he said. 'But I don't give myself airs. Now, be a good woman and go and get Master Marlowe some breakfast. I'm thinking he left home without any. And then, you can show us to a room where he can rest for a while before he goes to . . . where is it you're going, Master Marlowe?'

'A voyage,' Marlowe said. 'For my health.'

Eleanor Bull looked into his face and tutted. 'You do look peaky, now I come to look at you properly,' she said. She also took in the man's clothes; she hoped Ing and Nick weren't up to their old tricks. The last time they had tried that here the old gent in question had called the Watch and it had got very unpleasant, relatives in high places or no relatives in high places. 'You just take yourself upstairs and rest. I'll call when breakfast is ready and you can have a good wash. I'll send a girl up with some hot water. She'll wash you as well, if you want . . .'

Marlowe smiled wanly. 'Just the hot water, Mistress Bull, if you don't mind,' he said.

'She's a very clean girl.'

'I'm sure she is, but . . .'

'Master Marlowe has had the shit kicked out of him,' Skeres said, calling, as ever, a spade a spade. 'So some nice hot water and some breakfast would just do the trick lovely.'

'As you say, Master Skeres,' the ordinary-keeper said and bustled away, calling for girls, hot water and porridge.

When she had gone, Frizer took Marlowe by the elbow. 'I know the room she'll be thinking of, Master Marlowe,' he said. 'Let's get you comfy and we'll see what she can do about your clothes. This sleeve's a mess, look. Stiff with blood, it is. His?'

Marlowe twisted and stretched. Nothing felt other than bruised. 'I think so.'

'That's one good thing. The last thing you want on a long voyage is to be bleeding all over the decks. Them sailors don't like mess, I've heard. Lots of swabbing and such goes on, apparently.'

They had reached a door just off the top of the stairs. The climb had been more arduous than Marlowe had been expecting and he was grateful not to have to walk much further. Inside the room, the furniture was simple but clean and he had never seen a more inviting bed. With surprising gentleness, Frizer helped Marlowe off with his clothes. He didn't need a mirror to see the extent of the bruises. Frizer's face was enough.

'What did you *say* to him, Master Marlowe?' he asked. 'What did you *do*? You can see the print of his boot here. You'll be stiff by morning, and that's a fact.'

There was a tap on the door and a girl's voice told them there was hot water.

'Just leave it outside,' Frizer told her and they heard her pattens tip-tapping down the stairs. Along with the hot water there were clean towels, soft and thick, as well as lengths of linen, in case bandaging were needed. It was not for nothing that Eleanor Bull kept an Ordinary along a dock; she knew what sailors needed when they landed after a while at sea; women, drink and bandages, in that order.

Frizer was as experienced as Mistress Bull in dealing with injuries to the person and soon had Marlowe washed and dressed in a discarded nightgown of Master Bull's, may he rest in peace. Marlowe sat on the edge of the bed, feeling the cool linen beneath him and that was all he remembered until waking up with the sun high in the sky and the smell of roasting meat coming from a room somewhere below him.

Nicholas Skeres was sitting in a chair in the corner of the room, watching Marlowe through weaselly eyes. Marlowe had stopped noticing how like a rodent Skeres's face was but there was sudden realization in his sudden awakening.

Marlowe licked his lips and gingerly rolled onto one side. 'Nicholas,' he said, 'there was no need to watch me.'

'It's nothing.' Skeres got up. 'Me and Ing didn't like to think of you by yourself in a strange place. In case you had, you know, had a knock on the head or similar. How're you feeling?'

Marlowe flexed his neck, straightened his arms and legs, carefully twisted his back this way and that. 'Well, everything hurts, but it all works, so that's the best I can hope for. Can I smell food?'

Skeres laughed. 'Not much up with you, then. El kept luncheon late for you, seeing as you missed breakfast. I'll let you get dressed. She's done what she can with your clothes, she said, but you'll need some new ones when you get to wherever you're going. Where is that, by the way?'

'Just travelling to travel,' Marlowe said, enigmatically.

'We'll see you downstairs. One of our friends – not from the theatre, somebody you know though, I think – has dropped in. We thought we might play tables or something, fill in the time till you need to go.'

'There's no need,' Marlowe said, easing himself out of bed slowly and carefully. 'I can get down to the dock any time. The ship is there, waiting.'

'Waiting for you, now that's not something you hear of much,' Skeres said. 'Ships usually go with the tide.'

'And this one will,' Marlowe said, standing up and testing how his leg held his weight. Everything seemed to be working. 'That's why I can't be late.'

Skeres strolled to the door. 'See you shortly,' he said. 'Roast beef, it is. She's a good cook, is El.'

'I won't be long.' Marlowe eased his way gingerly into his clothes. His leg was not as painful as it had been at the time, whereas a knock he didn't remember getting on his left elbow was so excruciating that he could hardly get his arm down his sleeve. However, taken by and large and all in all, he was in not too bad a shape.

Downstairs, the table was laid with a joint of beef, with a knife sticking in it ready for the gentlemen to carve as they liked. There were spring carrots, greens and new bread, still steaming from the oven. Ale was frothing in a jug and Marlowe had a pang of pre-emptive homesickness. He had heard that the food in Scotland couldn't hold a candle to that in England; he wasn't a glutton by any means, but what he liked he liked a lot. And this food was just what he liked.

Eleanor Bull had even had the foresight to put a cushion on a chair for him. She stood at the head of the table, her hands folded in front of a snowy apron wrapped around her pleasant girth.

'Enjoy your luncheon, Master Marlowe,' she said and smiled. 'Your sleep did you good, I can see. You look twice the man you did when you got here.'

'Thank you, Mistress Bull,' Marlowe said, sitting down gratefully. He carved off a chunk of beef which was just the way he liked it, crispy on the outside and red in the middle. With a chunk of bread and some pickled vegetables, it was a meal fit for a king. He had taken one grateful mouthful when he heard the front door go and the sound of voices in the hall. Frizer and Skeres he recognized at once; their nasal whines had been in his ears off and on for years now and were unmistakeable. But the other he didn't know – he looked up and the food turned to dust and ashes in his mouth.

The newcomer smiled at Eleanor Bull and then at Marlowe. 'Good afternoon everyone,' Robert Poley said.

FIFTEEN

'It's been a long time, Master Marlowe, hasn't it?' Robert Poley pulled out a chair opposite the playwright and leaned his elbows on the table. 'I seem to remember the last time we met, you promised to kill me if you saw me again.'

Marlowe picked up his knife and carved off a piece of bread. 'I never break a promise,' he said. 'You've probably heard that about me.'

'That and much else,' Poley said. 'You're quite infamous in the circles I inhabit, as you probably know.'

'That depends on the circles,' Marlowe said, thrusting the knife deep into the meat and leaving it quivering there.

Skeres and Frizer sat one each end of the table and watched the men, as they would watch boxers at the fair. The only difference on this occasion was that there was no way of placing a bet, though neither man would have liked to guess how the match might go.

Poley smiled, thin-lipped and unconvincing. 'You know my circles, Master Marlowe. We are the same, you and I.'

Marlowe laughed. 'I had almost decided to break my promise, Master Poley,' he said, 'but say that again and I might change my mind. We are not and never could be the same. I have killed men, yes, but never in the dark and with a stab in the back. Anyone I have killed went to the other place of their belief with my face etched on their eyes. Can you say the same?'

Poley shrugged. 'That may be so, Kit . . . may I call you Kit?'

'No.'

'That may be so, then, *Master* Marlowe. But your dead are no more alive than mine. And I believe, if we had been keeping score, yours might be the higher number.'

Marlowe hacked off some more bread and chewed it slowly, making everyone wait. 'That could be true,' he said. 'But this isn't about a tally of dead men, is it, Master Poley? It's about whether and when and how I kill you.' He smiled around the table. 'Today may be your lucky day, however. I have decided on a change in how I live my life. This ducking and looking behind me all the time is wearing. I'm not yet thirty and yet some mornings I feel as old as the world. I need some fresh air, some fresh faces, some fresh voices. And so tonight, on the evening tide, I will go in search of all three.'

'Congratulations on that, Master Marlowe,' Poley said. 'Mistress Bull!' he called over his shoulder and the woman appeared in the blink of an eye. 'Oh, there you are. I thought you were further away than that. Bring some Rhenish. We need to toast Master Marlowe's journey with more than ale.'

The ordinary-keeper looked from one man to the other. 'How many goblets shall I bring?' she asked. She had had enough blood spilled in her house through arguments over the bill and forewarned was forearmed in her opinion.

Poley laughed. 'Four,' he said. 'My good friends Masters Skeres and Frizer are of the party. Oh, and could you get someone to set up the tables board? We need to amuse Master Marlowe until the tide and talk of mutual friends may not be appropriate.' He looked around. 'Tables?' Skeres and Frizer nodded. They liked a good game of tables. They had some handy ways to ensure they won, though probably using them against Robert Poley would be a certain way to get a one-way passage to Hell. Marlowe shrugged. He had never had much time for games in his life, but tables was better than quoits by a country mile in his opinion.

'I'll set up the back room,' Eleanor Bull said. 'Give me a few moments and it will be ready. Perhaps you would like the Rhenish in there too?' She liked to remind people she came from good stock. Putting a fine wine on a table with a joint of beef and pickles was not something her cousin Burghley would countenance, she was sure.

Marlowe looked up from finishing his meal. 'That would be lovely, Mistress Bull,' he smiled. 'And thank you for an excellent luncheon. I needed that.'

Eleanor Bull left the room and scurried to the kitchen. She wouldn't have been prepared to piss in Robert Poley's pocket if his pizzle was afire, but that Master Marlowe – what a lovely smile he had! And those curls! 'Quickly,' she said to her serving girl. 'Rhenish and the tables in the best room. Quick, now.' The girl jumped up. It wasn't hard work at Mistress Bull's ordinary, but sometimes, when her mistress used that tone, it was best to obey. As she scurried from the room, Mistress Bull called her back.

'Oh, and Abigail?'

'Yes?' The girl waited for more instructions.

Eleanor Bull had come over all maternal. She worried about poor Master Marlowe. She knew he knew her cousin Burghley from what Master Skeres had said when he came to arrange the events of today and she wanted to be spoken well of to her relation. She had yet to receive an invitation to his table, but knew that now it could surely only be a matter of time. 'Pull the couch over to the tables board. Master Marlowe has not been well and may be more comfortable lying down.'

The girl turned to go, rolling her eyes to Heaven. There might not be much to do as a rule, but when there was, there was too much! Pull out the couch? Had the old besom no idea. It weighed a ton and she knew the dust under it would shame the Devil. She would pull the tables up to the couch instead; that would be easier, though it might be a bit awkward for the gentleman when it came to getting up. But they could sort something out. She wasn't an ox that she could go moving heavy furniture around by herself, after all.

Mistress Bull herself saw to clearing the table. The gentlemen had made a good luncheon. She was pleased about that. She didn't run her ordinary to become rich. In fact mostly, she only just broke even. But she did love the gentlemen coming and going, she loved it more when they told her what a wonderful table she kept. She stood beaming in the doorway as they filed out, on their way to a friendly afternoon of tables.

'Thank you, El,' Skeres said, leading the way.

'Yes, thank you, El,' Frizer said, adding a smack on her rear, which she seemed to dislike less than Marlowe would have expected. 'Nice joint of beef.'

She simpered. 'I'll pack you some to take home, Ing,' she murmured.

'Lovely,' Frizer said, leaning in with a leer. 'Just the beef, or a little something to go with it?'

'Oh!' she shrieked. 'Master Frizer, you are a one!'

Poley simply stalked past her. Marlowe stopped and took her hand. 'You're very kind, Mistress Bull,' he said. 'How much do I owe you?'

'We'll sort all that out when you go and catch your tide,' Poley said over his shoulder. 'Don't worry about that now. We'll probably broach another few bottles before then.'

The room which Skeres led them to was clearly normally used as a private parlour. The walls were simple whitewash but clean and fresh. The floor was pitch pine boards, covered before the fire with a hand-woven rug. The fireplace was cold in the warm spring weather and Mistress Bull had put a jug of dried grasses in the hearth to make it look less bleak. Under the window, a couch caught the breeze coming in from the garden, along with the smell of lilac and early roses. The tables board was set up in front of it, with the counters neatly stacked ready for play. On the side trestle opposite the door was a bottle of Rhenish with the cork newly drawn and some goblets. A dish of newly shucked hazelnuts, the last from the previous season, was set out alongside some dried apricots.

Frizer looked at the nuts and fruit and made a rueful grimace. 'She's making a bit of an effort, Nick,' he said, concerned. 'You don't think she's been taking me seriously, do you?'

Skeres laughed. 'It's not for you,' he said. 'It's for Master Marlowe. She's taken a bit of a shine.'

'No reason to worry about why,' Poley said, shovelling a handful of nuts into his mouth. 'It all goes down the same way. Now,' he turned to the board. 'What's it to be, gentlemen? A groat a point?'

Skeres screwed up his face. 'We're just poor walking gentlemen, Master Poley,' he said. 'We can't afford that.'

'*Unemployed* walking gentlemen, Nick,' Frizer said. 'Don't forget the unemployed bit.'

'True,' Poley said. 'Let's play for the game, then. We'll keep a tally and settle up at the end. Losers pay the winner . . . what shall we say? Ten groats each?'

Skeres and Frizer looked at each other. That seemed

reasonable. They had no intention of winning – beating Robert Poley at anything never ended well – but ten groats each wouldn't hurt.

'Agreed,' Frizer said. 'Shall we cast lots on who goes first?' He smiled at Marlowe. 'Perhaps we could draw straws, Kit, eh? Like the old days at the Rose?' He surprised himself when his voice broke on the words. His days as a walking gentleman had begun as a means to an end, but now that they themselves were ended, he felt an unaccustomed feeling in the pit of his stomach. Any other man would have recognized it as sadness, regret and loss.

Marlowe lay down on the couch, resting his damaged elbow on the cushions. 'I don't mind going second,' he said. 'Let Master Poley play one of you two first and then I'll play the winner. Does that sound like a good idea?'

'A kind of knockout tournament,' Poley said. 'That sounds like a better idea than simply taking turns. Nick, I'll play you first. Ingram, you sit there,' he pulled a chair in front of the couch, 'and you and Master Marlowe can watch for fair play.' He laughed, a mirthless sound in that rat-trap mouth. 'I don't trust either of you two further than I could toss that couch with Master Marlowe on it.'

The men arranged themselves to play and watch as was their station and soon the only sound was the rattle of the bone dice and the hiss of Skeres's breath when Poley made a particularly good move, which was almost every time. Marlowe lay at his ease, secretly amused at Frizer's discomfiture as his friend made a mess of almost every turn. For a man of his proclivities, surely he had accepted from the first that it wasn't a good idea to beat Robert Poley? He may as well have handed over the ten groats first as last and not bothered with the game at all. Marlowe intended to give as good as he got but these men had more to lose than some money. Unlike Marlowe, they would have to live in London with Robert Poley for a while yet.

The sun was warm on the back of Marlowe's head and the bird song was soft in his ear. A blackbird was warbling what he would swear was a quatrain by Tallis, from long ago when he was just a boy singing in innocence in the cathedral at Canterbury, the high notes going straight to a God he no longer believed in. Under the birdsong was a hissing noise, like running water going over rocks. Marlowe could almost feel the cool kiss of the Stour on his hot skin. Then, a noise which was not part of his past woke him from his reverie. It was the sound of a chair being thrown back and it was followed by the scrape of three daggers being drawn in perfect harmony. His eyes flew open and he looked up into three tight faces.

'Well, Kit,' Ingram Frizer said, pointing his blade, 'what are you going to do now?'

AUTHORS' NOTE

According to the historical record, Christopher Marlowe, playwright, poet and 'university wit' was stabbed to death in an Ordinary, an eating house belonging to Eleanor Bull, on Deptford Green on the evening of 30 May 1593.

The next day, a sixteen-man jury heard evidence before the royal coroner, Sir William Danby, to explain how Marlowe died. The inquest, long forgotten and written almost entirely in Latin, was rediscovered by researchers centuries later and it raises more questions than it answers. This record claims that Marlowe arrived at Eleanor Bull's at about ten in the morning and spent the day drinking and walking in the garden in the company of three men – Robert Poley, Ingram Frizer and Nicholas Skeres. They played tables (backgammon) and after supper, a quarrel broke out between Frizer and Marlowe, ostensibly over who was going to pay the bill – 'the reckoning' – for the day's hospitality. Frizer was carrying a dagger in a sheath in the small of his back and Marlowe was lying behind him on the bed. Given to bursts of temper as Marlowe was reputed to be, he grabbed Frizer's dagger and hit him around the head with the hilt. The two men fought and it ended with Frizer's dagger being plunged into Marlowe's right eye socket. Death was almost certainly instantaneous.

Frizer was charged and imprisoned but released under the Queen's pardon in record time (twenty-nine days) and no further punishment followed. Today, most books on the period, even the well-written ones, contend that Marlowe was killed in a tavern brawl over a bill and that Frizer acted in self-defence.

All this would be acceptable if the three men with Marlowe in Deptford were anonymous travellers, but recent research has revealed that all of them, especially Robert Poley, worked for or on the fringes of Elizabethan espionage, as did Marlowe himself. There is nothing in Marlowe's character to suggest that he would lose his temper over what amounted to small change. He was almost certainly an atheist at a time when such beliefs, or lack thereof, incurred the death penalty by burning. He was undoubtedly a rebel – most of his plays were contentious and shocked polite society in his day and later. He may have been homosexual – and that 'crime' carried the death penalty too.

That Marlowe was a dangerous man cannot be doubted, but we have no idea why he was in Deptford at all. We know that he was arrested by Henry Maunder, the Queen's Messenger, on unspecified charges and that he had to report daily to the Court of the Star Chamber (in effect the Privy Council) in the weeks before his death. Coroner Danby worked for the Queen's government. He was a personal friend of Lord Burghley, the Queen's chancellor. Eleanor Bull, who kept the Ordinary, was Burghley's cousin. There is a sense of a net tightening on Kit Marlowe in May 1593 that makes the 'tavern brawl' seem an unlikely and superficial explanation.

Will we ever know what really happened at Deptford? Probably not, but today, Kit Marlowe is once again 'all fire and air', 'that pure elemental wit'. He is Shakespeare's 'dead shepherd' and the 'Muse's darling', he of the 'mighty line'. His ghost can be found in cobbled Canterbury, scholastic Cambridge, roaring London or anywhere where men's hearts and souls are free.

For more information, do read M.J. Trow and Taliesin Trow's gripping non-fiction account: *Who Killed Kit Marlowe?*